D0008222

# WHITE MALE INFANT

## OTHER FORGE BOOKS BY BARBARA D'AMATO

*Killer.app*
*Good Cop, Bad Cop*
*Help Me Please*
*Authorized Personnel Only*

# WHITE MALE INFANT

### BARBARA D'AMATO

FIC      D' Amato Barbara c.1
D'Amato, Barbara.
White male infant /                        2002

A TOM DOHERTY ASSOCIATES BOOK
NEW YORK

PROPERTY OF
HIGH POINT PUBLIC LIBRARY
HIGH POINT, NORTH CAROLINA

This is a work of fiction. All the characters and
events portrayed in this novel are either fictitious
or are used fictitiously.

WHITE MALE INFANT

Copyright © 2002 by Barbara D'Amato

All rights reserved, including the right to repro-
duce this book, or portions thereof, in any form.

This book is printed on acid-free paper.

A Forge Book
Published by Tom Doherty Associates, LLC
175 Fifth Avenue
New York, NY 10010

www.tor.com

Forge® is a registered trademark of Tom Doherty
Associates, LLC.

ISBN 0-765-30024-9

First Edition: June 2002

Printed in the United States of America

0  9  8  7  6  5  4  3  2  1

To Hugh Holton

A wonderful writer
A fine man
Goodbye, old friend

# Acknowledgments

Thanks to Lisa Chau for her good research.

To Pierre J. Meunier, M.D., professor of medicine, Department of Rheumatology and Bone Diseases, Édouard Herriot Hospital, in Lyon, France, for information on bone fluorescence.

To Betty Nicholas for the info on dachshunds.

To Vicki Zwart, supervising producer, WGN Morning News, who made many helpful suggestions about TV and reporting.

To novelist and video producer Libby Fischer Hellmann for all her good advice on video and her close reading of several sections.

To Susan Keegan for her knowledge and research about Ireland.

To Margaret Scotellaro, M.D., for helping me not make too many medical mistakes.

And to Hugh Holton, fellow writer, who was one of my wonderful, helpful writing group, whose insight made all my recent books better, and who before his death helped with the first part of this book.

# WHITE MALE INFANT

# CHAPTER ONE

WHITE MALE INFANT, HEALTH
PERF. 6 MO., HAIR BLND. EYES BL.,
BIDDING ENDS 1/19, AVAIL. 1/26

**TO CONTINUE CLICK <u>HERE</u>**

## 1

### Beekman Hospital
### New York City
### Early November

There is nothing stranger than a familiar place turned unfamiliar. Dr. Dooley McSweeney was in his accustomed place of work, which had been his home away from home five days a week for nine years, but today everything was changed. Dooley was a surgical pathologist at Beekman Hospital in Manhattan. Like most hospital surgical pathologists, he dealt primarily with tissue samples—chunks of necrotic tissue from patients in the emergency department, blobs of infected material, biopsy specimens, tissue taken from patients in operating rooms where the surgeon was looking for a tumor-free margin and wanted to know quickly whether there was any malignancy in the specimen, and hundreds of other diverse pieces of flesh from living people where his analyses made a difference to their survival. Hospital surgical pathologists generally didn't do lab tests—the chemical bench tests, hemocults, PSA levels, blood typings, and so on. There were thousands of chemical analyses these days. Surgical pathologists didn't do analyses for the medical examiner. Or exotic analyses, chemical or biological. These were sent to specialized labs around the country. What they did primarily was high-pressure work that had immediate life-or-death implications for real people present at that moment in the hospital.

Because Dooley had worked as a pathologist at Beekman for nine years, he had a lot of friends, a great deal of respect, intimate familiarity with the workings of the huge medical complex, and a certain amount of seniority.

Today, only the fact that he had friends was any help to him. He stood shifting from foot to foot in a minor surgery room in the pediatric wing. On the stainless steel table was his four-year-old son, Teddy, dressed in a blue-and-white surgical johnny. Dooley's wife Claudia had her arm around the little boy. Their pediatrician, Dr. Alison White, held Teddy's hand. A nurse and Dr. Felipe Fallot, the hematologist, busied themselves with a tray of instruments, which they had positioned behind Teddy, out of his sight.

Despite light sedation, Teddy sat rigidly upright, elbows close to his sides, hands in tight fists. He knew this wasn't going to be a good thing. Teddy looked tiny and vulnerable in the limp hospital gown. Dooley marveled at how much alike Teddy and Claudia were, an adult female and small male version of the same basic human form, with their curly red hair, pale skin, and green eyes. Big, frightened green eyes.

Dooley saw the figures in the hospital room as if they were a teaching tableau, frozen in time and place: patient, nurse, doctor, worried relative. Back when he was in med school, and later going through his senior rotations, he had treated many thousands of patients. Now that he was a pathologist, he dealt with tissues, not the people the tissues had come from. He was much happier this way. He hated hurting people. He thought possibly he had gone into pathology because he found it difficult to keep the necessary distance from patients so as to treat them objectively enough. You needed a certain blend of empathy and ruthlessness to do clinical work. Some patients had just stolen his heart, and his fear for them made it hard to do his job properly.

But it had never been as bad as this. This was his son.

Dr. Fallot had allowed Claudia and Dooley to stay here in the room. Their pediatrician, Alison White, had told them that Fallot usually let parents stay with their children for what she called "minor procedures."

"He believes having Mom and Dad around consoles them."

"Do we *have* to do the aspiration?" Claudia asked nervously.

"Yes, Alison, do we have to?" Dooley asked. "You didn't find any leukemic blasts in the smear." A blood smear had been done a week before and repeated yesterday. Maybe he could stop this, even now.

Fallot answered instead of the pediatrician. "I'm sorry. You know why we have to. We couldn't get a reading. The WBC was too low." His slight French accent made the words sound pleasant.

Claudia leaned closer to Teddy. Their red curls mingled. Claudia's arm was tight around the child's shoulders. Everything about Claudia's posture screamed fear. Dooley thought her rigidity made Teddy even more frightened. There was nothing he could do about that, though he took her hand and held it. In fact, he was more scared than Claudia, because he knew what was coming next. She had no way to anticipate it, not really. Claudia was a lawyer, not a doctor.

Dooley had seen a lot of bone marrow aspirations.

Dr. Fallot asked Teddy to lie down. The nurse swabbed the child's hip with betadine and placed a sterile drape over it. Then Fallot swabbed the area too. "This is a topical anesthetic," he said, and Claudia looked relieved. Dooley wasn't; he knew that would be very little help. "This is more anesthetic." Fallot injected anesthetic next to the place they would go in for the bone sample. Teddy gulped and began to cry.

"It'll be over soon, honey," Claudia said.

Dooley went to stand where Teddy could see him and be reassured. The nurse came closer to Teddy too. She wasn't there to console. She was there to help hold the child down.

"I wish we could give him a general," Dooley whispered to Fallot.

"You know we can't, Dooley. Every general anesthetic carries some risk. It wouldn't be ethical for such a brief procedure." He reached for the needle biopsy bone tool. With it he would punch into and suck out a specimen of Teddy's bone marrow.

Not brief enough, Dooley said in his head.

Claudia didn't know why Dooley was so upset about the procedure. She understood when Teddy started to scream.

"Mommy! Make them stop! Help me, Mommy! Mommy! Mommy! Mommy! Mommy!"

"Dooley, do something!" Claudia had shouted, making Teddy even more frantic. The thick needle ground into the bone like a drill.

"Please!" Claudia begged. "Dooley! Help him!"

Dooley wanted to close his eyes. Instead he did what he had to: he held Teddy, held him down so that it would be as quick as possible, saying, "It's almost over, pal. Hang on, Teddy, hang on there, kiddo."

"Daddy! Make them *stoooooop!*" And then he just shrieked and shrieked and shrieked and Dooley whispered words in his ear, thinking all the time that, if Teddy did have leukemia, there would be many, many bone marrow aspirations ahead for him.

# 2

The path lab was a long, bright room, with a lot of space for bench tests and high-tech equipment around the perimeter, in addition to the old standbys like microtomes and fluid baths to float sliced sections onto slides.

On a working day, Dooley might use most of these himself. Today he wouldn't be allowed near them.

"Go sit someplace, Dooley," Tony Groenington said.

Dooley sat at a binocular microscope station and stared at the bench top.

Felipe had allowed Dooley to come with them to the lab, on his promise to stay out of the way. Alison had come too. Dooley thought she had trailed along just to make sure he was all right, since as a pediatrician she would be no help to the lab techs or the hematologist.

Felipe Fallot carried the tray, covered with the sterile paper sheet, and, under that bland sheet, the precious bone marrow specimens. Dooley's colleague, staff pathologist Dr. Tony Groenington, had been waiting for them here in the lab.

Alison said, "I've got a feeling it's going to be all right."

"Then we shouldn't have put him through this," Dooley muttered.

It was a stupid and ungrateful remark, born of frustration and fear. Alison didn't even try to answer.

Dooley's whole body buzzed with tension, so much so that he could hardly see or feel anything outside himself.

He knew Alison meant well. She was a fine doctor. He knew she had to do what she was doing. She had to push him and Claudia, knowing they would have said, "Let Teddy alone. We'll wait and see what happens. Let him be a happy child." Of course she had had to push them. Acute leukemia had to be treated right away. The sooner you started therapy the more likely the child would survive.

The other docs would never ordinarily have allowed the father of a patient to accompany them to the lab. Not even Dooley, though this was *his* lab. Fallot, Groenington, and White must have been aware of how they would have felt in his shoes. Alison had a new baby daughter, chubby and perfect. Tony had two older children, healthy active boys aged eleven and fourteen. Dr. Fallot had no children, yet he had a perfect bedside manner for kids, both forthright and sympathetic; he was one of the most caring doctors Dooley had ever met. The fact that the three doctors didn't manufacture consoling phrases made it clear they understood how he felt—they knew that no sweetened words would have helped if the patient were their child.

Fallot had overheard Dooley's remark. "It's done now, Dooley," he said. "We'll know in a few minutes."

A few minutes was an exaggeration. They'd be lucky to take less than an hour at this, even though Tony would hurry preparing the slides. The favorite question of pathologists, who were often rushed by surgeons holding patients under anesthesia in operating rooms, was, "Do you want it fast or do you want it right?"

Dooley wanted it fast and right.

Tony immediately began to prepare the bone marrow as both sections for cellularity and touch-preparations for cytology. His assistant, who was following Tony's instructions, simultaneously ran up smears with less usual stains, Sudan black B, myeloperoxidase, para-aminosalicylic acid, and nonspecific esterase histochemical. Many hands make light work.

Fallot touched Dooley's shoulder. Dooley nodded his head to

acknowledge the encouraging gesture, but he couldn't utter a word.

Teddy's fevers and weakness had gone on too long.

When Teddy first started feeling sick, Dooley had thought it was just a virus. An FUO, he told Claudia, nothing to worry about, just one of the ubiquitous fevers of unknown origin, caused by one of the hundreds or thousands of viruses out there. In a few days it would go away.

But it didn't go away. Their little boy kept running the fever and his throat hurt and his lymph nodes were enlarged and still Dooley kept saying it couldn't be serious. Finally, they took him to his pediatrician, Alison White.

"Maybe bacterial," Dr. White said. She took a throat culture, but she couldn't isolate any specific bacterium. "Maybe infectious mononucleosis," she said. "These symptoms are pretty typical."

Claudia, already worried, asked, "Isn't mono something only teenagers get? The kissing bug?"

"Actually, no, not only teenagers, even though it's called the kissing bug a lot. Mono is an Epstein-Barr virus infection. We think half the children in the U.S. have had it by age five. Most of the time, it doesn't cause enough symptoms for anybody to notice."

Teddy was four.

His fever would go up in the afternoon, down in the morning.

"Well, then test him for Epstein-Barr," Claudia said. Dooley knew this wouldn't help. Claudia, of course, was not a doctor, and anyway by now he'd said too many reassuring things too often, so she didn't really believe what Dooley told her. He let Alison explain.

Alison said, "So many people carry the virus, Claudia, that finding it won't tell us whether it's the organism causing his symptoms. Although," she added cautiously, "if the test turned up negative, we'd know it had to be something else." If there were no Epstein-Barr antibodies, they'd know it wasn't mono. Something else like what? Alison said, "Let's wait and see."

It would leave them with more serious possibilities, maybe leukemia.

Alison ordered the test and the test discovered the antibodies. Dooley breathed a sigh of relief. Up until then, no one had actually uttered the word "leukemia" aloud, and since the test told them it might be mono, they could still feel hopeful.

But Teddy didn't get any better.

Three days ago, in a conference with Dooley and Claudia, Alison said, "We haven't nailed this down. We've got to go ahead with other blood work."

They did. Teddy's white cells were abnormal. He had mild leukocytosis. He had atypical lymphocytes and some of them were bizarre. Alison called in the hematologist. Dr. Felipe Fallot tried to be reassuring to Claudia and Dooley.

"This is pretty close to the textbook picture of mononucleosis," he said, in his precise French-accented speech.

Claudia said, "But?"

"But not exactly. I would like to aspirate some bone marrow."

"Dr. Fallot, what do you really *think*?" she asked tensely.

"I think it's mononucleosis."

Claudia was panicking. "If you really knew it was, you wouldn't ask for any more tests."

Fallot had just bowed his head.

# 3

Here in the lab, they were at the moment of truth. Dooley heard Tony and Felipe mumbling about the fixing and staining. They were making quick decisions, talking it through with the assistant and a pathology resident. At first Dooley strained to overhear them; even one word of optimism would have diminished the peculiar numb ache in his head and chest. Then he swung to the opposite extreme. Too frightened to let himself hear anything at all, he moved farther away. They were just talking about mechanisms anyhow. He was grateful that Alison let him alone in his silence for these moments, said nothing, just followed him, to be nearby in case he wanted to talk. Which he didn't. One more word of consolation would have made him frantic.

He still heard Teddy's screams echoing in his ears.

Dooley wondered whether Alison or Tony or Felipe gave a thought to the fact that Teddy was adopted. He knew some people believed you didn't care quite as much about an adopted child. Those people were so stupid. If anything, it was the opposite. An adopted child was such a wondrous gift.

Suddenly, his mood swung again. He needed speech, maybe he wanted to talk so he couldn't hear what the others were saying. He turned back to Alison and whispered, "When we first got Teddy, it was like the sun coming out. We wanted a baby more than anything else in life. We'd tried so hard. Claudia had gone through every infertility treatment there was. The treatments were debilitating. She felt sick all the time. And time after time, they simply didn't work. You think one more month—like gambling. She was utterly discouraged."

"I know."

"She felt worthless. Like she couldn't do something that almost every other woman could do. She didn't just *want* a baby; she *needed* a baby."

"I know."

"Then, when we started the adoption process, it was horrible. Months went by. Years. Six years! It seemed like there were no babies in the whole United States. Claudia wanted a baby that looked like her. Well, like us, I suppose"—he put his hand to his red hair—"except that it didn't matter to me at all whether the baby looked like me. It mattered to Claudia. Red hair, green eyes, and that pale Irish skin—"

Alison nodded. "I understand. Some of my patients' parents, people who've adopted, felt the same way."

"It sounds like ego. To want your child to look like you. Still, I guess maybe she didn't want it to be obvious everyplace we went that our child was adopted. I don't mean we'd hide the facts, but . . . whatever. It made me uncomfortable because I knew there were thousands of African-American babies in this country in foster care who desperately wanted a family. It's one of the nasty things about adoption that white babies get adopted more than black babies. It's not right."

"And also children who aren't 'perfect.' "

"Right. If they have a physical problem, people don't want them. Or mental disability. It's wrong."

Now he couldn't stop talking. He was just so tense. "I told Claudia all this and she sort of what I call 'went lawyer' on me. She argued that women all over the world give birth to babies that look like them. A Japanese woman expects a Japanese baby. An Ethiopian woman expects an Ethiopian baby. For that matter, when they adopt, that's what they adopt too. Why should she be different? Then we heard there was a chance of adopting an orphan from Russia, that they were finally letting some of their babies be adopted out of the country, and some of the babies looked like the child Claudia wanted—we—wanted. And then of course Claudia argued that a baby from Russia might die in an institution if they weren't adopted. Which is true. She said wasn't that better than adopting an American child who at least had a foster family and enough food and a house to live in. She had heard about this wonderful agency that was doing a marvelous job of finding babies for people. It was as if somebody had given us the gift of life. We went over there, to Russia. A man from the agency, a spotter, had heard a rumor about a red-haired baby boy in an orphanage. He thought he could find him and we might be able to adopt him. He took us to several orphanages, five, I think. It was like a treasure hunt, but very frightening in a way, because Russia is so chaotic now. You worry constantly that you might be breaking some law or other. There are police and soldiers everywhere."

"I've heard that."

"In one of the biggest orphanages he took us to, finally, there he was. He was so delicate and wonderful looking. Five months old. Very thin, but otherwise healthy. The orphanage was hideous. The babies had almost no care. And no love at all. It was pitiful. They were lying in their own waste. All of them had terrible diaper rash, actual bleeding sores. The staff changed their diapers just twice a day, morning and evening. The babies got no attention, no medicine, no sunlight, no stimulation, no cuddling or mothering. Not enough food. I felt like we ought to take them all. We couldn't, of course. I felt so bad, leaving the others. We were glad to get him out of there while he was still little and hadn't been . . . stunted."

"You've been blessed, Dooley. And so has Teddy."

He looked to where Tony and Felipe were working over the slides. "I hope so," he said.

"I believe Teddy will be well. Even if it's bad news, if it's leukemia, leukemia's not a death sentence anymore. You're a doctor. You know that."

"Yes. Yes, I do." It wasn't a death sentence every time.

"We're curing seventy-five percent these days."

Seventy-five percent go through hell—bone marrow aspirations, spinal taps, chemotherapy—and come out alive. Twenty-five percent die. Was he about to hear that his child had one chance in four of dying?

By now Tony had made up slides from the marrow in the trabecular bone, the spongy interior tissue. There were some minute discarded pieces of bone lying in the Petri dish, and a few slides that hadn't come out right, that had too much bone or were improperly stained. Dooley idly pushed the Petri dish with his finger.

"My child's bone," he said. "It's so cruel to do this to him."

Alison said, "It's awful, Dooley."

He picked up the Petri dish and studied the minuscule white and pink scraps. With a magnifying glass, he examined all the little pieces.

"Dooley," Alison said, "you can't tell anything that way."

"I know. I don't even want to. I'm trying to distract myself."

By now the slides were mostly completed, and Tony and Felipe were working at two different microscopes, double-teaming to get the answer sooner.

Dooley slid the Petri dish under the photographic equipment, but he wasn't intending to take a picture. He tipped it back and forth. "What sort of God made a world in which you have to drill bone marrow out of little children? Or leave thousands of babies wasting away without parents or love?"

He stuck the slide into the dark pocket under the fluorescing microscope, then drew it back out. Fidgeting, he ran it under again, then took it out and set it on the lab bench.

He was so absorbed that he didn't hear Tony at first.

"Dooley!"

He jumped, nearly upsetting the dish and the camera setup nearby.

Dooley, cold and too fearful to speak, looked at Tony. And he saw the smile on his face.

Felipe was smiling too. "Mononucleosis," he said.

"Oh God, oh God, really?"

"Really."

"Are you *sure*?"

"I'm sure."

Tony said, "You can take him home. Just don't let him bump his spleen for a few weeks."

Dooley threw his arms around Felipe, then Alison, then Tony. "We have to tell Claudia!"

Tony gestured to his resident to fill out the paperwork and clean up. He said, "Store the slides," to the assistant. Tony, Felipe, Dooley, and Alison bolted out the door.

But in the elevator, even while happy tears ran down his cheeks, Dooley asked himself why that tiny fragment of bone had fluoresced yellow-green. Fluorescence was characteristic of bone in patients who had been treated with the antibiotic tetracycline. Teddy had never been treated with tetracycline in his whole life in the United States. And there were no such medicines available to Russian orphans.

# CHAPTER TWO

I am a single woman and have been
denied a chance to adopt. I'm a
physical therapist, earning plenty of money
to take care of a child. I would
be a wonderful mother to your baby. Look
at the pictures of my house in
the cached accompaniment. There's a
sandbox all set up, and see the baby's
room inside. The walls are blue and white,
with clouds on the ceiling. You
may come and visit my home if you like.
Let me show you what kind of person I am.

**PHOTOS <u>CLICK</u>**          **<u>MORE</u> >**

# 1

Fifty-first Street near Park Avenue
New York City
Early November

Dooley, Claudia, and Teddy McSweeney arrived home just after lunch. Shrieking with delight, ignoring his sore hip, Teddy jumped out of the taxi. How quickly a child can put a bad experience behind him, Dooley thought, grateful for it. Claudia said, "Careful, Teddy!" and then put her hand to her mouth. "I wasn't going to do that. I promised myself not to let this make me overprotective."

"Me too."

"He's so excited to be home, you'd think he'd been in the hospital a week," Claudia said, smiling.

"Well, when you're that age, one day and one night maybe is a week."

"Let's go to the park!" Teddy shouted. "Let's go to the jungle gym!"

Claudia said, "Oh, honey, we have to be careful for a while. You're not supposed to hit your tummy."

"I won't hit my tummy. I *promise* I won't."

"We can't take a chance, honey," Claudia said. "Not yet."

"Why can't we take a chance?" Teddy begged. They made their way to the elevator.

Dooley said, "Because you're too important."

That held him for a few seconds. Then he said, "Why am I important?"

"Because you're so wonderful."

"Why?"

By now they were on their floor and then inside the front door. Dooley picked him up, careful not to squeeze him around the tummy, and held him in front of the hall mirror. "See? There's my Teddy. And as you can plainly see, he's extremely wonderful."

# 2

Teddy had put his I'll-absolutely-go-nowhere-overnight-without-it doll back where it usually lived on his bed. The utterly necessary doll was a very grubby, threadbare Raggedy Andy, and had it not been in the hospital with him, things would have been much worse. Claudia smiled at Teddy, smiled at Raggedy Andy, smiled at Dooley, and then whispered in his ear, "Thank God."

Teddy adjusted his collection. There was a bear wearing a Giants shirt. A yellow-and-black tiger. A floppy white plush beluga whale. Two plastic horses that Claudia didn't think should be in bed with him because they were so rigid they could poke the little boy, but nobody could get him to give them up. Teddy had just graduated to a "real" bed. It was blue, about four feet long, with small pictures of the Roadrunner on the head- and footboards, and he was enormously proud of it. He had a matching Roadrunner blanket. At night, when Dooley put Teddy to bed, they both would say, "Beep-beep!"

When Teddy started telling all the other animals what Raggedy Andy and he had seen and done in the hospital, Claudia and Dooley backed out of the room.

Claudia and Dooley sank into the living room sofa. For a minute neither spoke, and then Claudia said, "I wondered how we would feel the next time we saw Teddy's room. Would we have left him at the hospital and come home alone and terrified? Or would we be relieved and happy like now?"

"And exhausted," Dooley said.

"You do seem wrung out."

"Just totally tired. How about you?" Claudia was at the end of another round of hormone therapy, the end of still another go at fertility treatments.

"I don't feel so well, really. But I feel great too. Dooley, I just don't know what I'd do if we lost him."

"Me either."

"I'm glad we didn't tell Mom and Dad. They'd have worried unnecessarily."

Teddy appeared in the doorway. "Can I have some mepperpint ice cream?" he said.

Dooley jumped up. "Of course you can have peppermint ice cream. I'll go down to the store on the corner."

# 3

Seven hours later, at barely nine P.M., Claudia and Teddy were already both asleep. Dooley tiptoed into his office, actually a corner of the third bedroom. Their apartment was large by New York standards, small compared to apartments in the rest of the country. He had one half of the little room for his office and the other half was Claudia's office. Feeling sneaky, he dropped the Arts section of *The New York Times* in the doorway, knowing that if Claudia came toward the room and he didn't hear her, she would either step on the paper if she wasn't watching where she was going, or stop and pick it up if she was. Pick it up, most likely; no careful housekeeper like Claudia could see a newspaper on the floor and just let it lie there. Either way, he would know she was there before she got a chance to see what was on his screen.

Wait a minute. What was he worrying about? Even if she saw it, she wouldn't understand why he was researching fluorescence, would she? Claudia's background was law, not the physical sciences.

It made him feel better to leave the paper there in the doorway, just the same.

He began to surf the Net methodically. Because he was a doctor, he automatically went to the M.D.-friendly sites first, ones he was familiar with. The question was, did anything other than tetracycline make bones fluoresce?

An hour later, he knew very little more. Fluorescence happened when a source of energy, like X rays or ultraviolet rays, hit a specific excitable substance that absorbed it and gave back radiation of a longer wavelength. The excitation wavelength for tetracycline was 390 nanometers and its emission was 560. Because the lab's UV microscope gave off light at 390 nanometers it seemed to be right in the ballpark for making tetracycline fluoresce, even though he wished it weren't. What color light did tetracycline give off? Greenish-yellow, he was sorry to discover, exactly as the tiny chunk of Teddy's bone had done. That sickly color was a portent.

Dooley pulled Teddy's medical record from Russia out of his file cabinet. This was a translation they had been given, which they had been assured was complete. Dazed with delight at the time, he had only skimmed it. Now he read every word. There was a growth chart, showing the baby's weight and length gains over the first months of his life. There was an AIDS test, a test for the standard sexually transmitted diseases that infected mothers might pass on to their babies. All were negative. There was nothing about tetracycline or any other antibiotic, which conformed to his memory of the records. Nor was there any record of any illness that would potentially have required antibiotics. There was no reason for Teddy to have tetracycline in his bones.

Although his days on pediatric rotation were long behind him, Dooley knew that tetracycline was not usually given to young children. At the stage when teeth were forming in the jaw, tetracycline caused the enamel to darken permanently. Also, patients at any age are told not to drink milk when they take tetracycline, because the tetracycline binds to the calcium in the milk and loses a lot of its effectiveness. And since children need milk, or at any rate need calcium in some form, it wasn't the best choice. Still, there were times when tetracycline had to be used, even in young children, if other antibiotics aren't appropriate or have lost their potency against a particular bacterium. There was plenty of info in the M.D. websites on indications for the use of tetracycline. Plenty about side effects.

Maybe Teddy had never been specifically *given* tetracycline. Could he have absorbed it some other way? Maybe his mother in Russia had been prescribed tetracycline when she was nursing Teddy and Teddy took it in with his milk.

No, that wouldn't work. He and Claudia had been told that Teddy had been brought to the orphanage as a newborn, direct from the obstetrical wing of a Moscow hospital. "His mother was the poorest of the poor and she stayed just long enough after the birth to sign the papers," the director had told them.

Maybe his mother had been exposed to tetracycline when she was pregnant with Teddy. Would prenatal exposure pass the medication along to the developing bones? Probably. Would it last this long, four years? He just didn't know. And much as he searched the Net, he couldn't find the exact answers to those questions. He'd have to ask somebody. Even if unborn children could absorb tetracycline from their mothers, how could a poverty-stricken Russian woman get hold of the medicine, anyway? At a clinic? Everyone said the poor in Russia didn't have any medical treatment to speak of. At the time Teddy was born, the country had been in postbreakup chaos.

There had to be an explanation. He just couldn't imagine what it might be.

He took from his pocket the little discarded scraps of Teddy's bone and two of the finished slides that he had palmed at Beekman Hospital. They were wrapped in a Kleenex, as they had been since he left the hospital, but he could feel the little pieces of bone through the paper—or imagined he could—even though they were as small as grains of sand. He removed the Kleenex and placed the scraps in a clean specimen envelope. He deliberated for a few moments. The next step, he decided, was to call a pediatrician he knew from med school, a former professor who specialized in bone metabolism. His friends Benny and Abner would explain all this, and set Dooley's mind at ease.

# CHAPTER THREE

Orphan trains [hist.]—In the United States in the
mid 1800s, urban orphans were collected from the
cities, loaded onto trains, and run out to farm towns
where labor was needed. Farmers would come to the
whistle stop and pick likely-looking children.
Approximately 85,000 children were relocated
by orphan train. Some found good homes.
Some were abused.

—*Favorite Facts*, vol. 17

## 1
### Outside Moscow
### Early November

Eleven people stood in an uneasy clump in a cold office in a large,
featureless, public building in Russia. The floor was oak, marked by
years of spilled ink and winter boots. The desk was government-issue.
The Russians were mostly silent, waiting for the leader, the director,
to show them what to do next.

An American woman of thirty-five, bundled in a wool coat,
turned to a man wearing a purple parka. He was clearly an American
too, with his well-washed Levi's and L.L. Bean thermal jacket.

The woman, whose name was Gabrielle, said, "Got your backup
batteries? They're not lying in the case in the car?"

"Have you ever known me to fail? I *absolutely* have them with me," Justin Craig answered. This actually had nothing to do with batteries. It was their own private code. Gabrielle's question meant "Are these people lying to us?" and Justin's answer meant "Absolutely."

"Well, you've gone soft on me more than once," she said. Which only meant that she would soft-pedal her questions. Open-ended questions, nothing confrontational. She didn't need to rile these functionaries. What they told her didn't matter much, as long as Justin got his pictures. *Keep the goal in mind—a documentary with real emotional power in it, one that will make a difference. One with visual impact.* The more serious problem was the fact that the Russians would show her only the presentable parts of the institution.

It was like walking on eggs, Gabrielle Coulter thought, using one of her mother's favorite expressions. Gabrielle and her videographer were the only Americans in the bunch, in fact the only two here who weren't native Russians. Even the interpreter, a slight, smiling, dark-haired woman named Vlasta, had studied English in Moscow, and had never been outside the Russian Federation. Her English was perfect, idiomatic, and not overly formal. They must have given us one of the best, Gabrielle thought. *I wonder if she'd help us, tell us a little extra. Some insider viewpoints.*

In addition to the translator and director, there were three men and a woman who had been introduced only as "educators," two women doctors, and a representative of the Ministry of Labor and Social Development. Nine people to surround her and Justin on the tour. The director of the institute was in charge, and would tell Gabrielle what she could videotape and what she could not tape. This was one of the largest orphanages in the entire country. It was visited frequently by outsiders, but even so Gabrielle was sure there were many parts of it that outsiders never saw. If the *dom rebyonka* were not as secret as they had been under the Soviet regime, they were nevertheless close to it.

You just didn't know where you were with these people. Were they pro-Soviet Russians or anti-Soviet Russians? Were they eager to help the babies, and willing to do it by helping Gabrielle? Or did they resent the babies, as many Russians did, for using up scarce state funds? You had to try not to put your foot in your mouth. That was the foot you used for walking on eggs. Gabrielle almost laughed, but she realized it was the tension that was making her giddy.

They left the offices of the *dom* and entered a long hall. It was floored with dingy blue-green linoleum, cracked in places, making her think of seaweed in a dirty backwater. The walls were painted an odd shade of dark aqua. From all sides, Gabrielle could hear babies crying. Like so many Russian buildings, the windows in the hall near the front door were small and few. More important than the view, more important than style, Muscovites first of all wanted to keep out the Russian winter.

The director of the *dom* spoke in Russian for three or four minutes without stopping, completely ignoring any courtesy to Vlasta, as if any effort to make her job easier showed weakness on his part. Self-important government functionaries are the same the world over, Gabrielle thought. She caught Vlasta's eye and smiled just slightly. She actually got a smile in return.

One small step forward. Maybe this would all work out.

During the director's speech, Justin leaned patiently to one side, countering the weight of the Sony digital SX camera, audio and video cables, and three "bricks," the five-pound camera batteries, stuffed into a cloth bag. He had left several other batteries in the car. Still, photographers needed strong shoulders. Usually, he and Gabrielle had a third person on board, making up the customary two-man crew plus reporter. Today Gabrielle was the other crew member, carrying a box of mikes and some extra cassettes.

The director talked on and on, uncaring, until he came to the point where he wanted to stop.

Vlasta translated. "The director says that when a Russian baby is abandoned, which is usually soon after its birth, the hospital keeps it for several days, while they give it a physical examination. Then it goes to a *dom rebyonka*, a baby house such as this one, where it will live for four years. During that time, its mental and physical health is assessed. At the age of four, it goes to one of two places. A children's home, run by the Ministry of Education if it is a well child, or the *dyetskii dom*, a total institution run by the Ministry of Labor and Social Development, if it has severe physical or mental problems. That is for those who are *imbetsily* or *idioty*. Those well children who are in the children's homes go to school with other ordinary children and leave the institution at the age of fifteen."

"And the others?"

"Oh, the defective ones cannot learn much in any case. The *dyetskii dom* teaches them basic self-maintenance skills, dressing oneself, feeding oneself, washing, if they are able to learn these tasks at all."

"The care of children must be an extraordinarily large undertaking," Gabrielle said cautiously. During her thorough research in preparation for this shoot, she had read the U.N. reports on Russian orphanages, which estimated that over a million children were in state care. A hundred and thirteen thousand Russian children were abandoned each year according to Human Rights Watch. She would not baldly ask the director how many children were in their care, though she thought of it. You tried to surprise an unguarded response from an interviewee. But the director would surely deny that the number was so large. And an aggressive reporting style might get them thrown out before they got their pictures. Mainly, she wanted to get him talking, so she could do the noddies, bobbing her head to encourage him.

He produced a spate of Russian. Vlasta said, "The director says yes, it is a large and important undertaking, as we must make as many as possible of these unfortunates into productive Russian citizens."

"I am told," Gabrielle said cautiously, "that before the breakup of the Soviet Union, many of these children would go directly from the orphanages into the army."

Vlasta translated to the director, then his reply. "Yes, it is much more difficult now."

They had reached the door to a large room on the north side of the building. Babies' cries came from the room, but then babies could be heard crying behind several other doors as well. There was a smell of stale diapers, milk, milky vomit, and under it all a distinct smell of paint. *They're going to show us a spruced-up room.*

Twenty iron cribs lined each of the two long walls of the room. The cribs were freshly painted white. The walls were freshly painted white. The floor was old brown linoleum. A single small window penetrated the thick wall at the far end of the room. Justin immediately flipped on his camera and began a slow pan of the room, working for smoothness. Nobody stopped him.

Gabby took off her heavy outer coat and placed it on the floor near the door.

Justin meanwhile would be assessing the light. Unlike the days of film, they could tape in low light, but there were always contrast problems. There would be pools of darkness and too much contrast, the light patches near the window too light, the shadows too dark. She trusted Justin to handle this. Color balance was a problem in low light too. She saw him fiddle with his equipment. *Wonderful, wonderful,* she thought, *to have him and not to have to worry.*

In each bed lay a baby. The oldest looked about a year old, the youngest possibly two weeks. Some rested on hands and knees, rocking rhythmically forward and back. Some lay still and silent, staring at the cracked ceiling. Some cried. The blankets laid over the children were freshly washed. However, underneath was uncleanness; Gabrielle could smell diapers that hadn't been changed in hours, the urine fermenting to skin-irritating ammonia.

There were no cheerful colors here, no pictures on the walls. At first Gabrielle had noticed the sound of crying. But now she noticed the comparative silence. There was crying, yes, but not very much of it, given the large number of babies, and what there was sounded more like keening. She knew the sound of healthy, angry babies, and she didn't hear it in this place. Most of the infants were silent. There was too much silence, no cooing, no babbling, no music, no stories being told, no lullabies sung, no one talking to the babies.

Since Gabrielle and Justin had not been able to see the orphanage earlier and plan their shots, they had decided that she would do stand-ups in locations Justin thought would give good visuals. Now he gave her a go-ahead, pointing a finger at a spot in front of one of the cribs. Gabrielle began to speak. She had only half her brain on what she was saying, mentally checking the room, knowing that Justin had the sense to get whatever background they needed of the children and the environment.

For now, she put aside most of what she'd learned in her research and tried to recap roughly what the director had told her, since that was what the Russians wanted to promulgate. She could always do a final stand-up later with different content. Or she could delete sections, lower the natural sound, or lay in a voice-over once they got home.

Justin began to shoot her with a bed and a baby just off center of the shot, angling himself so that the long row of iron cribs stretched beyond her. She said, "I'm in a *dom rebyonka*, a baby house, just outside Moscow. The *dom rebyonka* system, with two hundred and fifty such houses in the nation, is run by the Ministry of Health, to provide care and housing for orphaned babies. Most of these are infants who were abandoned at birth. A child will remain in a baby house until he or she is four years old."

Gabrielle walked slowly past the babies, stopping for a few seconds at each crib. Justin trailed, working to keep it smooth. Gabrielle was still developing the format for the documentary. Somewhere in it she thought they might build a montage of dozens and dozens of babies, to illustrate how many orphaned children there were.

She continued her stand-up, pausing at another crib. "By four years of age, the toddler will have been assessed on mental and physical characteristics. Those who are educable will likely be sent to a children's home, run by the Ministry of Education. Ordinarily they will attend regular public school with other, nonorphaned, children for nine years."

She now stood near an infant with long, fine, blond hair, possibly a girl, lying on her back. The baby looked about six months old, and smiled up at Gabrielle, but did not try to move. Gabrielle gently touched the child's cheek, but the infant scarcely blinked.

"The children classified as disabled, called *debil*, will go to one of the *spets internaty*. In an *internat*, the child receives six years of schooling and vocational training if he or she is able to use it." Did she have that right? These were Russian words she had just recently studied. She started walking again, coming back up the other side of the room. The officials and Vlasta were trailing, keeping silent. Gabrielle was starting to notice more, now that she had adjusted to the impact of the children. There was a toy in every other bed and one large red-and-white plastic ball on the floor. The toy in the bed she was passing was a sharp-edged metal dump truck, the kind you would never leave in a crib with an infant. In the U.S. it would be labeled "for children three to eight years old" or some such age range. The next bed, when she reached it, contained a baby and a large, fussily-dressed bride doll still in its plastic wrapper. Where were the infant-appropriate toys?

One changing table was at the end of the room, a covered bucket near it. One table for forty babies? Was that enough? There was a big white porcelain sink with one faucet. Gabrielle knew what that meant. If there had been two faucets, she would have thought maybe they had hot water. But with one, there would only be cold. To wash a baby's bottom in cold water in Russia in the winter! Gabrielle shivered at the thought, but she was still speaking. "The more seriously disabled child, called *idiot* or *imbetsil,* will go to a closed institution run by the Ministry of Labor and Social Development. When such a child reaches adulthood, he will be housed in an asylum, an *internat,* for life."

Conditions in those closed institutions were said to be hideous. The children were sometimes left in unheated rooms for punishment, or controlled by older children in the system, who beat and tormented them. Gabrielle knew that she would never be shown such places. Her video essay was going to be on babies anyway, not children, so it didn't so much matter that she couldn't get into those institutions. She felt anguish for the children there, but she knew she needed focus in this documentary if it was to have power.

As she came to the last crib, near the door, she reached a conclusion. These toys were window dressing, nothing more. So was the big red-and-white ball. Little babies did not play with that kind of toy. If these toys had been in here yesterday, she was Brad Pitt. She'd talk about this in her voice-over when she recorded it at home.

The camera was off. She picked up her coat. Back out in the central hall, she half listened to another lecture about what the infants were fed. This was given by one of the physicians. Justin photographed the doctor. The little pod of officials surrounded her and Justin, herding them toward the front doors. Just coming in the front doors were two men in suits. *State inspectors,* she thought, judging by their stiff wool suits. She nodded as they approached, and said, "Good afternoon, gentlemen. I'm Gabrielle Coulter and this is Justin Craig. We're from the U.S."

They had not been planning to talk with her, but now the orphanage director said their names hurriedly. Vlasta translated. "May I present Mr. Krysigin and Mr. Lupov, of the Russian Ministry of Education." Justin triggered his camera and photographed them.

The director hurried Gabrielle and Justin along, past a set of double doors on the left. As Gabrielle passed the doors, a janitor came out, carrying two buckets filled with wet diapers. Behind him were the cries of little children. Not babies, children.

Gabrielle turned and stepped over to the door, saying brightly, "Oh, more babies?"

Justin double-stepped after her.

"Ah-ah-ah!" one of the officials said, followed by a spate of loud Russian.

"No taping! No taping!" Vlasta translated.

The official put his hand over the lens of Justin's camera, but Gabrielle was already in the room. The room was dim, and the thick, feces-clogged air was filled with moans and cries.

She stared down into the face of a small child lying passive on an unpainted concrete floor. He was the size of a two-year-old but from her research on disabled children she decided he was probably three. And so sweet, so mild, so sad. He looked like a little elf. A few feet away was another similar elf-child.

This was the characteristic face of prenatal alcohol damage. Fetal alcohol syndrome they were calling it now. The thin upper lip, the short, flat, low-bridged nose. The flattened midface. The small, shallow jaw. Low-set ears. Eyes like slits. Drooping eyelids. Russians were said to think it looked like an Asian face and regarded these children with suspicion because of a national fear of Asia at their back door. Gabrielle thought it was a sweet and lovable face. They were cute little elves, Cabbage Patch children. Big eyes, little chin, the most lovable child's face in the world. So sad. The child was probably brain damaged. A matron stood by, looking sympathetic but exhausted.

One of the educators, a man who had not yet spoken, sputtered out something in Russian. Vlasta looked at Gabrielle. When she didn't translate, Gabrielle said, "I'm sorry. What?"

Vlasta pressed her lips together, making it all too clear what she thought, and then translated, "He says this baby is defective. It is a waste of state money keeping him alive. He is using up valuable state funds to no avail."

How dare they hold this damage against the child? What were they thinking? The Russians knew alcohol caused this hideous damage as well as Gabrielle did. They *knew* it. They made stupid Russian jokes about it. How dare they blame it on the baby?

And then as her eyes adjusted to the dimness, she became aware of the other occupants of the room. With a lurch of horror, she thought at first they were huge, wriggling maggots. But they were children, all lying on the floor, tied in unbleached cotton gunnysacks. The sacks were roped in at the waist and neck. Several of the children were also roped to pipes along the walls to hold them in place.

Another long burst of Russian came from the representative of the ministry. Vlasta pursed her lips.

There was a silence after he finished. Then he made a go-ahead gesture to Vlasta, as if shooing a dog. She said, "This is called a lying-down room. They are all *debil*. When a woman gives birth to a disabled child, the doctors encourage"—she glanced at the official and her chin came up a fraction of an inch—"they put great pressure on the mother to give him up. To forget about him. He is damaged goods. The parents will be ostracized if they keep him. No one will adopt him, the ministry says. It is not in the interests of the state to spend money correcting cleft palates or clubfeet. It is better to keep them sedated on humane medications to control their bad behavior. The Russian state is based on order and discipline. The state replaces the family. The socially useless are not fit to be considered good Russian men and women."

When she had finished, ending in a monotone, the man from the ministry rumbled out a short phrase that sounded to Gabrielle like "boojet kutz," and then he laughed uproariously.

Gabrielle looked at Vlasta, puzzled.

"It is a phrase from your country, he says."

"I don't understand it."

"He said, 'budget cuts.'"

## 2

As they left the orphanage, Gabrielle had to shake hands all around. So did Justin, and he did not look happy about it. Vlasta walked them toward the car, where their driver waited. When they were still far enough away so that the driver couldn't hear, she seized Gabrielle's hand, smiled, nodding up and down as if saying just an ordinary good-bye.

"Charitable agencies send toys to the orphanages," Vlasta said in her clear, slightly formal English. "Or they bring them." She fixed Gabrielle with a straight stare. "The next day one may see the toys in the market stalls. For sale."

# 3

The room in the Russian hotel was quite large but drab, with narrow metal-framed windows and concrete walls. Despite the lack of big windows, it was drafty. Gabrielle constantly felt cold here. She had tried to sleep but couldn't. When she heard the knock on the door about midnight and Justin's voice saying, "Are you awake?" she got up gratefully and let him in.

"I dubbed the tapes," he said, handing her three cassettes.

"Good." Most of the video equipment was in his room, with a bit of overflow in hers. This was not an efficient studio-away-from-home, but they'd put up with far worse in other countries.

"Couple things I want to show you on today's footage when we get a chance."

She said, "Sure."

"Man, oh, man," he said, looking around her room, his hands on his hips. Justin was big, heavily muscled, with dark hair and dark eyes. "These guys really don't go in for interior decoration, do they?"

"No." She had wrapped herself in a scratchy gray blanket to answer the door, which she now closed and locked.

"I mean, they got two architectural styles, Catherine the Great's wedding cake or 'Stalag 17—Return to the Gulag.' From the sublime to the hideous."

She laughed. Some of the most glorious architecture on earth was in Russia. And some of the most hideous. The hotel was called the

Metropole, which was also the name of a famous bakery in central Moscow. Gabrielle could not decide whether the hotel name had been chosen as a sort of wry joke, because the food in its restaurant was so dreadful, or as a naive attempt to make the hotel seem better than it was. Having found little humor in Russian officials anywhere, she decided it must be the latter.

The Metropole had been built around 1950, not a stellar year for architecture in the Soviet Union. The Cold War was growing more frigid all the time. A military base was just a couple of miles away—one large building of which was now the orphanage—and the Metropole had been built as a billet where visiting army functionaries and various inspectors could stay. The highest-level army personnel, however, did not use it. It was much too Spartan for generals or major politicians. They stayed in hotels in central Moscow and were ferried to the base in luxury automobiles.

The hotel manager, Mr. Gabovitch, reminded Gabrielle of a large egg on legs. His face was round and usually shiny. His neck was fat and his body rotund. He smiled a lot, but looked worried underneath the grin. He had given Gabrielle and Justin separate rooms before she had even tried to specify what she wanted. Gabrielle thought this was just as well; they should maintain an illusion at least of sleeping separately. You never knew where you were with Russians. They could become very straitlaced when you least expected it.

Many old-style Russian hotels still used the *dezhurnaya* system, not giving the guests a key but just an I.D. card with the guest's name on it. The *dezhurnaya* was a lady who guarded your floor. She was the keeper of the keys and watched the arrival and departure of every guest in her charge. When you went to your floor, she handed you your key. When you left your room, you gave the key to her to keep. A lot of people who had visited Russia had warned Gabrielle about the *dezhurnaya* system, feeling their privacy had been intruded upon, even though the woman would also provide services like arranging for laundry to be done or getting hot water. Still, it would have been embarrassing in a way, Gabrielle thought, to have some woman noting that Justin had come to her room. She was pleased that there were no floor ladies in the Metropole.

"Maybe we shouldn't talk about the Russians," Gabrielle said.

"Why?"

"Maybe the room is bugged."

"Really?"

He wouldn't have thought to worry about it. A lot of her colleagues believed Justin was a little dim-witted, or at least naive. In fact, he was extremely bright, but he was a visual thinker, which was hardly surprising for a cameraman. He was quicker to spot the telling camera angle than anybody else she had ever known. He was completely focused—not a bad word for a photographer—on what his eyes saw. He was sweet-natured, which some people read as stupidity. They ought to see him when he ran out of tape. He was able to vent then, and had a big vocabulary of multinational curse words to prove it.

Gabrielle and Justin had worked together for several years now. Ordinarily she reported from trouble zones for major television news stations, the last few years for CNN. Justin had been the cameraman on one of her first foreign assignments in Bosnia. She had seen right away that he had a good eye.

He noticed now that she was trembling.

"Are you sick, Gabby? What's wrong?"

"Those babies."

"I know. I know." They sank down on the bed together and he pulled a second blanket over both of them.

"I thought of this documentary as the accomplishment that could make my career."

"And that bothers you."

"Of course. Because children are dying. And I was trying to build a career on them."

"You talked to me about orphan children before you even thought of doing a documentary. How else are you going to help them? Won't showing the world what's going on do some good?"

"Maybe so. I certainly hope so."

Gabrielle had made a name for herself in a highly competitive business. Lately it seemed to her that being a media star was useless if she didn't turn it to some good works. But she was self-aware enough to question her own motives.

She was a known face on CNN, reporting from all over the world. People often recognized her on the street, but she was not in the Christiane Amanpour class. Amanpour made at least half a million dollars a year, if rumor was correct. Amanpour put herself in harm's way, going into any trouble zone. But then, so did Gabby and Justin. So did Amanpour's photographer, of course. And staff.

"Justin," Gabrielle said, "when reporters go into danger, the public sees the tapes and thinks how brave they are. But the public hardly ever realizes that they wouldn't be seeing them at all there unless there was a cameraman standing right there too."

"Naturally."

"Doesn't that make you angry?"

"Curse of the profession," he said, leaning back comfortably. "You're the pretty face. I am the invisible man."

She didn't think her face was so wonderful. Like a lot of on-screen women reporters, she had rather large features—a broad mouth, big dark eyes, wide face, and thin nose. All her childhood she had considered herself ugly. In high school, she had been the too-tall girl, gangly and awkward, with the big bones and big face. Her straight hair was a chestnut brown color, which she considered undistinguished. She had longed for curly blond California surfer-girl hair. Instead she had hair inherited from her grandmother, who had come to the United States from Belarus. Oddly, the reddish brown hair photographed rich, dark red. On camera her face looked chiseled and elegant. She was a striking figure—on film. Now and then, somebody meeting her in person would say, "On television you look so much—" and then the sentence would screech to an abrupt halt, before the speaker could say "prettier."

Gabrielle said, "Our lives are so easy. We have food and families and a warm place to live. These children have nothing."

"Come on. There's misery in the world. All the reporting you've done, Gabby, wars and famine, you know a lot about misery. That doesn't mean we're not entitled to live our lives."

"But how can we be happy, knowing all the time these babies are suffering?"

"Help where you can, when you can."

"All our talk about getting married and having children—"

"Two. Two children. And take them every place we go to see the whole world with us."

"How can we justify having children of our own when these children are dying? I wouldn't even buy a puppy as long as there are dogs in the pound waiting for homes."

Justin got up, took two more rough blankets from the closet, and carried them to the bed.

"Gabby, you're tired. I'll turn out the light. We can think about this tomorrow."

# 4

When Gabrielle woke up the next morning, she put her feet to the floor, screamed, and jumped up and down on one foot. The floor was so icy, it hurt.

Justin sat up. "What's wrong?"

"Just cold. I'm sorry. I didn't mean to wake you."

Justin leaped out of bed and grabbed her up in his arms. Then he started dancing from foot to foot, shouting, "Yipe! Yipe! That's really cold!"

"Put me down, silly," she said, giggling.

He danced her over to her pile of clothes and lowered her enough so she could grab up her thick socks and pull them on as he held her in the air.

He said, "Now I know where they get that cossack dance where they squat down and kick out one foot and then the other."

They both fell back onto the bed laughing. Gabrielle put her feet under the covers for a couple of minutes, then reached out and took her clothes from the varnished wood chair. She hurried on two shirts, Levi's, and her shoes.

She said, "Would we be suffering like this if Sam were here?"

Justin said, "Sam's the one who got us this hotel."

"Well, location-wise it's pretty much the only hotel that makes sense to be in."

Sam Bielski was their field producer. Producers do all the work or not much, depending on the company, the shoot, and the producer. On shoots outside the United States, producers usually did a lot of work. When Gabrielle and Justin decided to take several months off to make their own documentary, Sam agreed to help out from home and to go on the actual shoots whenever he could.

Producers usually did all the unappreciated work, all the business end of things. Sam had set up the itinerary and located some of the sources, although Gabrielle had used some of her contacts as well. Ordinarily Sam would handle most of the money and the bribes to local officials. Bribing local officials was so commonplace that they had a separate item line for it on their expense forms. A lot of places you had to bribe officials to let you into the country and then a second time to let you take your equipment out at the end of the shoot. Bielski also dealt with visas and all the other paperwork. Fortunately, he'd done most of that before he got sick. Bielski had contracted listeriosis from a piece of contaminated soft cheese. He had been very sick. When Justin had said to Bielski's doctor, "If it's just food poisoning, won't he be over it in time to go to Russia?" the doctor had made it quite clear that it wasn't *just* food poisoning although it was a foodborne illness.

"Listeria is not an upset stomach. It's got a twenty percent mortality rate. Mr. Bielski will be very lucky if he's back on his feet in three weeks."

Bielski, even though he was feeling horrible, was mostly outraged that he'd been all over the world, eating food swarming with all kinds of unfamiliar bacteria, and he had to be felled by a bit of Brie from a restaurant just off Park Avenue.

Gabrielle got into her coat, scarf, and mittens. She said, "I'm going down the hall to the bathroom and then out to get hot tea. And rolls."

"Let me go," Justin said.

"No. I'm all set."

"You're a saint. This isn't the sort of place where you call for room service."

"No."

"I'll go for the rolls tomorrow. And when we get back to New York I'm going to take you to the Russian Tea Room. Leave a good taste of Russia in your mouth."

"By going home to eat?"

"Why not?"

"Tomorrow at noon we get to leave for home."

Justin heard the relief in her voice. "Don't like it here?"

"It's just so depressing."

"A couple of weeks editing and postpro on this and you'll be ready to go again, do the last two countries."

"China first. I'm looking forward to it."

"You were looking forward to Russia before we actually got here."

# 5

The street in front of the hotel ran east-west. East led to the orphanage, less than two miles away, which made this the perfect hotel to stay in. It was also the only hotel for quite a stretch. West led to several nearby small shops, including a wonderful bakery. The Metropole served breakfast, but the breads were cold and dense. Two days ago, a well-meaning traveling merchant staying at the Metropole had encouraged her to try *kumys*, which he said was a breakfast typical in the eastern part of the old Soviet Union. *Kumys* smelled like sour yogurt and was lumpy. Gabby had not liked the taste of it, and could not imagine how Russians could bear the thought of it on a cold winter morning like this.

There were delicious smells from the bakery, which Gabby scented even from three blocks away. As she walked, she reflected on the bad and the good news. The bad news was that the hotel rooms were cold. The good news was that outdoors was about the same temperature, so you had no shock to the system when you stepped outside.

There was a line at the shop. There were always lines in Russia. This one was shorter than most, maybe twenty-five or thirty people. Gabby suspected that the prices here were too high for most Russians.

In general, the food wasn't bad in Moscow, even though the dining room at the hotel was very poor. Gabby had been told by half a dozen Russians that in the big cities the days of nothing but borscht and kasha were long gone. It made sense, because it was the big cities where most of the emmigrants from other parts of the former Soviet Union had settled, and as a result you could find restaurants serving good Asian, Siberian, or Baltic food. If you were particularly homesick, Moscow even had a McDonald's and a Taco Bell.

Still, the Russian ways were old-fashioned enough not to be conducive to fast food in local stores. Gabby waited in line over half an hour just to get inside, into the warmth where the baked goods were. Then she had to decide what she wanted. She could not just ask for it and pay. She had to get in line for the sales clerk and request the price. The clerks spoke a bit of basic English, but that didn't make the process any faster. Having arrived at a price, Gabrielle had to get in a new line for the cashier. After a wait, she reached the elderly woman who worked the register. She announced her intended purchase and the price. Sullenly, the woman punched up a receipt, and after Gabby paid, she moved to yet another line. Here there was another wait, then she surrendered her sales slip and the final clerk handed her the pastries—*zavyvanets*, which were a sort of crumb bun, and *pampushky*, which were like doughnut holes. Gabby had a brief instant of misgiving, thinking of eating warm bread while the children in the orphanage were receiving the minimum ration of food, probably cold formula.

With her purchases rolled into a sheet of newspaper, she clutched the fresh-baked breads to her chest to help keep warm while she walked the three blocks back to the hotel.

At the hotel, she stopped in the lobby, a cavernous, grim square room with one small window. She had brought two thick coffee mugs from her bedroom, carrying them in her big purse along with her phrase book and passport and visa and money and extra digital camera and tapes and cosmetics and so on. Now she filled the mugs from the flimsy plastic and steel dispenser of hot tea that the hotel was so proud of. It was in the travel guides: "Hot tea served from a samovar in the lobby throughout the morning for the convenience and delight of our guests." Somehow it sounded better when you were 4,681 miles away. Samovar indeed!

# 6

Balancing the mugs on top of each other while holding the clumsy newspaper package of breads was hard enough. When she tried to get the room key out of her purse, the tea threatened to spill. She dropped the wrapped bread gently to the floor while she groped for the metal room key.

It twisted in the lock and she pushed the door open.

It was the wrong room. Hers had been dreary, gray, and, except for their equipment, barren. This one was painted red. With sparkling—

—broken glass. Pieces of video gear. Ripped clothing. A pile of red clothing.

Justin was the pile of clothing. His face was red. A wound in his throat had spurted across the walls and a pool of red had flowed across the bare floor to the door.

Gabrielle moaned and jumped back, stepping on the parcel of bread. The mugs of tea fell forward, spilling down her leg and into her shoe, burning her. One mug cracked on the floor with a sound like a shot. She jumped over the mugs and ran to Justin.

He was warm to her touch. Despite the huge quantity of blood, she desperately hoped he was still alive. Gabrielle put her ear to his chest, trying to hear his heart. There was no sound. She touched the artery in the left side of his neck—the right carotid had been slashed—and found no pulse. He wasn't breathing. She yelled, "Help! Help! Help!" through the open door of the room, then she blew into his mouth, as she had been taught to do in CPR classes. His chest rose as she did so. Then fell, and didn't rise until she blew again.

Some hotel guests appeared in the hall, peeking in the still open door. She screamed, "Get doctors! Get doctors!" Some of these people must speak English. "Get doctors! *Medecins.* Doctors! Please!" she screamed again and one of them said, "Okay," and ran.

She blew into Justin's mouth, then gave him five chest thrusts, then repeated this over again and again. After several minutes, she picked him up to listen for a spontaneous breath, pressing her ear to his open mouth. No sound. The deep gash in his throat was covered in a scarf of blood, but blood was no longer flowing out of it. Gabrielle laid him on his back and started chest compressions again. One, two, three, four, five, then blow in the mouth. One, two, three, four, five, then blow in the mouth. One, two, three, four—

Ages later, somebody put a hand on her shoulder. A slender man in his twenties gently moved her aside and took over. Gabrielle now had time to look into Justin's wide-open eyes. Wide open, dilated, and unblinking.

# Chapter Four

Faline is a darling baby from Central America. She
has chubby cheeks and brown eyes and black hair. At
the age of two and a half, she is giving and patient.
She would give you much love too, if you could be a
family to her.
Phone us at . . .

## 1

### New York City
### Mid-November

Dooley arrived at Children's Hospital early for his meeting with
Benny Batali. Benny was a guy Dooley had always kind of envied. In
med school, Benny had an easy manner with women, never seemed to
feel ugly or awkward, like Dooley often did. The funny thing was,
Dooley knew that objectively speaking Benny wasn't any more movie-
star, leading-man handsome than Dooley was. Dooley considered
himself pleasant enough looking, and that pretty much described
Benny too.

The other odd thing was that, even though Benny had dated all
the great-looking women in their med school class, as well as the class
ahead of them and the class behind them, he didn't really care about
sex and women all that much.

Benny wanted to fix sick children. It was all he seemed to want in life. A couple of mutual friends said he had no other life. They said it as a criticism. Dooley thought Benny was a truly happy man. He had asked Dooley to meet him in the cafeteria at Children's Hospital today, because he refused to take more time off than the minimum necessary for their chat.

"So what is this question you have?" he asked Dooley. "You stayed with pathology, right? You're not going into pediatrics now?"

"No, no." Dooley had it all worked out that he would pretend he was asking for a friend. The friend lived abroad with his son. There was this problem he couldn't find out about in a foreign country. And so forth. Off the beaten track. Tibet, maybe. Now that he saw Benny face-to-face, though, he couldn't lie, but he couldn't tell him the facts either. Right now he feared there was something terribly wrong with the adoption, and he didn't dare have people wondering whether it had been legitimate. "Benny, can I just ask you about some stuff and not explain?"

Benny closed one eye, turned his head, and regarded Dooley as an owl might. "Sure, pal. Go ahead."

"I know you don't usually give tetracycline to children because it stains their teeth. In young babies the teeth are still forming in the jaw, so they're especially vulnerable. Still, is there *any* reason you'd give it to a child under seven months?"

"Well, sure, sometimes. If you think other antibiotics won't work. Or if you tried them and they weren't effective. You'd do a susceptibility plate testing first. I mean, no sense exposing a child to the problems if it isn't going to work on whatever bug they have anyway. You ever seen tetracycline-stained teeth?"

"I don't think so. Not even in med school, as far as I can remember."

"Doesn't happen much anymore. They're a really yucky grayish, dirty-looking yellowish-greenish-brown."

"Do they use tetracycline on children in other countries around the world?"

"Some. Everything is always different in different countries. What's the real problem here, Dooley?"

"Wait. Tell me. For what diseases?"

"Rocky Mountain spotted fever, typhus, tick fever. Brucella. Some *E.coli.* Tetracycline is the treatment of choice for gingivitis. In *adults.*"

"Well, when exactly would you give it to an infant?"

"Say you had an infection that isn't responding to whatever you've been using. God knows, what with overusing antibiotics, we're developing a hell of a lot of drug-resistant strains of perfectly ordinary organisms. Yeah, then you might try tetracycline."

"Despite the staining."

"Well, there comes a point where if an infection is life-threatening, the teeth just don't seem so important anymore."

"I can believe that."

"Anyway, say you've got a child with an infection resistant to other antibiotics. You run a Kirby-Bauer with a thirty-microgram disc of tetracycline against your organism. You're looking for a dead zone nineteen millimeters around it to show that the stuff works. You certainly don't want to use it if it doesn't kill the little buggers. Is this child we're being so careful not to talk about allergic to the penicillin family?"

"Uh—I don't know."

"Well, that's another possible reason. Also, if it's a brief use for an overwhelming infection, say a week or so, staining the teeth isn't so likely. It's long-term use that really discolors them. We sometimes use tetracycline for sick preemies, and when we do, the growth of the fibula is slowed down. But the leg catches up after you stop the drug."

Was Teddy allergic to penicillin? Dooley didn't know. He'd been perfectly healthy since they had him. Nothing worse than a couple of colds. Up to four weeks ago at least. And anyway, if there was so little medicine in Russia to begin with, would the Russian doctors have given him penicillin and then when they saw it didn't work switched him to tetracycline? It made no sense. Plus, he'd now repeatedly studied Teddy's medical records from Russia, which covered his life from birth to the moment he left the country with Dooley and Claudia, and they showed no use of any antibiotic whatsoever.

"Dooley?" Benny said. "Later on, when whatever this is has blown over, will you tell me what it was all about?"

"Yeah, Benny. I will."

# 2

Dooley's former professor, Dr. Abner Gerdman, was sixty-seven years old, and a midget.

Abner was exactly four feet, two inches tall. He was not a small person, he was a real, genuine midget, or had thought of himself that way all his life. Recently the term "midget" had gone out of favor, being considered offensive, and people with his body type in size and shape were now called proportionate dwarfism, although he personally stuck with midget. Proportionate dwarfs had a body proportioned like the average person, but much smaller. The condition was caused by a hormonal deficiency, and if he had been born twenty years later, he could have been treated medically. The more common type of dwarfism, achondroplasia, was produced by a gene. An achondroplastic dwarf had legs and arms that were shorter than most people's, a large head, a large forehead, and an average size torso. There was no treatment, except for some controversial, painful, bone-lengthening surgery that was fraught with complications and sometimes didn't work.

Abner had a beard, which he let grow long. His lab assistants, with the irreverence of medical people, called him Rumpelstiltskin. Dooley thought Abner liked the nickname very much.

Abner belonged to the Little People of America society, subscribed to little people's newsmagazines, belonged to the Dwarf Athletic Association, was an activist for dwarfs, and when he was out on the street, he didn't take any guff from anybody. If somebody made a stupid remark about his size, and people made stupid remarks all the time, he was likely to say, "You there, brontosaurus boy—big body, tiny brain." If they didn't get the point, he would say, "Everybody's the same size with a Tec nine," and pat his jacket. He didn't carry a Tec 9, but he carried a lot of combativeness.

And a big heart. Dooley thought it was curious that Abner had not gone into endocrinology, since dwarfism was traditionally considered to be a condition dealt with by endocrinologists. However, his interest was bones.

Abner was a leading figure in bone research. He was well funded and so internationally prominent in his field that St. Vincent's Hospital had been happy to give him the perfect lab. Table surfaces were fourteen inches lower than in most labs. Light switches and the cranks on the windows were lower too. His assistants had no problem with this. They did a lot of work sitting down that people in other labs usually did standing up. And they liked it that way.

Abner met Dooley at the coffee bar called the Brew-Ha-Ha across the street from the hospital. Dooley noticed that Abner's hair was much grayer than when they last met.

"How long has it been, Dooley?"

"I hate to think. Four years maybe."

"We ought to get together more often." Abner cocked his head. Then he pointed at Dooley's espresso, said, "Too much coffee will stunt your growth," and laughed uproariously. "Actually it won't. So— I think this isn't a social occasion. What do you need from me?"

"I have a bone specimen that fluoresces. It's from—"

"Yellow-green?"

"Yes. How did you know?"

"It's tetracycline."

"Well, yeah, I guess so."

"Who's the patient?"

"A boy. Four years old."

"So he's been treated with tetracycline. What's the problem with that?"

"The problem is it appears he's never been treated with tetracycline. What other kinds of things could make bones fluoresce?"

"Nothing."

"Nothing at all?"

"Nope."

"Pollution? Ionizing radiation? Heavy metals?"

"Nothing, Dooley. If he's fluorescing, he's been treated with tetracycline."

"He *can't* have been!"

Now Abner studied Dooley with caution. "Who is this child?"

"That's not important. Abner, what about prenatal exposure?"

"Well, that's not impossible, of course."

"Could you tell from a bone specimen when the child got the tetracycline?"

"Possibly. If the specimen had a little variety of bone in it."

# 3

Twenty minutes later in Abner's lab, under the watchful empty eye sockets of a mounted human skeleton hanging from a hook, Dooley was listening to a lecture. As he spoke, Abner studied the scraps of bone in a fluorescing microscope, then switched to a standard light microscope.

"You realize," he said, "that an unborn child has bones that are largely uncalcified. They are mostly cartilage and quite pliable. Put another way, a baby's mostly rubber. A human's bones ossify slowly, over a period of years. They aren't really fully ossified until a person is in his twenties. That's one of the ways forensic pathologists tell the age of skeletons. As a doctor, you're aware of this yourself. Dooley, why do you give me this story?"

"What story? It's true. It's important to know how old he was when he got the medication."

"Dooley, come on. You bring me this specimen. You act like you're James Bond. Your slides are unlabeled. You've got little flakes of pelvic bone in a bag. You're nervous or frightened, I can't tell which. And I can't for the life of me imagine what could be so important about whether or not somebody had been given tetracycline at a specific age. Was the patient allergic? Is this a malpractice case? Are the child's teeth stained? Are you being sued?"

"It's nothing like that. Please, Abner. Just tell me."

Abner sighed theatrically. "Do you know the way the pelvis develops?"

"I haven't thought about it even once since med school. After I passed the exams I didn't need to know it anymore."

"Typical. Thousands of researchers, decades of study, the glory of the human body revealed, and students forget it on the way out the door. Okay. Look over there. Remove the femur." Abner pointed to the skeleton. The pelvis formed a shallow bowl, somewhat tilted, capable of holding up the abdominal guts. On the left and right outsides of the pelvis were the sockets into which the upper leg bones fitted. Dooley unhooked one from its small hook-and-eye attachment.

"The pelvis ossifies from three principal centers. At birth most of the pelvic girdle is still cartilage. As I said, most of a baby's skeleton is cartilage, not bone. Easier to be all curled up in utero. Easier to be squeezed through the birth canal. And easier for a child to grow if everything isn't set in stone, so to speak."

"Which is why the long bones ossify at the ends first, and make their fast growth in the middles."

"Ah! He remembers something! Who says there are no miracles? The pelvis develops hard bone essentially from three centers—here at the top of the crest, here at the top of the pubis, and here at the ischium. There are smaller centers as it goes on, but that's the gist of it. They come together where the head of the femur goes in."

"I see." There was a little Y-shaped seam in the socket where the final joining up had taken place.

"At birth they haven't come together yet. By the age of seven or eight, the bottom of the pelvic girdle has united. By the age of twelve or thirteen the crest is starting to fuse with the pubis. The whole pelvis combination isn't totally hard bone until the age of twenty to twenty-five." He stopped talking, studying the bone and slides more carefully. He tapped the slide with his forefinger. "This is from a biopsy, possibly to determine whether the child has leukemia?"

"Yes. He hasn't. It was mono." Dooley remembered his relief, which he still felt and would always feel, no matter what happened now.

"And the biopsy was done in the usual site?"

"Yes. Right here." Dooley pointed to the crest.

"Okay." Abner came back and sat down. "When the baby is new-born, this area is mostly cartilage. Infants sit up around six months. They stand around nine months. They walk at a year to a year and a half. Each of these stages is accompanied by some necessary additional solidification of the bone. You can understand why."

"Yes. Of course."

"So each stage requires the deposit of more calcium. And since tetracycline binds to calcium, they're laid down together."

"Tetracycline can be passed to an unborn baby from the mother, can't it?" He hoped he didn't sound as desperate as he felt.

"Oh absolutely. Dooley, listen to what I'm telling you—the question is where in the bone the tetracycline is laid down. It's a marker of bone growth. In the lab here, we often use tetracycline to measure the rate of bone formation. We can do a bone biopsy a few months after we give somebody the antibiotic, and you can look at the bone in UV light and know exactly where the patient is laying down bone and where he isn't."

"The tetracycline should fade away after a while, though, shouldn't it?"

"Nope. Once it's bound up with calcium in the bone, it's there essentially as long as the bone lasts. If your patient were mummified and entombed in an Egyptian pyramid, five thousand years later his bones would still fluoresce."

"Then—when was this tetracycline laid down?"

"It's in bone that formed in the baby sometime around the sixth month after birth. Possibly as early as four months and not later than one year of age."

# CHAPTER FIVE

Senator Philbert:            I resent that implication. What exactly are you implying?

Investigator Sample:      I am implying, Senator, that your committee has made no effort to task the FBI with apprehending baby-selling cartels.

Senator Philbert:            I must remind you, Mr. Sample, that there is no federal law against baby selling.

## 1
### Moscow
### Mid-November

"When did you leave the hotel room?" the police interpreter asked Gabrielle.

"I want to talk to somebody from the United States Embassy."

There was an exchange in Russian. The interpreter was a very thin middle-aged man with spare hair and a sunken chest who spoke to Gabrielle absolutely without emotion. The policeman was much more like the popular notion of a Soviet detective, and given his age was probably a man who had worked under the Soviet regime with all of its harsh methods. He had retained a lot of its mannerisms even though the Soviet Union had not existed since 1991. Before she left for Russia, Gabrielle had been told by a friend, "Don't expect that all the KGB agents have just evaporated." The police station, too, had a very Soviet look about it.

He was square-bodied, built like a cinder block, with a five o'clock shadow and wiry dark hair on the backs of his hands. He looked angry. The translator, the cop, and Gabrielle were in a plain office in a room on the second floor of police headquarters.

"The embassy has been informed," the interpreter told her, after translating her words for the policeman. "When did you leave the hotel room?"

"The employees in the bakery saw me." *Am I in real danger? Should I say nothing at all, or tell them the truth and hope they'll believe me and let me go?*

"How long were you in the bakery?"

"Almost an hour. I want to talk with a representative of the United States Embassy. Now." Gabrielle was adamant. She had been in twenty or thirty countries as a reporter and had worked in the news business all around the world for thirteen years, most recently for three months in Afghanistan. She knew what her rights were, not United States rights, which didn't apply here, but her rights as a foreign national. She also knew that those rights would not necessarily be honored. However, the Russians no doubt appreciated the fact that she was a person with a certain amount of renown. She could wait them out.

Where was Sam Bielski when you needed him?

"Why did you go out of the room?"

She didn't answer. *Isn't it obvious? To get pastries! To get pastries! Maybe I should tell him everything. He's just badgering me for his own enjoyment. He knows I'm not involved in Justin's death. Doesn't he? Doesn't he?*

"Was Mr. Justin Craig dead when you left him?"

She didn't answer, instead folding her arms across her chest. The cop was angrier and barked a question at the interpreter.

"Why was Mr. Craig in your room? He had a room of his own." The interrogator looked stern.

"I want to talk to the American embassy."

"Did you and Mr. Craig have an argument?"

She didn't answer. There was blood on her hands, blood on her knees, blood on her face and mouth where she had given Justin CPR. She wanted to cry for Justin, and she would, but not right now.

"Why did you not call for the police immediately?"

Firmly, she said, "I was giving him CPR."

"Was Mr. Craig dead before you went to the bakery?"

# 2

If she had been cold last night and cold this morning, she was now chilled to the bone. They left her sitting in the interrogation room. Three hours went by. A pale boy who looked twelve years old came in with lukewarm tea in a glass and she was grateful for it. It stopped her shivering for a while.

Sometime during the fourth hour, one of the other police officers led in a man wearing a dark suit, white shirt, and blue-and-red striped tie. He blinked when he saw the amount of blood on Gabrielle's clothes, face, hands, and hair. "Henry Stover," he said. "I am first assistant to the ambassador."

The big police officer barked out some Russian. Stover translated. "The women at the bakery verify that you were there a long while." More Russian.

"Also, certain other hotel guests heard sounds," Stover said, "bumping and such, and place the time during the period that the women say you were at the bakery."

Gabrielle said, "If they heard the attack, they should have called somebody. They should have called the manager."

Stover said more gently, "It would take a lot more than a few bumps and thumps for anybody to call anybody around here. I've lived in Russia quite a while, and I can tell you that for certain."

The police officer growled out several sentences. He sounded grudging.

Stover said, "He says you have a great deal of blood on you, but none of it is spattered. It is all consistent, he says, with your story of trying to revive Mr. Craig. Whoever killed him would have been extensively spattered." He hesitated, apparently out of a sense of delicacy, and then must have decided that he was obligated to translate fully. "The way the walls were spattered," he added.

"Thank you, Mr. Stover." Gabrielle was careful to keep her voice firm. The police must hear that they hadn't frightened her.

"They are returning your purse. Or bag."

"Good."

Her shoulder bag was carried in by a short woman with hair dyed a strange henna shade. Stover said without inflection, "They've been through it thoroughly by now. Trust me on this." After a couple of seconds, he added, "Thoroughly."

"Can they do that?"

"Of course. They could in the U.S. too."

"They could search my property in the U.S. if I'd been arrested. But not if I'm just a witness."

"We'll be happy—we *are* happy—that they now consider you only an important witness."

She took his point. "Right. Well, there's nothing illegal in my purse. Or in anything else of mine."

She looked into the bag, nevertheless, to see whether everything was there. The three digital cassettes looked as if they had been viewed. One was put into its sleeve backward. But apparently they were intact. Three thirty-minute cassettes, an hour and a half of raw footage. Enough for the Russian segment if she ever finished the documentary.

"They want you to go to your hotel room with them and see what's missing."

Gabrielle hesitated.

Stover said, "I can tell them that to do so would be cruel to you. They can't make you do it. I could tell them you'd draw up a list of whatever was in the room."

"No! I'll go. I want to see what those killers did to Justin. And me."

## 4

"Where is Justin?" she asked, the instant they entered her hotel room.

Stover translated the question and then answered her. "They've taken the body to the medico-legal institute."

"Of course," she said.

She had been so focused on the possibility of seeing Justin's body where she had left it that she had hardly noticed the room. But now the amount of damage leaped to her eye. Her clothing had been thrown around on the floor. The video equipment she had kept here, just a backup camera, some extra tapes, a Polaroid for checking scene layouts, and a Polaroid CU-5 for small details she might want to show in the finished documentary, her own cellphone, chargers, and cables, all had been destroyed, the equipment crushed, the cables cut. Forcing herself to keep her mind on the condition of the room rather than on the thought of Justin, growing cold in some concrete morgue, she tried to guess how much noise this destruction had made. And she decided maybe not too much. Most pieces of their equipment looked as if they had been stepped on. Only the clothes had been thrown around.

The room smelled of old blood.

On the walls were swags of blood. Drips had trailed down from the swags, but they were dry now and the color had changed from red to rusty brown. Blood was everywhere.

"Why so much blood?" she said to herself.

But Stover responded, "They said he had a throat wound. It must have spurted."

She nodded. She already knew that, better than any of them. "Tell them I don't see anything missing. Justin's wallet is there on the table. If his money is in it—"

"How much money?"

"We had about two hundred dollars American. We got money from an ATM when we needed it. We have a policy—had a policy not to carry a lot."

While Stover translated, one of the police officers checked the wallet. Gabrielle believed he was doing this as a show to intimidate her, which was *not* going to work. She saw that there was whitish fingerprint powder on the dark leather wallet. Somebody had already investigated it.

The officer held out the money for her to look at, fanning it. But not giving it to her.

"That looks about right," she said.

As she turned to study the rest of the room, she recoiled. "What's that?"

There were spray-painted words in Cyrillic letters on the back of the room's door.

Stover told her, "It says, 'Go home. Do not make our country look bad.'"

"Do they mean our documentary?"

"I imagine so."

Gabrielle felt sick. But these police officers would never know it. Making fists of her hands to keep focused, she demanded, "I'm here. I've looked around. Now, is there anything else I have to do?"

Stover translated the question and the reply: "You need to look at Mr. Craig's room."

It too, had been trashed. The equipment was destroyed, the tripod bent, the laptop computer eviscerated, the Panasonic portable editor filled with glue, the camera smashed, batteries split open, and the cassettes of the orphanage were piled in the room's small sink, soaking in water and soap. "Our work," Gabrielle said. "All our work." She took one cassette and started to lift it from the water, but the police officer barked, "Nyet!" and she dropped it. It was evidence, she supposed. And what difference did it make to her now? It was ruined, it was hopeless.

Unlike hers, this room stank of battery chemicals, but at least not of blood. On the door of this room was the same message as the one in her room.

"I want to leave now," Gabrielle said. Stover translated to the policeman, who waited a full minute, then nodded and turned his back on her.

"Will I be able to leave Russia?"

"Probably not right away," Stover said. "Will you want to accompany his body home?"

"Oh. Of course I will."

"Then you have to expect to wait several days."

Gabrielle shivered. "Can you find me a place in a safer hotel?"

"I think so."

The lead investigator said something.

"He says 'Just a minute.'" Stover listened and then translated, "He wants to ask you about something."

The policeman pulled a VHS tape in a cardboard sleeve from his coat pocket.

"He says what do you know about this tape?"

Gabrielle stared at it. "Nothing. I don't know anything about it. It's not the brand we use. See?" She pointed at the boxes from their destroyed tapes, which littered the floor. "What you have there is ordinary Fuji VHS. We use digital cassettes. They're much smaller." Gabrielle narrowed her eyes at the officer. She knew he couldn't understand her, but she challenged him directly. "Why? What are you trying to do?"

Stover didn't translate her words to the officer. Pointing to the Fuji tape, he said, "Ms. Coulter, they found this tape in your room."

"That doesn't make sense. It isn't ours."

"And they want you to come back to the police department and view it."

# 5

"The idea," Stover told her half an hour later in the office, "is that you are to explain to them what you think of the content."

"Why would I be able to explain it? I told you, it isn't ours. What is the tape of?"

"I don't know."

"You haven't seen it?"

"No and they won't tell me anything."

# 6

The big officer had lowered the room lights.

*They're watching me. They're watching me watch this, because they want to see how I react. I won't give them the satisfaction.*

When the video began and she realized what she was about to see, tears began to run down her face.

The tape was in full color but without sound. The camera moved down the hall of the Metropole Hotel, following a man seen by the camera only from behind. The picture swayed a little; the camera was handheld. The man approached the door of Gabrielle's hotel room and knocked. Nothing happened. The man knocked a second time on the door. He wore a heavy khaki-colored coat, gloves, and, like most of the population this time of year in Russia, a thick black knitted cap. At the third knock the door began to open. Justin's arm and shoulder were visible in the opening. As the door opened wider, the intruder, still seen only from behind, pulled the cap down over his face. It was a ski mask with holes for eyes and mouth.

Justin must have been expecting Gabrielle. He must have thought she couldn't carry the tea and pastries and open the door too. He was barefoot, half dressed, and looked cold. When he saw the masked man at the door, he stood up straighter, surprised, his mouth a big O that might have been comical if the situation hadn't been deadly.

The man in the ski mask pushed inside. As he got farther from the camera, more of his body was visible—lean and of medium height. The cameraman followed him into the room. The masked man shoved Justin hard toward the far wall and very methodically swept the video equipment to the floor, where he carefully stepped on each piece. Justin leaped forward as the man approached their extra SX camera. The man backhanded Justin across the face, but Justin was a big man and he rebounded with his fists up and punched the man in the stomach. The man doubled forward.

When the masked man straightened up, he was holding a box cutter. The blade reflected the room light. Seeing this, Justin backed away, but the man pursued him step by measured step until he had backed Justin into the wall. Then he slashed. Justin had his hands up, the left hand fending off the attack. His right hand punched the man in the face. But the box cutter was sharp, slicing through Justin's left forearm, severing the muscles on its underside. Without the muscle tension on both sides of the arm, the hand flopped upward, pulled by the upper side muscles.

Justin blocked with his elbow. He was bigger, but he was essentially one-handed now. And the element of surprise had crippled him too. The man sliced at Justin's right wrist, hitting the fingers instead, and as Justin recoiled, sliced across his neck.

Justin staggered back, spraying blood. The spurts were visible as pulsing red streams. His blood went everywhere, gouts and jets in time with the pumping of Justin's heart.

The masked man now turned and ignored Justin, who crumpled

to the floor a couple of steps from the bed. The camera followed the masked man as he took a can of bright red spray paint from his pocket and sprayed the back of the door with Russian letters.

Then the video ended. The big cop gave an order. Somebody turned up the lights. Gabrielle heard one of the police officers spit out a word she had no need to translate. "Hooligans!"

Gabrielle demanded, "How could you have questioned me like a suspect? You had this tape all along?" But when the cop simply shrugged, she realized they would say she might have been behind the attack in some way. From their point of view, she had been so conveniently out of the hotel at the important time.

She discovered that she was holding her breath, holding in her rage at Justin's terrible death. Taking a deep breath, she commanded them, "You find those men. You go out there and find those men!"

# Chapter Six

In the late 1800s, the Chicago Nursery and Half-Orphan Asylum helped many children. However, it would not accept "children of unworthy families" such as children of the irremediably unemployed or the children of alcoholics.

—*Favorite Facts,* vol. 23

## 1

## New York City
## Mid-November

Dooley had been on evenings that week, three to eleven. Generally the surgical pathologists at Beekman took late shifts in turn. There were far fewer surgeries in the evening, of course, most of them emergency operations, so the staffing was cut back. Sometimes Dooley was the only board-registered surgical pathologist in the unit. This was both the good news and the bad news. The good news was that he didn't have to act happy for his colleagues. The bad news was that it gave him time to think. He seemed to turn the same worries over and over and never resolve them.

The schedule was a help at home though. Since nanny Annalise was in the apartment to ride herd on Teddy during the day, Dooley had time to web search while Claudia was out of the house at her nine-to-five job at the United Nations. Two days a week, Teddy went to playschool in the mornings. Annalise shopped for groceries and then picked him up.

At work, when there was a tissue sample to analyze, Dooley was able to force his mind to stay on his job; his years of training stood him good stead. He was well aware that if he made a mistake in diagnosis, a human being could die. When the surgeon was looking for a tumor-free margin, slowly paring away more and more tissue after the original mass had been cut out, taking more and more flesh until no sign of malignancy remained in the removed pieces, Dr. Dooley McSweeney's word was what guided the surgeon's hand.

He must not have looked quite himself though. Two or three of his colleagues in recent days asked him if he was all right. Of course they expected him to be ebullient about Teddy's good health. Looking as pensive as he did seemed inappropriate. By way of explanation, he mumbled, "I'm fine. It just makes you think. How valuable life is." This wasn't even really like him. He tended to be self-deprecating, to make jokes when he was upset.

They accepted his excuses. When he took his midshift "lunch-break," which was usually around seven P.M., instead of staying at his desk with his head in his hands as he felt like doing, he was careful to go to the cafeteria and sit chatting with a couple of staffers. Act as normal as possible.

During the days, he was at home at noon for the real lunch hour. Claudia was at work; she didn't often come home for lunch. The U.N. was eighteen blocks away.

Dooley was ashamed that he was so glad to have the whole day without Claudia around. Since his discovery several days earlier and his follow-ups with Benny and Rumpelstiltskin, he found it even harder to keep up a happy front for her than for his work colleagues. Certainly he couldn't tell her about his suspicions that there was something wrong about Teddy's adoption. He didn't know enough facts yet, but that wasn't the main reason. Dooley had an uneasy sense that she wouldn't react the way he had to the horrible situation. She would probably want him to stop his search and keep quiet. He wasn't sure how he guessed that. Nothing remotely like this had ever happened to either of them. They'd led a very blessed life so far. But now he saw catastrophe looming ahead for both him and Claudia. What if Teddy had been kidnapped from perfectly good, legitimate parents? Would Claudia insist on keeping him if she knew he belonged to someone else?

And for that matter, would he?

Would she take Teddy and run? Disappear with him, with nobody knowing where the two had gone. Other parents had done exactly that, rather than give up a child.

As he walked home about eleven P.M., going east on Fifty-sixth Street, he tried to consider the possibilities methodically. That should have been no problem. He was methodical in his work. You didn't just wing it in pathology. He was a moderate man, careful with his life. He usually considered options before jumping into things or making a rash decision.

For days now he couldn't think straight.

The nights he was on the late shift, Dooley went to bed the moment he got home at eleven-thirty, and he woke up around eight A.M. That gave him a chance to play with Teddy. The last few days he'd been sleeping badly, either having nightmares or waking too early.

He forced himself to stay in bed until eight o'clock so as to appear normal, but today when he heard sounds from the kitchen at seven, he got up to eat breakfast with Teddy and Claudia. Claudia was making waffles, one of Teddy's favorites.

"You're up early," Claudia said.

"Oh, I didn't notice the time," he lied.

"What are your plans for the day?"

"Doing some studying at home. Why?"

"Maybe we could have dinner out, in the middle of your shift. Annalise's willing to stay. Say seven?"

Dooley's heart sank at the idea of sitting with Claudia over a nice dinner and keeping up a brave face. "I'd like that," he said. "But I'm not sure who's covering. I mean, I'm usually supposed to be within pager distance."

Maybe he should just tell her his fears. No, he should wait until he knew more.

"No problem," she said. "Let's go to Orso's."

Orso's was a block from Beekman Hospital. It was a favorite of the staff. He was trapped. His heart sank. "Great idea," he said.

"And don't forget, we have that benefit we have to go to at the U.N. on Friday."

Claudia left, Annalise arrived, and Dooley went to his in-home office. He took with him a mug of coffee, a glass of water, and four aspirins, all of which he swallowed immediately.

His fears were a jumble. This made Dooley furious with himself. You didn't go to medical school, four years of study, then interning and residency, and the rigors of pathology, a field that was nothing if not detail-oriented, without being able to organize material. This had to be analyzable. If Teddy had not been the Russian orphan he was supposed to be, he was something else. Was he not Russian? Or did it matter exactly where he was from? Maybe what mattered was whether he was an orphan at all. Yes, certainly that was the important thing. If he wasn't the child he was supposed to be, maybe he wasn't an orphan.

He was probably Irish, at least in some sense. The research Dooley had done on the Net confirmed a fact that he had heard years before. If you had red hair, you had at least some Celtic blood, which was precious little help. The Irish had traveled all over the world.

If Teddy was not an orphan, he had parents somewhere. Had his parents sold him to the—to whom? To the director of the orphanage, who sold him to Windsor House, the agency that facilitated their adoption? Possibly. How much would the parents have been paid for the child? How much had the agency? Teddy was a particular sort of child—red hair, green eyes, that creamy Irish skin. They could get quite a lot for a child like that. Why was he even guessing? He knew how much they had paid. Ten thousand dollars to the lawyer for "fees." Fifteen thousand to Windsor House Adoptions up front for "office costs." That was what Claudia had said. Then the bribe money in Russia. Altogether, he thought it was about $35,000.

He *thought*? Why had he put it that way in his head?

Because Claudia had done most of the arranging, that's why. She was a lawyer; it made perfect sense for her to handle the paperwork, didn't it? Still, there had been times when she seemed evasive about just how much money one or another set of papers would cost. The final total had never been clear.

Claudia had her own money, from her grandparents. She could have paid more than she told him and he would never have known. He had been poor as a child, and still thought of money in terms of what he earned at the hospital, his take-home, not investments.

Fifty thousand dollars for Teddy, adding up everything Claudia had told him—could it be that much?—split between the agency and the parents or perhaps just between the agency and Teddy's unwed mother? It would have been a fortune for an unmarried woman, alone and desperate.

It would be even more of a fortune for the agency if they just snatched a child, sold him, and kept all the money for themselves.

His thoughts were making circles again. *Get a grip, Dooley!*

Dooley started to surf the Net.

In a matter of minutes, he found five sites that specialized in "missing and exploited children." Two of the sites included pictures of the children, and in many cases there were additional "aged" pictures of how the children would look today, the aging depending, of course, on how long the children had been gone. Dooley's heart ached at aged photos of young adults whose families had last seen them as toddlers. The National Center for Missing and Exploited Children in Arlington, Virginia, maintained a web site anybody could log onto at no charge. You entered your missing child's description. Dooley just lurked, surveying the site for children lost. He hoped there was no way anybody could trace his contact with the site back to him, but he believed not. He was looking for people who had lost a child like the child he possessed, a fact that he couldn't explain if anybody traced him and asked.

There were so many missing children.

Dooley was looking for children born approximately four years earlier. When he and Claudia had adopted Teddy, they were told he was five months old; the papers from Russia gave his birthday as October 19, 1998. Dooley now felt he couldn't trust that information. At the time, he hadn't questioned it, so he now had to search his distant memory. Had Teddy appeared any older or younger than five months? He had enough knowledge of human development to have been aware of any large discrepancy. In fact, if the agency was deceiving them, they probably wouldn't go far from the truth, knowing he was a doctor.

To the best of his recollection, Teddy had really looked five months old. He was thin—all the Russian orphans were thin—which might have made him appear a bit younger than he really was. Dooley doubted, though, that Teddy could have been as much as seven months. Malnutrition can make a child small and developmentally delayed, but there are still physical characteristics diagnostic of an infant's age. If he had been a large baby, he still couldn't be younger than four months—maybe three and a half?—no, four. A three-and-a-half-month baby just looks different in too many ways.

Dooley printed out all the male children in this age range who went missing in mid-March 1999. Hundreds and hundreds of them. Then he sat down with the pile of paper and methodically began to cross out the impossible ones. Those of a different ethnicity, or those with an unalterable birthmark or birth defect. He hesitated at the many, many children presumed to have been abducted by one parent from the other, custodial parent. When both the child and the presumably abducting parent had vanished, wasn't that conclusive evidence that the baby wasn't Teddy? Should he cross those off his list as well?

He decided not to. It was possible that a parent had gone missing coincidentally around the time the child did. It wasn't very likely, but he wasn't going to be sloppy and make hasty, lazy decisions at the outset.

Then he realized he had to make another decision, this one about the timing of the abduction. Could he assume that Teddy had been abducted just before he turned up in Russia? No, he couldn't. He could have been taken months before. He could have been abducted at birth. Dooley shouldn't have restricted his search to children who went missing around March 1999.

He changed his parameters to early October 1998 through March 1999.

The longer he worked, the more daunting the task became. A million children, he discovered, went missing in the United States every year. By far most of them proved to have just wandered off. A very large number of the others were taken by the noncustodial parent during custody battles or later. Most of the children were later found, but there was a small but significant number who never turned up. The pieces of data on the missing children painted a sad image in his mind, a long, long line of children alone, babies who had vanished from their strollers, a very small number of babies stolen from hospitals, babies vanished from bedrooms and cars and church socials. He knew he wasn't even considering the toddlers and older children.

After two hours, he threw down his pen. Certainly there were police agencies that could do this search much better than he. He could get the FBI to give him a list of missing children in his target age group.

*The FBI!*

What was he thinking? He wasn't looking for a child, he already had a child. Suppose they came and asked him about his "missing" child? *Good God!* If he told them about Teddy, they might take him away. He wasn't ready to risk that yet, if ever.

What exactly *was* he ready for?

Admitting it to himself, he desperately hoped that he would find that Teddy's parents had died, and Teddy could be theirs always, with no guilt. Second best would be that the parents had been abusive, horrible people, child molesters who in all good conscience you would not send a child home to.

He wasn't proud of himself for thinking these things. But he couldn't put the whole situation out of his mind, either, and just live with it. He must at the very least find out who Teddy's parents were. He could not accept not knowing. As soon as he pictured himself trying to forget about Teddy's parentage, he realized he would think about it every hour of every day for the rest of his life.

Oh God, he thought. *I can't do this.*

*Wait. What's the best outcome for Teddy? Isn't it best for Teddy to stay with the only family he has ever known? Wouldn't it be unbearably painful for him to be uprooted and given away to a stranger?*

And yet Dooley knew that if he found Teddy's parents and they were good people, he would have to give Teddy back. He would have to.

Maybe he should go back to Windsor House Adoptions and demand an explanation. *No. Not yet.* If there was a scam going on, they were the people perpetrating it. He decided to save confronting them as a last resort.

By noon he had thirty-five serious possibilities, a full page of data and his own speculations on each, and a pain in his chest. And of all the big questions there was only one small thing he knew he had to do. He picked up his daily notepad and wrote, "Get more paper."

# 2

Teddy was cutting some kind of animal-like figures out of brown construction paper when Dooley walked into the kitchen at lunchtime. Annalise, the nanny, said, "Look, Dr. M, what he can do."

Studying the figures, Dooley said, "Those are great, Teddy," but he exchanged a glance with Annalise that asked her to give him a clue. He didn't want to tell Teddy what wonderful fish he was cutting out if in fact they were meant to be dogs. They looked quite a bit like pregnant brown guppies with scalloped tail fins.

"And just in time for Thanksgiving," Annalise said, smiling.

"Wow! I don't know when I've ever seen better turkeys. We can tape them up all over the house."

Teddy giggled.

"Annalise, if you wanted to go shopping or take a break, I'll have lunch with Teddy," Dooley said.

## 3

Dooley wanted to watch Teddy cut more paper turkeys, but Teddy wanted Dooley to cut them. He cut one for Teddy, making it look exactly like Teddy's did. Dooley had always been ambivalent about whether he should do things more like adults did them, to show Teddy "the right way," or assume that Teddy's way was right for him.

"How about snowflakes?" Dooley said after the first turkey. "I'm better at snowflakes. And it's winter now; we should be getting some snow soon."

"Snow soon, snow soon!" the little boy chanted. Teddy was sitting on the floor with his legs sticking out, wearing denim shorts and a T-shirt. His legs were still chubby, like big sausages. His tummy was plump under the shirt. He was losing that baby fat little by little, now that he was running and climbing and doing little boy things instead of baby things. His green eyes glowed behind pale lashes and plump cheeks.

Dooley got some white typing paper. He cut a sheet into a square, then folded the square into a rectangle, the rectangle into a smaller square, and the small square into a triangle. This would make an octagonal snowflake, not hexagonal, he observed irrelevantly, still trying to distract himself.

As if Teddy would care.

He'd make the next one hexagonal, the way a perfect snowflake ought to be.

Unfortunately, his hands could do this and his brain could still whirl and worry. Teddy was watching, fascinated. Dooley had made lots of these cutouts before with him and he knew what was coming.

The snowflake was done. He had cut little curves and triangles into the sides of the triple-folded sheet. "I can unfold it, Daddy," Teddy said. He especially loved to unfold them because you couldn't quite tell what they would look like until you opened them up.

Very, very carefully, the child unfolded the paper. "It's beautiful, Daddy."

There were little bits of paper all over the floor. In the past he had told Teddy they'd pick the scraps up and keep them in a box and use them for confetti at a special celebration. "More comfetti!" Teddy said. "I'll get the box. Some day we'll have a big, *big* celebration."

## 4

It wasn't until two o'clock, with Teddy and Annalise out at the park and Dooley getting ready to go to work, that he realized he had forgotten to search the Web for sites about the rest of the world.

How stupid! He'd been searching Web sites in the United States. But where better to abduct an Irish-looking baby than Ireland? There was also Canada, the U.K., and every other country in the world to which Irish people had migrated. Or visited, come to think of it. Maybe the child of a medical missionary in, say, Honduras had gone missing. How would he ever find all these children?

And what about Irish-looking people? Were there red-haired Serbs, for instance? Belgians? Portuguese? Did they have some Celtic genes?

The irony of his search wasn't lost on him either. Here were all these families looking for their missing children, while he was doing the reverse. They were trying to discover where their child had gone, desperate to find out. He was trying to discover where his had come from, and he didn't really want to know.

# Chapter Seven

FRANCO IS A LITTLE ANGEL, BORN
VERY PREMATURE ON JANUARY 2.
HE MAY REQUIRE EXTRA LOVE AND
ATTENTION TO DEVELOP HIS FULL
POTENTIAL, BUT IS NOW GAINING
WEIGHT WELL.

**RACE: CENTRAL AMERICAN**
**DISABILITIES: NONE KNOWN AT THIS TIME**

## 1

### The next day
### The Long Island Expressway

Dooley thought rain was hitting his windshield, but the pellets made a tapping sound, like ice. Probably a mixture of both, and chillier to walk in than snow.

He was cold anyway, because he was scared. He'd got Peter Evans, a colleague, to work an hour past the end of his shift, picking up the first hour of Dooley's. Dooley then had left home an hour and a half early, telling Annalise he had some library work to do, just in case Claudia asked. Although, why would Claudia ask what time he left home? He was still on the three P.M. to eleven P.M. shift and Claudia, as usual, worked nine to five. When she got home, why on earth would she ask Annalise how long Dooley had been gone?

He had now got himself into the position of having to work an hour for his colleague Peter Evans some time in the next week or so, which would probably have to be explained.

No it wouldn't. Claudia would never ask. If he had to stay late to cover for a friend, what of it? It happened all the time.

The whole problem was that he felt guilty. And because he felt guilty, he was patching together excuses he would never need. The wicked flee where no man pursueth.

He liked honesty. With Claudia, with Teddy. He'd been frank with Teddy that his illness was serious and had to be looked at, even though he also tried not to be too scary. Claudia and Dooley both had been honest with Teddy about his adoption. Dooley had no experience in deceit. That was certainly changing.

One missing child on the list he put together had sounded so much like Teddy.

The case had just jumped out at him. The story of Michael Destiger, who had lived with his parents far out on Long Island, near Yaphank, New York. Michael had been five months old that Saturday in March 1999. The weather had been unusually warm, in the low seventies by noon. Long Island had a mild climate for its latitude, and Michael had been taking naps outdoors most days since mid-February, except when it was raining. Michael's mother always placed him in his baby carriage on the roofed porch outside their back door. It did a child good to get a little fresh air each day. Michael's mother had checked on him frequently, but she had been busy inside too. People from the city drove out here in fine weather, buying herbs in pots at local greenhouses and having lunch at country restaurants. This had been one of the first sunny Saturdays, the newspapers said. When Mrs. Destiger checked on Michael at 4:10, the carriage was empty. The baby boy had vanished into thin air and had not been seen since.

From Manhattan Dooley took the Queens Midtown Tunnel heading roughly east into Long Island on the Long Island Expressway. Most Manhattanites weren't familiar with Long Island, other than the Hamptons, if they knew even that much, and many had never been east of the East River. There was a decreasing amount of the island that was still agricultural. Cattle and potatoes, Dooley thought.

After he'd been driving three quarters of an hour on the L.I.E., Dooley discovered he didn't know Long Island so well either. It was bigger than he remembered. He couldn't possibly make it out there and back in two hours. He was going a couple of miles past Yaphank, which he now realized was more than sixty miles from Manhattan.

He wanted to give this whole trip up. For that matter, he wanted to give up the whole quest, but instead he called the hospital on his cellphone. Peter would work another hour. "But you owe me," he said. Dooley fervently agreed.

He got off the L.I.E. on something called the William Floyd Parkway. After half a mile on a small crossroad he started to scan for the address, which he expected to be an old farmhouse or maybe, given the encroaching exurbia, a new house in a housing development. What he found, to his surprise, was a little crossroads and in it a shop called the Baked Potato. The shop part was the ground floor of a very old house with the old-style narrow wood siding and a gingerbread-decorated porch that went all around four sides of the house. That must be the porch from which Michael had been stolen. The shop looked a bit too cute, but given the age of the building, it had earned its cute. The upper floors, a full second floor with gables and a half-floor under the sloping roof, appeared to be living space. There were ruffled blue-and-white curtains at the second floor windows and despite the chill of the day, one of the windows was open an inch or so. Probably upstairs was where the Destigers lived.

The little crossroads was composed of only eight or ten shops. All shop fronts wore garlands of green and red light strands, and the bushes between shops were decorated with lights, ready for the holidays. There was a doll shop with a sign that said DOLL HOSPITAL. A sweets shop had a red-and-white striped candy cane, six feet tall, in its front yard. Dooley wondered how little shops like this managed to stay in business. Probably the proprietors owned the little wood houses and probably each holiday through the years was the occasion for a change of theme. He could well imagine red, white, and blue at the Fourth of July. Today there were no shoppers on the sidewalks. The dreary cold weather would keep them away. And it was midweek, after all.

Dooley parked, but sat frozen for several minutes in his car. This was terrible. What horrible perverse thinking had made him come here? His emotions were a mess. He wanted the Destigers to be Teddy's parents and he wanted them to be unpleasant, cruel people so that he wouldn't have to return him, would never think of letting him go live with them, and would never experience any guilt about it. That way he could lay all this hideous experience to rest for the whole remainder of his life.

He made himself get out of the car. He made himself march up the three green-painted wooden steps in the cold rain to the porch and open the door. The last step creaked. A bell over the door dinged, as he had known it would.

He stepped inside. It was all just like he knew it would be from seeing the outside—tea, dried flowers, scented candles, jars of potpourri, fragrances to put in the bath, to burn, to leave on a windowsill, or to touch to your neck. Boxes of fudge. Local pottery, most of it really beautiful, which was sort of a surprise.

More of a surprise was the pig. A man in farmer's bib overalls, with a leather jacket worn open and a baseball cap on his head, its bill backward, was paying for his purchases. He accepted his change and a big shopping bag. Around the wrist that held the shopping bag was a leather leash. It went to the collar of a large, dark gray pig that stood patiently nuzzling the man's leg, for all the world like an affectionate puppy.

The man said, "Thanks, Mort." He touched his hat politely, said, "Come on, Bratwurst," and headed toward the front door. Dooley held it open for him, since the man had his hands full.

The man said, "Thanks."

As the door swung shut, Dooley turned to see the middle-aged shopkeeper at the cash register smiling pleasantly at him. Behind the man were freezer cases of potato casseroles, potato puffs, and stuffed potatoes of several types—cheddar cheese, broccoli, chili with onion, spinach, garlic, double garlic, tomato—judging by the color pictures on the wall above the coolers.

"New here?" the man asked. "Or passing through?"

Dooley said, "Passing through."

Matter-of-factly, the man nodded his head toward the departed duo. "Local character. Nice guy, nice pig too."

"Was that one of those potbellied pigs?"

"No, regular pig. Just the runt of the litter."

"Huh."

"Old Bernie comes in twice a week for our stuffed potatoes. Loves the garlic stuffed. Locally raised potatoes, you know."

The man didn't seem to be trying to sell his potatoes particularly, just passing the time of day. Trying not to rush Dooley. The man, whose name Dooley assumed from the news reports was Mort Destiger, Michael's father, reminded Dooley of one of the seven dwarfs, the one called Doc. Doc was jolly and a little bumbly. He was the one who got the other dwarfs to wash their hands before dinner, when Snow White insisted. Mort had curly red hair and pale skin. Dooley's heart sank at the realization that this man could actually be Teddy's father. At the time of the kidnapping, he and his wife had been separated, and he had been working a few miles away at a canning factory. He had been briefly under suspicion in the kidnapping, then proven to be at work when it happened. More than thirty people had seen him on the line at the factory.

"Kind of sad too," Mort said about Old Bernie. "Alcoholic, you know."

"Bernie is?"

"Both of 'em, matter-of-fact. Bernie gets beer delivered by the case. Drinks three six-packs a day. Been giving the pig beer in his water bowl for years. The two of 'em sit around drinkin' beer together. Tells me the pig drinks one six-pack a day."

"I guess then the pig's not really an alcoholic," Dooley said.

"Say, I guess you're right."

Before the man could ask, "How can I help you?" Dooley said, "I'm not exactly here for potatoes, although now that I've seen those casseroles, I'd like to take some back with me. I'm here because—uh, see, my name is John Destiger."

"Oh? No kidding."

"Destiger is such an unusual name—I've been looking around on the Net and so on, trying to see if I can find some family." Dooley stopped for a moment, uncomfortable with lying. "You are Mr. Destiger, aren't you?"

"Yup. Mort Destiger. I didn't think there were any other ones of us around here. Where you from?"

"Upstate. Rome, New York. You know, it's not far from Albany." *And don't let Mort Destiger know anything about Rome, New York, please Lord.*

"No kidding. Come all this way to find a Destiger?"

"Well, not entirely. My wife wanted to come to the city. See a couple of plays. Today she's"—Dooley made one of those faces men made at times like this—"shopping. So I figured I'd get out of town."

"Good thinking."

"So, do we Destigers have other relatives you know of? My dad is dead and he didn't have any brothers or sisters."

"Well, John, there's my dad and mom. Dad had a brother named Henry, but he died in the war. Vietnam War. Way back. I have a sister, Esther, who lives in Salt Lake City."

"Esther have any children?"

"Four. That's about the most anybody in our family's had for yay generations."

"You have any kids, Mort?" Dooley almost couldn't utter the words, but he'd come here and he couldn't go back without knowing a lot more. *I hate myself. I hate myself.* He held his breath, trying to be cold-hearted.

Mort took a couple of beats before he spoke. "Ah—no. No children."

Dooley got hold of himself. "Well, I guess the Destigers just seem to be a rare species, huh?"

Dooley had not planned much past this point, believing that he would know immediately whether these parents looked like Teddy, so when he heard footsteps, he turned around, hoping the missing child's mother was coming.

For a moment, he couldn't tell the source of the sounds. There was nobody entering from the side room. Then he realized that at the back of the store was a staircase. Of course—he had thought when he came in that the owners probably lived above the store.

A woman's legs appeared, moving slowly. The woman descended, slumped and quiet, dressed in a shapeless sweatshirt and Levi's. Her red hair was curly, like Teddy's, but pushed up in back as if she had been sleeping and forgot to comb it when she woke up. As she got closer to them, Dooley noticed that her eyes were puffy too, like a person just awakened.

"Louise," Mort said, "come meet a Destiger."

"A Destiger?" she asked, but with no real interest.

"This here's John Destiger from upstate. He was looking around for relatives."

"Well, it's nice to meet you," she said, holding out her hand.

Dooley shook it. "Good to meet you, Mrs. Destiger."

"Where's your family from originally, John?" she asked politely enough.

"Canada as far back as I can trace."

"Oh."

Quite suddenly, Dooley had a flash of realization. The woman's eyes were blue, a washed-out blue but definitely blue. So were Mort's. And Teddy's were green. My God! What had he done, Dooley thought, coming here and bothering these people? At the same time he was relieved, so much so that he felt breathless. They couldn't be Teddy's parents.

"I think I'll go take a nap, Mort," Louise Destiger said, and she walked back to the stairs, dragging her feet. She vanished bit by bit up the stairs.

"I'm sorry," Mort said, in his matter-of-fact way. He was well aware, Dooley thought, that his wife looked like a person who had just awakened but was now going back to bed. "She's not feeling herself. We had a . . . a loss in the family a little while ago."

*A little while ago. A little while like three and a half years!*

"Oh. That's too bad. I'm very sorry to hear that." Dooley smiled at Mort and added, "Well, I'd better get back to town. But let me get some of those stuffed potatoes. They really look good."

"You're gonna heat 'em up in a hotel room?" Mort said.

"Well, we've got a little kitchenette in there with a microwave," Dooley said, thinking fast. "Kitchenette about the size of a checkerboard. Be a help not to pay New York restaurant prices for one night."

# 2

Dooley got back on the L.I.E. and headed toward Manhattan. The raindrops with ice inside them had changed to little snow pellets that were now coming down hard, bouncing on the hood of the car. For a while as he drove, Dooley thought the windshield had steamed up inside, but he soon realized it wasn't the windshield. There were tears in his eyes.

He felt so guilty, so slimy, so dirty, so *wrong*. He had lied to Claudia by omission and he lied straight out to the Destigers. He was keeping a secret that he wanted to blurt out, but he didn't know how to bring it up or what would happen if he did. Somewhere out there might be another couple like the Destigers, but who were really Teddy's parents.

A woman mourned for three and a half years for a missing child. A man was so traumatized he couldn't admit his son existed. Would they be as damaged as this if the child had died?

If Teddy went back to his birth parents, would he and Claudia mourn forever like the Destigers?

Green eyes. Blue eyes. The news accounts of course hadn't said anything about the Destigers' eye color, and although the missing child information had said that the baby's eyes were blue, Dooley had assumed that a lot of babies had blue eyes at first, which later on became the real color.

Dooley knew that a person's eye color was inherited fairly simply, not like more complicated things like height and skin color. It used to be thought to be completely simple, although it was now known to be more polygenetic than people had realized. In the simple theory, every human being carried only two genes for eye color, one he got from his mother and one from his father. When a person produced an egg or a sperm, that cell had only one of the parent's two genes, generated randomly. The resulting baby then had one from each parent. If you had one blue-eye gene and one brown-eye gene, you would have brown eyes, because brown was dominant. If you had two brown-eye genes, of course you would have brown eyes. You would only have blue eyes if you had two blue-eye genes, because blue eyes were recessive and any other color trumped them. It was now known that there was interaction between the genes and more than one from each parent that determined eye color. Still, two parents who showed pure blue eyes most likely had two genes for blue eyes. So both Mort Destiger and Louise Destiger must each have two genes for blue eyes. The chances that they would have a baby with intensely green eyes were very, very low.

Therefore, they were not Teddy's parents.

# 3

Out over the Atlantic, a 747 bound for Kennedy Airport from Moscow was descending out of 33,000 feet, approaching the far eastern end of Long Island. It covered the entire length of the island in the time it took Dooley to drive two miles against the thickening snow. After the plane, invisible to him, had passed over Dooley's car, three miles from Kennedy, TRACON handed the aircraft over to ARTS, the local area radar tracking system. The plane glided into its runway approach.

Gabrielle sat in a window seat, clutching her shoulder bag to her chest. Somewhere underneath the passenger compartment was Justin's body. She wondered if the coffin was in a cold or warm place.

The paperwork needed to get out of Russia with Justin had taken ten days. It was normal to have problems getting out of a country, sometimes as much trouble as getting in. You had to have your equipment *carné*, which lists every piece of equipment you brought in with you. Otherwise, you might never get it back out. This time, it was ironic that when she didn't have Sam Bielski to help, she didn't need him. This time, there was almost nothing left of their shoot, except the three tapes in Gabrielle's bag and her extra cellphone. And sadly there was Justin's body to deal with. The medico-legal institute required a full autopsy—which was no surprise and would have been the same in the States. But the procedure kept being delayed. Nobody would tell her when it would be finished, and after a while she stopped asking. Paperwork was an endless burden all over the world, but in Russia it was the worst of the worst. That was the time she most wished she had a producer along, riding shotgun for her.

Mr. Stover had found Gabrielle a well-guarded hotel just half a block from the embassy. People involved with various foreign legations stayed there, so the staff screened visitors carefully. Gabrielle had immediately found two women at the embassy who liked to do fitness walks and who were flattered that a famous reporter would like to walk with them. Gabrielle passed the time walking all over Moscow with the women. Gabrielle was used to being in dangerous locations, and was certainly willing to take chances for a story. But she was also assertive about finding people familiar with the locale who could show her the ropes. She needed to walk off her anger and grief. She did not need to take stupid chances. Someone had killed Justin. She did not know whether the killers would strike her too.

Gabrielle had talked with Justin's parents by phone several times. Every time, she ended by crying and so did the Craigs. Justin had a younger sister, Katie, who had recently turned seventeen and apparently hero-worshipped her big brother. Every time she got on the phone she asked, "Why? Why did they kill him?" over and over.

Mr. and Mrs. Craig were meeting the plane. Gabrielle had warned them it would take the airline a while to get the coffin out of the storage hold or wherever they put it. All Gabrielle knew about coffins on large airliners was that the company didn't load them using the baggage loading ramp that the passengers in the terminal could see. In Moscow she had watched for it and never saw it go on. She supposed that airlines didn't want the passengers to know they were flying with a corpse, although one of the airline officials told her that many flights carried coffins.

When the plane came to a halt at the gate, people pushed into the aisles, eager to get off, glad to stretch their legs after hours cramped in their seats. Gabrielle continued to sit.

Let everybody else get off first. There was no hurry whatsoever.

# Chapter Eight

I'm of English extraction, in good health, expecting a
baby girl in June. My boyfriend is a Native-American
male in good health, but we are both seventeen and
can't raise a baby. Please send photos of yourselves,
your home, and a letter about why you want a baby.

Inquiries to Box 2217, the *Press*,
all information held confidential.

## 1

### New York City
### Mid-November

The Boss was feeling great. He dropped his briefcase casually
onto the conference table and lowered himself into a soft leather
chair. The chair swiveled slightly as he sat. He turned it to face the
table squarely. The chair mechanism moved with satisfyingly expensive
silence.

Life was good.

Three other men had followed him into the conference room.
The smallest of the three, Gordon Ridley, winced when the Boss's
brass-cornered briefcase hit the glossy walnut of the table. Solid
wood, with heavy leaf-and-grapevine detailing around the sides, its
legs carved in the forms of griffins, the table had come from the

library of the Guggenheim estate. It had cost roughly as much as an Aston Martin. Ridley was the company CFO and he knew these things.

The Boss noticed Ridley's small reaction, and didn't care. As founder and CEO of a very lucrative company, the Boss could pretty well call the shots with his staff. But he'd chosen the top men with specific talents in mind, and he let them run with their ideas as much as he thought was wise. Ridley, the CFO, was a genius at business math but as rigid as a minus sign. He was wearing a stiff Sulka-clone pinstripe, uncomfortable Bally-ish shoes, and a rep tie that said, "Hello. I'm sober and responsible." At the same time, however, Ridley had laid out quite a few bucks for the ensemble.

But not as much as Jean Sippolene. The Belgian, all lanky, casual, and laid back, slid into a buttery leather chair and crossed his legs, displaying Belgian loafers perfect in their inappropriate-for-business flavor. A molten-lead-gray jacket floated on his body. The Boss guessed it was Miyake because the seams were sewn with red thread, which you could hardly see unless you knew enough to look for it. Sippolene was Publicity and Public Relations.

Sigmund Rutgauer, COO and Security, was a German—East German—who had been brought into the company by the Boss because of his knowledge of Eastern Europe. He spoke fourteen languages, including Hungarian, Polish, and several Serbo-Croatian dialects that hurt your eyes just to look at them written on a page. The Boss thought fleetingly of a remark some television comic had made: the United States was sending aid to Eastern Europe—vowels. He chuckled and the others looked at him. He felt no need to explain. Rutgauer wore an austere, dark Sulka suit, and held his head high with his sharp nose in the air.

The Boss himself wore a continental-cut suit that he had chosen carefully—neither boxy British nor ordinary Armani style. The fabric was his favorite Dormeuil cashmere that upped the price of the already pricey Armani suit by two thousand dollars. He wore Lobb Brothers riding boots. These boots were made to measure on custom-carved lasts. Occasionally, in the company of certain people, he crossed his legs in such a manner that they could see the soles of the boots; people who knew where to look would see the way the rubber cut across the heel and would *know*. He didn't do that now, however. There was no point. These four men knew each other well enough.

The secretary entered with a tray of frothy mochaccino in tiny cups, then immediately withdrew, closing the soundproof door behind her.

"Go right ahead, Ridley," the Boss said to the CFO. "Time is money."

Ridley said, "As you all know, I have only the Q3 figures, since we are only halfway through the fourth quarter. But we've enjoyed better than expected earnings, even though our expectations were high." He smiled at the group in a conservative fashion, no teeth exposed.

"I have devised a little chart that might give a clearer picture. This is the past twelve months, which of course doesn't represent our fiscal year. Fiscal 2002 will be prepared the first week of January. When the last quarter figures come in." He clicked a remote and a chart appeared on the wall screen.

"Very nice," the Boss said. The chart showed virtually straight upward growth, rising in little steps across the twelve months, except for July. "A veritable stairway to paradise, Ridley. But what happened in July?"

"Well, we try to keep inventory to a minimum, and we just developed a bit of a shortfall of product. Some of our licensing agreements fell apart."

"Our inventory runs around how much?" asked Rutgauer.

"On hand at any one time? Rarely more than two to three million dollars' worth."

Rutgauer said, "Good."

"I'm wondering, though," the Boss said, "whether the market downturn, particularly in the tech stocks, means our customer base will shrink."

"Yes. A lot of dot-com millionaires have become dot-com thousandaires," Rutgauer said, chuckling.

"I've been thinking about a way of dealing with that," the Boss said. "But forge on, Ridley. We'll come back to it."

Ridley forged on, his flow altered, but not broken. "Now here is a summary of our past four years. Despite stock market fluctuations, we grow quite steadily. I'm not sure we're all that economy-dependent. The demand for product is really fairly constant."

"And of course," said Jean Sippoline, breaking his silence in his Flemish-Belgian accent, "we have a high level of customer satisfaction."

"We have absolutely *no* returns," Rutgauer said, "which means excellent word-of-mouth, particularly with a lot more product out there every year. Our reputation can only continue to grow. We now are getting twenty-eight percent repeat business."

"Amazing," Sippolene said.

Ridley clicked his remote. The screen went off and he pulled a stack of papers from a folder. "All right. I have here our P-and-L for the past six-month period. I'm giving each of you four sheets with all the numbers. There's a full breakdown—"

"Ridley," said the Boss, looking at the third sheet, "our unit cost has gone up."

"Yes, average unit cost is seven thousand five hundred, as compared to seven thousand two hundred last fiscal year, but our average sales price has risen even more. Of course, the higher costs are on our special product. Ordinary product runs much less. Our special product constitutes less than ten percent of our merchandise, but thirty-three percent of our profit. Cost runs eight point seven percent of average sales price, which I think is better than the standards in almost any other industry on earth."

"That's for damn sure," the Boss said. "Sigmund, what about employee costs?"

Rutgauer said, "I'm going entirely for independent contractors in the new 'hires.' That way we don't have monthly out-of-pocket costs for them. They get paid for what they actually do. Very few of our people are now hanging around drawing payroll checks when they're inactive. And of course, we don't have to give them benefits."

"I like that," Ridley said.

"The surveil people are a little pricey, but they're on jobbing rates too. They are our insurance policy."

"Plus, they spot-surveil, right?"

"Right. So almost everybody is indep contractors. With the exception of our tech guy. He's absolutely pivotal. We couldn't survive without him, and not only is he on salary, I recommend giving him a raise."

"I think you're right," Sippolene said.

"Well," the Boss said, clapping his hands. "Now to my question. We've always been the Cadillac of the business. A splendid market, but narrow. Do we want to expand?"

"Expand into what? And why?" Rutgauer asked.

The Boss steepled his fingers. "We've become high profile lately because of our high price. People know about us and tell their friends. This is good. While we have absolutely no customer dissatisfaction, and therefore no complaints whatsoever, I think we should hedge a bit. We don't want to attract the wrong sort of attention."

"We haven't," Rutgauer said.

"You charge top dollar, people start talking."

"No way around that," Rutgauer said.

"There is one way. We could start thinking of a midprice product line as well."

"What we lose on percentage we could make up on volume," Sippolene said.

Ridley, the CFO, said, "Many's the company that's tried that and was caught short trying to make up a loss per item on volume. And found to their surprise that a thousand times a one-dollar loss was a thousand-dollar loss."

Rutgauer said, "In other words, we could be victims of our own success."

Ridley said, "If life isn't fair, business is far and away not fair."

The Boss went on. "We're going to have to think seriously about this. If we were gonna be Wal-Mart in addition to Neiman Marcus, we'd need a different name."

Sippolene, the PR man, said, "Goes without saying."

Rutgauer, sketching a little head-bow to the Boss, said, "Windsor House Adoptions was absolutely brilliant."

Sippolene said, "Elegant."

Sigmund said, *"Anmutig."*

"But what if we want to go the midprice route?" Ridley asked. "All the cuddly names are taken. Names with 'heart' and 'caring' and 'love.'"

"So, we'd need something warm but distinctive."

Sippolene said, "Pine Grove Adoptions?"

"Sounds more like a cemetery," the Boss said.

"Walnut Grove?"

"Sounds like health food."

"Small Blessings?"

"Belittles it. We don't want 'small' in it anywhere."

"Snuggle Time?"

"Sounds like herbal tea."

"Heir Apparent."

"I think it's already a brand of maternity clothing. We need something that says *quality*. In a low-cost way."

"Quali-babe?" Sippolene drawled, with heavy irony.

"Sounds like cheerleader training camp."

"Reliable Adoptions?"

"Too much like the Roadrunner."

"What do you mean?" Rutgauer asked.

"You know, like Acme Birdshot Company."

Sippolene said, "Well, then *you* think of something."

"How about Families in Formation?"

"Sounds like the Partridge Family marching band."

"I've got it!" said Ridley.

The Boss said, "What?"

"We'll hold focus groups."

"Oh, for heaven's sake!"

"How about Golden Angels?" Rutgauer suggested.

The Boss said, "Possible. A little tacky. Like those cherubs with big eyes. I like tacky in a midprice name. Ridley, check out its availability."

"But I certainly hope we're not actually going to go ahead with cut-rate product," Rutgauer said. "It's not necessary. We can handle any investigation. We're bulletproof."

Sippolene drawled, "I have some reservations myself, you know. I don't see how adding a product line, even if we rename it, is going to make the Windsor House line any less exposed. Unless we fold the special products part. They're the big risk, after all. But I don't think you want to do that."

The Boss said, "Certainly not."

"Well then?"

The Boss clapped his hands. "Another line would make more money in a less obvious way."

"In that case, I don't see the need for two entities."

"Well, we'll meet back here in a week. Be thinking about it."

# Chapter Nine

FEES REDUCED: Child No. 261: White female,
four months, clubfoot, normal mental development.

## 1

## New York City
## Mid-November

Claudia stopped in front of her closet door wearing just her underwear, slip, and shoes. She could hear the bumblebee hum as Dooley in the bathroom put the finishing touches on his shave. Annalise was staying over, and would sleep in the full-size bed next to Teddy's child-size bed, in Teddy's room.

Teddy was thrilled. "I'm having a sleepover!"

Claudia picked up her dress and let it slide down over her shoulders. It was her favorite, a dark ruby red. The organizers of the U.N. benefit had urged in the invitations that everybody wear either red or black. This would make the evening, which was just six days before Thanksgiving, "seasonally festive" they said. Claudia rarely wore red because it made her red hair look orange, but this particular blood red worked for some reason. Now she studied herself in the mirror and was almost satisfied. She added a silver necklace and silver bracelet. Just a touch of lip gloss and she was ready to roll.

She glanced at the bathroom door. Dooley had shut off the razor; she heard him slapping shaving lotion on his cheeks. Claudia frowned. There was something wrong with Dooley. She'd been aware of it for several days now. She'd begun to wonder whether he was having an affair. He seemed secretive and remote from her. A couple of times she had come into their combined offices unexpectedly and he'd shut off his computer monitor. Maybe he had been e-mailing a woman.

And yet he didn't have the manner she thought a man having an affair would. Instead of being secretively gleeful, he seemed like a sad person pretending to be happy.

When exactly had all this started?

## 2

"Claudia. At last!" a bulky man in a fuzzy camel hair coat exclaimed, gesturing broadly as he stood filling one of the U.N. doorways. "It wouldn't be a party without you." He had thick woolly bear eyebrows that moved as if of their own free will as he spoke.

The big man seized Claudia and hugged her, air-kissing both sides of her face. "And this," he said, "is Doogie."

"Dooley," Claudia said.

"Bertrand Cartier," the man said, holding out his hand to Dooley. "We met just once, I think, a couple of years ago."

"And this fall as well," Dooley said. Claudia realized her husband was annoyed but being careful to sound pleasant. She watched Dooley as he smiled at Bertrand and thought again that, courteous as he was in the face of the man's casual rudeness, he still didn't seem like himself.

They were standing in the entryway, blocking new arrivals. The three moved farther inside together.

At least two hundred people milled around in the atrium. The occasion was the kickoff fundraiser for a United Nations–related group called Medical Helpers. Brochures piled on small tables explained that its first chosen goal was to buy AIDS drugs for sub-Saharan Africa. Recently, Squibb, GlaxoSmithKline, Merck, and Boeringer-Ingelheim had agreed to provide drugs that would treat an AIDS patient for a couple of dollars a day. Treatment that ordinarily would cost tens of thousands of dollars for a standard three years of meds would be provided for $700 to $1,500. Unfortunately, most of the nations involved couldn't pay even that amount, the organizers' invitation had explained. In Ivory Coast, for example, a million people were estimated to be HIV positive. With luck, the government might be able to give treatment to two or three thousand. Many infected people all across Africa refused to be tested because they knew that finding out their HIV status meant nothing but added fear. There weren't any drugs available. Nobody would help them. The Medical Helpers organization planned to collect money and beef up the treatment programs in Senegal, Rwanda, Uganda, and Ivory Coast.

Claudia had nothing to do with the Helpers group personally. She worked in the office of the United States ambassador to the U.N. But a lot of her friends were interested in Helpers. To get into this rather posh fundraiser, you had to have contributed at least a thousand dollars. Claudia had contributed.

The United Nations lobby was often used for fundraisers. The space was dramatic, with draped windows four stories high and flooring of large tan and cream squares. As the guests entered the atrium they saw to their far left a photo gallery that housed a variety of exhibits throughout the year, right now poster-size black-and-white portraits—the many faces of humanity from around the world. Beyond the photo gallery was a terrace frosted with snow, overlooking the East River. Far to the right in an alcove was an illuminated Chagall window. Rising in front of the guests were three curved balconies fronting the three floors above and a matching curve at the top, beneath the distant ceiling. The decor throughout the building was very 1950s.

Someone had brought in two dozen blue spruce trees in pale clay pots. The trees were just about the height of basketball players. Tiny red and white Christmas lights were strung through the branches of the trees, which marched in a line away from the front doors, past the *Apollo 14* moon rock in its glass cover, and led the visitor past a bank of coatracks to the refreshments table. On a dais at the far end of the atrium, to the right of the photo gallery, was an internationally known string quartet called Van Gogh, donating their talents to the cause. Their dais was studded with tiny red bulbs, and the band, in honor of the occasion, had left their traditional black-and-white dinner wear at home and wore instead red-and-black jumpsuits in a diamond motley pattern.

Dooley turned from Bertrand when Bertrand was accosted by a thin blond woman. Dooley sighed audibly.

"Glad to get away?" Claudia asked.

"Do you really like that guy? He's impossible."

"Nope. Don't like him, but can't escape him."

Dooley took Claudia's coat and handed both of theirs to the coat-check attendant.

"They must have spent a lot of money on champagne and munchies," Dooley said, choosing a shrimp from the long buffet table. Red and white lights surrounded red and white candles down the center of the table. "Why can't everybody—"

"Just send in the money so the organization can keep all the funds for the charity?"

"Do I say that every time?"

"Only every time we go to one of these charity donation things."

"You know me too well." Dooley laughed. Then he sobered up abruptly and Claudia wondered again what was wrong with him.

She had little time to think about it. She and Dooley had just half a minute to investigate the array of cheeses when a slender woman with a cloud of curly black hair tapped Dooley on the shoulder. She was on Claudia's legal team. She said, mock-flirtatiously, "How's the Gruyère, handsome?"

"Hi, Betsy. Haven't tried it yet," Dooley said. "The Brie's good. But personally I like good old Wisconsin cheddar."

"And how is your little angel?"

"He's a big boy. Making cut-paper turkeys now."

"We took some new pictures," Claudia said casually. She didn't want to show how much she doted on her son. Then she blurted out, "Actually, I have the pictures right here."

Betsy might have winced slightly, but if so she hid it well, and Claudia already had the photos out of her tiny formal silver bag. "They're almost all I can fit in this little thing."

"That's why God made husbands with pockets."

Claudia showed Betsy three photos—Teddy on the dining room table, holding two plastic hammers and wearing a red plastic hard hat, Teddy trying to skate in Rockefeller Center, and a close-up of Teddy, smiling at the camera. Claudia noticed that Dooley turned away as she showed them to Betsy. Embarrassed, Claudia thought, that she was so proud, forcing pictures on people who didn't really care.

In fact, she was a little embarrassed at herself.

"Well, I shouldn't push my child at you," she said, laughing.

As she spoke a tall, bony man stopped and nodded at Claudia. "Are you well, my dear?" he asked, putting an arm on her shoulders.

"Hi," she said. "Happy Holidays! Have you met Betsy Bergen, an attorney in the office of the U.S. ambassador to the U.N.?"

Releasing Claudia rather slowly, the man bowed deeply toward Betsy.

"And my husband, Dr. Dooley McSweeney—"

The man was graceful and very expensively dressed. He shook Dooley's hand, looking down from dark eyes over a bony nose.

Betsy, who still held the photos in her hand, said, "They have the handsomest son."

"So I have heard. Are those photos of him? May I see them?"

Because people so often said, "Why, he looks just like you," making Dooley feel awkward, he said, "We adopted him from Russia a few years ago."

"Ah! You did a good thing there. Children die in those orphanages." He had an accent that sounded to Dooley somewhat like Dutch.

Dooley said, "No, we didn't do a good thing. We *got* a good thing."

The man held up one index finger. "No. You did a good thing. What everybody should do. We all feel guilty. *Everybody* feels guilty. Pretty much everybody in the world knows there are babies dying. And most of us are not adopting babies, even though we could afford to, and even though we are well aware some of the unadopted babies will die. Even people who've adopted one or two or three still feel guilty."

Dooley said, "That's true."

"You felt it too?"

"When we were there, I wanted to take them all home."

"Small lives winking out," the man said. "We should make it a point to tell people."

Dooley said, "I'm sorry, I didn't get your name."

"Pardon me. It is Sigmund Rutgauer."

"My fault entirely," Claudia said. "Sigmund is a member of the German delegation."

# 3

Dooley and Claudia walked home in the cold. November was usually damp in New York but tonight the air was crisp. Dooley was very quiet. She took hold of his arm, not for protection since the street was familiar to both of them and not dangerous, but for companionship. She looked into his face. He smiled at her vaguely, as if he were thinking of something far away.

"I feel so good tonight," she said.

"I'm glad, honey."

"I think I know why too."

"Because you look so beautiful?"

"No, silly. Because I'm off the fertility drugs. We came to the end of this sequence and I'm trying to decide what to do now." She remembered seeing photos in one of Dooley's medical journals of a normal human ovary and one that had been treated with fertility drugs and forced to ovulate. The normal ovary looked about the size of an almond. The stimulated one was as big as a misshapen lemon, engorged and lumpy. No wonder she hadn't felt well. She had been taking daily hormone injections, which meant leaving work every noon and going to the doctor's office on her lunch hour, skipping lunch and making up for it with a granola bar. Then when her ovaries had swollen and produced eggs, her doctor inserted a tube into her abdomen, sucked out the eggs, fertilized them with Dooley's sperm, and inserted the embryos into her uterus. In vitro fertilization was a painful and expensive process. The results, time after time, were zero, nothing but disappointment. All the embryos died.

She knew Dooley was very conscious that the stress, physical and emotional, was mostly hers and not his. He was always very careful about what he said to her. "You need to do what *you* want about it, Claudia. I'll go whichever way you want."

"I know. Thanks." She touched his arm.

"We've had this discussion before," Dooley said.

"And we never resolve it. How much longer should we fight this? The infertility. We have Teddy after all."

Dooley didn't respond. This was unusual for him. He liked to walk and talk. When they were first married, they walked and talked whole weekends, it seemed.

Claudia had a sudden flash of certainty. Possibly it was the reference to Teddy that triggered the thought. More likely it was just the strange way that ideas come to you out of the blue. She knew now when Dooley had begun to behave strangely. Right around the time that Teddy got sick.

They walked in silence for a while, passing their favorite restaurant, PastaPasta, and then a pocket park, dusted with snow.

Dooley said, "Claudia, do you ever think about Teddy's parents?"

"*We're* Teddy's parents."

"All right. His *birth* parents. Do you ever wonder whether they're wondering about him? Where he is? What he's doing?"

"I guess I have at times."

"They'd be happy, don't you think, that he's healthy and growing?"

"I suppose. Dooley, do you feel sorry for them?"

"Sure. In a way. They're missing all the events in his life."

Claudia kept walking, her boots making snapping slaps on the sidewalk. Finally, she said, "Really I don't. Feel sorry for them. I don't care what they wonder about. Maybe they don't wonder at all. They shouldn't have had a baby if they weren't going to take care of him. I mean, it isn't necessary; these days everybody knows about birth control. Russia may not have much in the way of medical services right now, but it's not the back of beyond either."

"Maybe they couldn't afford birth control."

Claudia was walking faster and faster. "Then they shouldn't have been having sex. That lovely child may have been given away within days of when he was born. He was dumped in one of those horrible state orphanages and he could have died there, easily. Lots of them die."

"I know that."

"Unless the mother was raped, she should have known better. At the very least, she was irresponsible. And the father doesn't seem to have stepped up to the plate, either, does he? Took his pleasure and left. No skin off his nose."

"You can't know what problems they had."

"Whatever problems they had, they were willing to let Teddy face worse problems. Neglect. Deprivation of basic mothering. Malnutrition. Disease. You don't *get* to do that to a child. To have one and just dump it! When some people in the world can't even *have* a baby!"

## 4

It had become depressingly obvious to Dooley that he didn't have the expertise to track down all the people on earth who could have been Teddy's parents. Even if he could narrow the quest down a lot, the number was still too huge and he might miss a lot of possible cases. And even if he had the expertise to do a thorough Internet search, it would take him too long. The search alone would take hundreds of hours with his barely adequate knowledge of databases. Traveling God knew where to actually look at the possible parents would take much longer than that. He'd been made well aware by the horrible Destiger trip that news accounts were sketchy and full of inaccuracies, although they were sometimes valuable supplements to the missing children data on-line. If he had to go see the parents of even the most likely children, it would make him absent from work so much that co-workers would notice. He might even lose his job. And Claudia would be aware something was going on long before that happened.

Plus, the more he tried to narrow the possibilities to only the most likely ones, the more chance that he would overlook the people who really were Teddy's birth parents. He supposed he could start with the most likely and work down from there, but still—

His first thought was to hire a private inquiry agent, the sort who was an expert at doing Net searches and had access to all kinds of arcane databases, especially secure government databases that he didn't know how to get into. This person could put a really thorough list together, with as much physical data about the child and the parents as possible, and then Dooley could prune it down himself. The thought had no sooner crossed his mind, though, than he realized he would have to tell such a person too much. It wouldn't take a genius to guess that since Dooley wanted him to search for a male child with red hair, green eyes, etc., etc., born between August 1998 and early December 1998, and abducted from his home or hospital between, say, August 1998 and March 1999, and since Dooley had a child of exactly that description and age, there had to be a personal connection. But why would the investigator know about Teddy? Because he'd make it his business to find out. Dooley was certain that one of the first things these investigators did wasn't to research the subject, it was to research whoever they were working for. It would be a simple matter of self-protection.

Once the detective had deduced that Dooley was worried about his own son, what was to stop him from blackmailing Dooley? Dooley thought if he were challenged, he could claim that he was trying to find the parents with the intention of giving Teddy back. Therefore there was nothing to blackmail him about. He could claim that was exactly why he had hired the investigator.

Oh sure, and then he had a bridge to Brooklyn he'd like to sell. The investigator would know in an instant that Dooley would have gone to the FBI if that was really his intention.

*Was* he going to give Teddy back to his birth parents? *Don't go to that question yet.* If they were good people, he would have to, wouldn't he? Again, he thought maybe they were dead. Again he put off the decision.

Maybe he could work through his lawyer to have the databases searched. *Your lawyer had to keep your conversation with him confidential, didn't he?* And lawyers used inquiry agents and researchers who were bound by the same rules of confidentiality. He thought.

He would go to Roger Nederlander. That would work.

So he left the apartment early on Thursday, with an appointment with Roger already set up.

As soon as the handshaking ritual was over, he said, "You're my lawyer, right? So anything I tell you is in confidence?"

"Yes, generally," Roger said. "Let's sit down." While not a very pedantic man, Roger had a tendency to steeple his fingers, which Dooley found irritating. Roger had recently grown a little toothbrush mustache too. But Dooley knew Roger to be straightforward, up-to-date in the law, and smart, which were the things that mattered.

"Generally?"

"Well, if you told me you were going to rob a bank or murder your grandmother, I'd be obligated to go to the police. But if you told me that you had robbed a bank or murdered your grandmother ten years ago, I would have to keep that confidential."

"Okay . . ." Dooley said slowly. He was getting uneasy, though he wasn't quite sure why. He wanted to go the "I have a friend who has a problem" route, but he doubted a friend would have any presumption of confidentiality unless he came to the lawyer himself, and since the friend didn't exist, he was hardly going to make an appointment. Not to mention that Roger would see through that tired old ruse. Dooley reflected that Roger was one of those people, woefully fewer than they should be, who was precise and schoolmasterish, but also kind. He could count on Roger to be sympathetic. Maybe Dooley should throw himself on Roger's mercy. But he was impeccably honest too, which now began to seem to Dooley like a two-edged sword.

"Look, Roger, I need an investigator to find out something for me. If I tell you what I'm looking for, as my lawyer, it's confidential, right? That confidentiality would apply to your investigator too, wouldn't it?"

"Yes."

"Roger, I need you to know one thing. The original crime—I don't even know whether there was a crime in the first place. But *if* there was, I didn't do it. I didn't even know about it."

"All right."

"But I can't explain exactly what it was unless I know for sure it won't go beyond this office. Except maybe to the investigator."

Roger steepled his fingers again. "Now look. I need to know a few things myself first. Did the original crime give rise to any ongoing crime? Is any crime going on right now?"

*Oh, God, that was it, what was in the back of my mind. If I'm harboring a kidnapped child, I'm committing a crime right now, today. And I intend to go on doing it tomorrow. Therefore—*

*I can't tell Roger anything.*

Dooley said, "Maybe. Maybe. Look, all I want is somebody to do some database searching. And not tell anybody about it."

"Are you asking me for a slightly shady investigator, who won't report whatever it is to the authorities?" Roger studied Dooley's eyes, which Dooley could imagine showed a world of pain and confusion.

"Yes, Roger. I guess I do. And frankly, I need somebody who also won't blackmail me later."

Roger sighed. He spent several long minutes looking at his fingers, then at the telephone, the fax machine, and the pen set in its marble base. Finally he said, "I think my own investigator knows somebody who might be good for your problem. He's used this person for things he didn't want to do himself. The man in question is honest, as far as that goes. He's not a crook. He's more like"—Roger hesitated and then said really quite disapprovingly—"like antiestablishment."

# CHAPTER TEN

Recognizing that the child, for the full and
harmonious development of his or her personality,
should grow up in a family environment, in an
atmosphere of happiness, love, and understanding. . . .

—The Hague Convention on the Protection of
Children and Cooperation in Respect of
Intercountry Adoption of 1993

## 1
### Washington, D.C.
### The J. Edgar Hoover FBI Building
### Mid-November

Edward S. Bettenhausen's office in the Hoover Building was about
as high up as you could go in Washington, a city that permitted no
buildings to be taller than the Washington Monument. It was a
stripped-down office, though, reflecting Bettenhausen's earlier career
in the U.S. Navy. The floor was low-pile carpet, and three of the four
walls were bookshelves. His desk was shiny bare wood, except for the
keyboard and monitor. The computer hid under the desk in the knee-
hole.

"Sir, you can't pull the plug on this investigation!" Walter Sexton
paced across the room, spun around, and paced back, trying to resist

bunching his hands into fists. You didn't challenge your boss this way; he was well aware of that. And to make matters worse, there were three other men in the room, who watched him from their chairs.

"Because you're getting somewhere?" Hector Brassich sneered.

Bettenhausen said, "All right, Walter. Give it a rest. Sit down."

"Damn." He grudgingly lowered himself onto a hard wooden chair. "Okay. Now I'm sitting."

"Fine, so exactly what do you have?"

Walter Sexton had walked into the office of his boss, Ed Bettenhausen, with no notion that he was here to do more than report on the job so far and explain that he needed more investigators. He'd been summoned, yes, but you were summoned all the time. Orders were what passed for conversation around here. But as soon as he saw Hector Brassich and John Marriolara, he knew there was trouble. And within seconds, all three had told him his case was going nowhere.

John Marriolara was a wiry, rangy guy with a bad attitude. His ticket, or area of expertise, was financial crime. He had devoted a lifetime to fraud, scams, and cons. Therefore, he was senior adviser on the adoption agency cases. Hector "What can we allege?" Brassich was a big-shouldered former prosecutor turned FBI in midlife, an authority on prosecutability—whether a case was likely to be winnable in court—but whose real talent was picking holes in whatever anybody said. Brassich and Marriolara were classically handsome, elegant-looking men, even though their body types were different. They wore good suits, had their hair styled weekly, and walked as if they owned everything in sight. Both had what Walter thought of as upper-class hair, Brassich's white and silky, worn combed back en brosse. Marriolara's was still dark and lush, with just enough white around the temples to give him authority. By comparison Walter felt short, slight, big-nosed, small of eye, kind of a dachshund-person. Come to think of it, dachshunds had been bred lean and pointy so as to follow badgers down into their burrows and catch them. Maybe he *was* a dachshund-person. Useful to the higher-ups, but not glamorous. It amused Walter that Ed Bettenhausen looked very similar to Walter, and yet was the boss of these two Brahmins. Walter would never have said word one about it, of course. Ed Bettenhausen was not a bad boss; he was smart, fair-minded, and understood the problems of agents in the field, but he wanted results and he was budget conscious. He wanted his results in exchange for a reasonable amount of staff hours. He waited for Walter's reply.

"Results? Not much yet," Walter said.

Brassich, the blocky prosecutor, immediately jumped in, never mind that Bettenhausen was senior to him. "You've had six guys and six months. Why nothing?"

"People won't talk. None—not one—of the adoptive parents will say a bad word about Windsor House."

"You got withdrawals from their bank accounts. Amounts that are more than 'reasonable fees.'"

"You bet. Bank withdrawals. And stock sales. In a couple of cases big real estate sales. They were raising serious money. No question."

"Then you threaten their ass. Get me something to *go* on."

"Hold it a minute here, Hector," Bettenhausen said. "There's this little problem of the adopting parents not being criminals. You can't go around threatening the citizenry. And you know it better than the rest of us. I hope. We allowed Walter to go into their bank accounts, and even that is questionable. He didn't have probable cause."

"Then find out the new customers and search them when they leave the country to go abroad. We know they've gotta be carrying more money than the ten-thousand-dollar limit."

"Attack desperate couples whose only crime is that they want to have a baby? Not good press."

"Don't let it get to the press. You say they're not criminals, but they're breaking federal law carrying that cash out and we can scare the shit out of them for bribing foreign officials. It's not like we want to prosecute them. We want to use them."

Marriolara said, "We could get them as they're coming back."

"They have legitimate papers on the baby when they come back."

"Who are we kidding? They take out a pile of money, go to Europe, come back with a baby but without the money."

Bettenhausen said, "Let me make a few things clear. What they do in Europe we can't get them on. We can't arrest them if they go to the Netherlands and do cocaine. We can't even arrest them if they go to, say, Spain and murder a Spaniard. *Spain* can arrest them. We can't."

"We don't *want* to arrest them. All we want is their testimony," Marriolara said.

Walter Sexton said, "Windsor House operates in the States."

"You bet it does. So given enough proof, we can go after Windsor House. But say some U.S. couple gets a proper home study according to the rules of their state, study finds they would be okay adoptive parents, they go get a baby that has legit papers from the country of origin, says the birth parents are dead or gave him up, whatever, baby has no communicable diseases, they bring the baby back, they are A-OK under the laws of any state in the union. Matter of fact, under the new federal law, that baby is an instant U.S. citizen."

Marriolara leaned forward, his eyes narrowed. "Walter, why are you so hipped on Windsor House specifically? The U.S. is full of adoption scams."

"Piddling ones. Like some woman tells ten couples that she's pregnant and all they have to do to get her baby is send her money for medical and living costs. Which of course is legal. Legal for the couples to do, I mean. Maybe she meets with them. She looks pregnant.

And they all send money, and then she disappears and oh, gee, by the way, she was never pregnant in the first place. The couples are victims. The woman is a criminal. She does this across state lines it's federal. It's cruel. But it's still piddling."

"But why Windsor House, Walter? Why do they get up your ass so badly?"

Walter Sexton took a couple of seconds to think. "They're the biggest of the shady agencies. They grew surprisingly fast. They make the most money, and what I think is really important, they make the most money per dollar invested. Their profit margin is huge. It's really uncanny what they're able to do. They charge a fortune for a baby and they get their price. Word on the street—well, on the baby market—is that if you pay Windsor House, you get a baby. But not just any baby, you get the kind of baby you want. Exactly the flavor you ordered and healthy too. Nobody can do that. *Nobody.*"

"Statistically *some* agency has to be the best." Marriolara was acting like a man playing devil's advocate. "Acting," Walter thought, was the operative word. Walter could tell that Marriolara, like Walter, sensed there was something nasty behind Windsor House.

"Of course statistically somebody is always number one. But not this far ahead of the others. It's not an easy business."

Marriolara nodded. "Exactly. I can buy that. It smells." Walter sighed in relief.

Bettenhausen said, "Smells isn't good enough to spend a fortune chasing it down."

Walter said, "There's something really wrong here, sir. If you've ever trusted my instinct on anything, do it this time. Give me just a month more."

Hector Brassich said, "If you haven't got anything in the past six months, how's one more month going to help you?"

Walter didn't even look at him. He held his boss's eyes and said something he usually hated to utter. "Please."

"Okay, okay. You and I'll discuss it. John, Hector, you've made your points. No need to wait around."

# 2

After they had left, which was quickly, since they knew their boss meant what he said, Ed Bettenhausen announced, "Actually, I think I'm going along with you."

Walter let out a breath.

Bettenhausen held up one finger. "But you're going to do this thing my way."

Sexton said, "Of course," thinking, *Sure, sure, anything you want.*

"We're going to give up this pointless panting after satisfied adoptive parents and run you in as a ringer."

"In? In where?"

"You will become a man eager to adopt. You and your wife will approach Windsor House—"

"I don't have a wife."

"I'm aware of that. We'll give you agent Pepper Smith."

"Pepper Smith! Pepper? That can't be a real name! And I don't work with a partner. I work solo or I run a team."

"Not this time, ace. This time you work with a partner, if you want to catch them. Otherwise I've got other assignments for you."

"And I don't work with women. Especially not with women."

"This time you do."

"And it'll take weeks to work up a background. Windsor House could check up every element of this couple's life. And very easily. Not just whether I was a real person. If they can get into the state database, they'd know that the home study of the parents—this Pepper person and me—hadn't been done, for instance. And I'm damned sure that one thing they're super-great at is getting into government databases. I'd need an identity and a state of long-term residence and then I'd have to apply for the home study—"

"Wisconsin."

"What?"

"The study's been done. INS form I-600 is ready, except for the country of origin's verification about the baby. You and Pepper are going to replace some real-life people. You're going to be George and Sylvia Carroll."

"Who are these people?"

"I'm glad you asked that. Here's the tale." Bettenhausen swallowed coffee, then leaned back in his chair. "In Madison, Wisconsin, lives a sort-of-young couple named Sylvia and George Carroll. Sylvia is a professor of sociology at the University of Wisconsin. George is a thoracic surgeon. They have no expenses to speak of except a small dinghy they sail on those lakes up there; they work practically all the time, and as a result they've accumulated a fair amount of money, even though they are only in their midthirties. To be specific, George is thirty-eight and Sylvia is thirty-four. They are childless and very upset about it. They've wanted a baby for the last five years at least. My impression is that before that they were too busy with their careers to care. Thought there was plenty of time. When they decided to forego their contraceptive, nothing happened. They went through the usual medical tests and fertility treatments. Nothing worked. During the last year, they have been trying to adopt, but haven't had much luck there either, partly because their requirements are too specific. And it is my impression that they are not very patient people. They want to adopt *now*, not when some agency gives the go-ahead."

"And so?"

"So they ask around, get on the Net, and to make a long story short, eventually they hear that Windsor House is the Cadillac of adoption agencies for out-of-the-U.S. adoption, and they can get you whatever kind of baby you want. So they make contact. Windsor House is very upfront. First, they tell the Carrolls they have to come up with fifteen thousand for the search and twenty thousand for fees, including the lawyer's fee. Well, they expected that. They're experienced, professional people. They've done their research. Fees up to a point are permitted by law; it's not considered baby selling. Other people who adopted abroad have paid big fees, and the Carrolls have money. They want a baby. They want a baby right now. They say okay.

"The lawyer tells them they will have to go to Romania or Russia themselves when a possible baby is located. A finder who arranges adoptions in that country will take them to several orphanages and let them look at a few baby candidates. They are to take a lot of cash with them, hidden on their bodies, fifty thousand to be exact, plus another thirty thousand in traveler's checks, and be prepared to spend it all. The officials in charge of the orphanages need to be paid. 'Bribed, you mean,' George says. The agent says, 'Yes, but that's the only way to do it. You want it or you don't want it?' And they do want it, so they agree. They'd heard in advance about this too, from other couples.

"But then they start talking it over between themselves. What if Windsor House had a recording device and their phone call was on tape? They didn't exactly agree to anything criminal, they hoped, but yet in a way they did. They'd be taking an impermissible amount of money out of the country. They agreed to bribe an official of a foreign country. Maybe that was a crime there. Maybe that was a crime here. Even if it wasn't, did they want to get involved with people like this? Maybe the Carrolls would be arrested in Romania or Russia and all their money taken away, and maybe they wouldn't even get a baby. Or maybe this adoption group wanted a tape of the conversation to hold over their heads if something went wrong with the adoption, so they wouldn't complain. Sometimes if a child has an unexpected defect—it's not politically correct, of course, to call it a defect—or is sick or shows some weird behavior problem, the parents want to return it. The more the Carrolls thought about all this, the more they got cold feet."

"And came to us? That seems unlikely. How did you find them?" He tried to keep the annoyance out of his voice. There was an implied criticism here—after all, he was the expert on the Windsor House case and he hadn't found them.

"Didn't. They found us. Really. George Carroll decided to go to a guy he knew. He had more or less saved the man's life a month earlier when some cardiac stent got loose in an artery or clogged up or whatever the damn things do, and George did an emergency snuffle-out job. The man was an FBI agent. Naturally, I immediately thought of you."

"And I'm supposed to do what?"

"Go to New York with Pepper as the Carrolls, meet with as many of the agency people as possible, pay them big money, get staff fingerprints when you can, photograph all of them, tape them advising you to take more than the permitted ten thou out of the country, go on to Romania and Russia—"

"Wait a minute. All Windsor House has to do is inquire around Madison, Wisconsin, and they'll find the Carrolls are still there."

"Nope. The Carrolls plan to leave in three weeks on an extended tour of the Yucatán Peninsula, studying several interesting Maya ruins."

"Anyway, they'll know what George and Sylvia look like."

"They may. As it happens, George looks a whole lot like you. Same height, same face, same nose, forehead, and hairline, anyway. Chins are a little different. It took us a while to locate an agent who looked like Sylvia. Pepper does. Especially now that she's had her hair dyed and added ten pounds. She's been on a cheeseburger-and-shake diet for a week now."

"Oh God."

"Actually, we assigned her two quarter-pounders with cheese and fries for lunch and a bucket of KFC for dinner. A chocolate shake before bed. Fixed her right up. You should have heard her complain. Most people would have thanked us."

"God."

"And as for you, George is going to start growing a beard today. So are you. Today. In two weeks, George will have his picture taken at a conference in Madison for a new cardiac intensive care unit, and the picture will be prominently displayed in the city news section of the local paper. So if anybody is really interested in him they can find the grainy news photo of him sporting his hairy chops."

"Swell. You've been planning this for a while."

"Couple of weeks."

"Why not tell Hector and John?"

"No need. Actually, I would prefer we didn't have to send you abroad, but I've given you as long as I can to get the evidence some other way. If you can't get it, nobody can."

"Flattery? Now I'm suspicious. Anyway, what about the paperwork? You can't just run out and bring home an infant."

"The Carrolls had already completed the paperwork. They had the home study by a social worker that Wisconsin requires before you can adopt a baby."

"Nice of them."

"You'll pop down to Quantico and spend about two weeks learning how to act like a cardiologist, just in general conversation, at least in the sense of speaking the lingo, knowing the names of the major drugs, and so on. It would be a real embarrassment if somebody asks you whether you think nitroglycerine is useful and you say it makes really great bombs."

"Be a real disaster if somebody has a heart attack and I don't know how to defibrillate."

"All you need to know is to add doctor-style confidence to your basic CPR. For more exotic stuff you'll have to say you're traveling on business and don't have your gear."

"This Pepper person is going to be trained in sociology?"

"Majored in it in college."

"Oh great!" He sneered. "Perfect."

"So, right after Thanksgiving you two go to New York as George and Sylvia, prepared to travel. And then the two of you will go to Romania or Russia or wherever Windsor House sends you."

Walter stared in horror. "Travel for days in a foreign country with this woman? Stay in the same room?"

"What are you complaining about? You've been wanting to get inside Windsor House. And you get to sleep with a lovely young woman. Or at least in the same room. Of course, you won't have any law-enforcement authority abroad."

Most people believed that the CIA operated in foreign countries and the FBI only within the geographical confines of the United States. Walter well knew that wasn't true. The FBI had no jurisdiction outside the United States, of course. Other countries were sovereign powers. But the FBI maintained investigatory staffs, liaisons, and legal attaché offices called LEGATs, in every major nation on earth. There were at least forty countries where the FBI maintained resident agents.

This did not mean they actually had authority in any of these places. You go and try to arrest somebody in Canada, say, you could be arrested yourself, and the fact that you were a U.S. FBI agent wouldn't help you. If you were carrying a firearm in Canada, you were in very big trouble. Russia would be worse.

Walter Sexton said, "I don't like this whole idea. We're not exactly popular out there."

"Oh come on," Bettenhausen said. "Since September eleventh, Russia and the U.S. are best buddies."

"Remember Moonlight Maze?" Sexton said, referring to an Internet crime incident. "Russia ever so kindly let us in, and then gave us zero help."

"Ukraine actually invited us in to help determine if that corpse with no head was Georgiy Gongadze. They often make use of our expertise."

"That was a propaganda move. The point I'm making is that the Russians can't possibly want somebody like me to come in and find out where their orphans are going. Never happen. Headless corpses are one thing. But international adoption is sensitive. There's something you're not telling me."

"Right. I was coming to it. I'll admit we've already asked Romania and Russia about Windsor House."

"And?"

"They don't see anything wrong."

Sexton folded his arms. For a few seconds he fought against the rush of anger he felt, and he finally beat it down. "So I'm going to be trespassing. Investigating on foreign soil without the approval of the local governments."

"Um—actually without the *knowledge* of the local governments."

"Oh great. In other words, without any backup from the local police. So Windsor House, which is probably in bed with local officials anyhow, can strike back at me and Pepper if it finds out we're ringers?"

"It's an adoption agency, Sexton, for God's sake, not the effing Mafia. They won't have squads of enforcers. They're not violent."

"Right. What could possibly go wrong?"

# 3

As Walter stepped outside into the gray light of a Washington, D.C., November, he felt disenchanted with the FBI. Not for the first time, he wondered why the Hoover Building had been designed to be so dispiriting. Maybe it was a sly comment on J. Edgar Hoover himself, with its square dullness and repellent exterior. The windows were recessed in a honeycomb pattern framed in gray concrete. The cement ceiling of the entry courtyard was also gray honeycomb concrete. The entry hall was heavily barred, the flooring gray and mottled, and even where the interior was carpeted, somebody had chosen a drab, speckled institutional low-pile rug.

The place looked like a prison, even though it wasn't one. This amount of dreariness must have been intended as a statement.

Walter shrugged. He crossed the street and paused outside the Caucus Room, a restaurant where FBI agents in a hurry sometimes ate.

Despite reservations about his assignment, Walter had left the office with a great feeling of relief. He'd resented being under such tight scrutiny, and he was uneasy about it too, because Bettenhausen was an acute observer of people. He hadn't got to his present position by letting agents put scams over on him. Walter knew he was burning much too hot on this case. He would be astonished if Bettenhausen hadn't seen that.

But it wasn't the emotion invested in the case that Walter was keeping to himself. Not really, even though he'd like to appear judicious.

What he wanted to keep to himself was what he thought lay behind the success of Windsor House Adoptions. Letting that idea out of the bag would make him seem like a raving paranoiac.

# 4

Bettenhausen watched the door close behind Walter Sexton. He deliberately let five minutes go by and then punched a button on a display of two dozen on his desk pilot.

Almost immediately, Hector Brassich came back in. "How'd it go?" he said.

"He's on board."

"Yeah. But is he under control?"

"For now. He's really the man for the job," Bettenhausen said, thinking that you had to use the human supplies that were available. One part of his job was placing people into their most useful positions. The fact that you were then accused of using people was really a statement that you were doing your job right.

Brassich was his next-in-command, not his superior. Nevertheless he said, as if giving permission, "Well, I guess we'll go with that. I agree."

"You'd better."

"Yes, sir."

"It's going to give the CIA fits when we trump them."

"Don't you love it."

Bettenhausen was comfortable with the setup. He had put plans into motion to keep track of the situation. Sexton was an unguided missile. He needed watching.

# CHAPTER ELEVEN

I'm in graduate school at a superior college and am
three months pregnant. The baby is a boy. His father
is a professor of mathematics. I want a family that
can provide only the very best in life for my son.
I expect to maintain a permanent relationship with
that family.

*Bids will be accepted through February.*
*This one will go fast. Press 1101.*

## 1

### New York City
### Mid-November

The flies tell you whether the baby is dead. But not just any flies.
The nagging little black flies that burrow in around your mouth and
eyes and seem to want to eat teardrops—those don't mean death. The
burrowing flies that bite to make sores on your skin and then lay their
eggs in the raw flesh so their larvae can suck your juices to their heart's
content, those didn't mean death either. It was useful to recognize
which were the flies of the dead, because the living children were often
so weak you couldn't tell them apart from the dead. But the flies could
tell.

The little Sudanese boy lay on a piece of cloth, which was all that
separated him from the red-ochre sand. Gabrielle squatted next to

him, holding a bottle with a nipple on the end. In the bottle was a nutritive drink the relief workers supplied for the starving children. The aid workers had separated the older orphans from the infants so that they could bottle-feed the babies. The older children sat or lay dying in a meadow a quarter-mile away.

Gabrielle put the bottle to the child's lips and he sucked. Even though he was at least two, he was too weak to hold the bottle or to eat solid food.

She put the bottle down on the ground when the child faded off into a kind of coma. She looked at the camera and began to speak.

Now in her studio in New York, Gabrielle watched herself in the segment. The sound on her monitor was off. Gabrielle remembered when they had shot the part with the feeding bottle. She could almost hear the buzzing of the flies, and she saw them now on the screen, one species hovering around the child, waiting for him to die, other types eagerly boring in around his eyes, to make lunch of the flakes of skin around his eyelashes.

The camera zoomed out slowly, showing Gabrielle and the two-year-old flanked by two other babies. One was about a year old and one, to her right, was a tiny infant. The infant was dead. Gabrielle knew that because the flies on his eyelids, lips, and those moving into his tiny nostrils were different from the flies that buzzed around the child she was trying to feed. The dead-flies, one of the nuns said, feasted on the corpses. But one of the U.N. aid workers said the flies that came to the dead were not eating. They were blowflies, he said, and they were laying their eggs. They were *Chrysomyra*, he said, and there were members of their large family all over the world.

You were supposed to watch for those particular flies and when you saw them you called for the dead cart, a farm wagon hitched onto the back of a jeep. It was very important, the nuns said, to collect the dead and remove them from the living before they could spread pestilence. The refugees already had dysentery and malaria, but they would have more serious disease if the aid workers allowed the dead to lie among the living. The dead cart took them several miles away.

With the Polaroid CU-5, Gabrielle had photographed three different types of flies in close-up. She thought she and Justin could use the close-up stills in the documentary.

Justin's camera started in close on the face of the dead baby and the flies. Then the camera backed slowly away, discovering that Gabrielle and these four were surrounded by two more rows of children, one behind her and one nearer the camera.

There was a cut. Justin had stopped taping here. In a new shot, the faces of Gabrielle and the children on either side of her filled the screen. Then the camera tilted up and widened out, showing the children behind her and in front of her, then it widened more and dollied farther away, showing Gabrielle and many nuns and aid workers utterly outnumbered by a sea of starving infants and children. Higher and higher, farther and farther away it moved, until the fields of the starving in the distance looked like dots on the rose-colored land.

Gabrielle froze the last shot. She could hardly bear the pain of watching. The video had been shot four months ago, when she and Justin had just begun work on the documentary. Gabrielle had been overcome by the numbers of the dying, the big doomed eyes of the children, and the smell of death, feces, and rot, all stewed together in the heat rising from the plains.

She remembered that day, holding the child, telling Justin that they had to take the experience back somehow and show people. But she was also desperately frustrated because of the impossibility of conveying how many children there were. "We can't walk from one child to the next. There are hundreds! Thousands! The video would go on for hours. But if we don't show it, nobody will understand!"

Justin had been drooping from the horror of it too. They both knew, though, that standing there stunned would not help anybody. And more and more starving people were coming to the camp all the time. Twenty or thirty aid workers trying to feed a few at a time would hardly help. The horror would never end unless the world resolved to end it.

That their contribution could stir the world's compassion was hardly likely, but they had to try. Surely they could reach some people's hearts.

"I know," Justin said. "We'll do a *Gone with the Wind.*"

"What do you mean?"

"You know that scene that begins with a few injured Confederate soldiers, Scarlett's looking for somebody, Ashley maybe, no, the doctor, and then the camera dollies and pans and tilts up and you see more and more soldiers, just fields of dead and dying soldiers."

"Oh. Yes."

Gabrielle had been whipsawed emotionally for a few moments. It felt coldly analytical in the midst of all this pain, Justin's mind going immediately for the most effective visual. The best camera angle. The most impact. But he was right, of course; she also felt an overwhelming need to *show* the world what was going on. You couldn't convey this horror adequately unless you did it superlatively. And for that matter, Gabrielle herself had done the same when she photographed several types of flies with the Polaroid. The point was to make the situation vivid, wasn't it?

Their producer, Sam Bielski, had been with them on the shoot—fortunately, since the whole area was extremely dangerous, rife with marauding soldiers from both sides. Sam had found one of the aid mission's helicopter pilots willing to take Justin up, with just a little money donation for several days' worth of fuel. And here was the result.

Look at this film! she thought. He was *so* right.

Staring at the frozen image, Gabrielle began to cry. She missed Justin. She hadn't helped those children or any children. Not yet. Most of them were probably dead by now. But she could finish the documentary.

Without Justin?

It would not be as good without Justin. Not even close. She could put together the words, but he had the eye. Nevertheless, this was the way it would have to be.

## 2

The funeral, two days before Thanksgiving, had been dreadful. A lot of Justin's friends from CNN came, and a lot of people from his high school, particularly the ones who still lived in the town where he grew up. Justin's parents introduced her as his fiancée.

The church was the same one where he had been baptized. There were actually ancestors in the cemetery, something Gabrielle, with her lack of family, had never seen outside of a movie.

The coffin was made of beautiful golden oak—and how awful *that* was, to think that this beautiful wood would be lowered into the ground to rot, and Justin, who had been a beautiful man, would rot also. And the grave was a real grave, dug in the earth. Why hadn't she ever realized how deep they were? Six feet was terribly far down. She saw with a shudder that the hole was dark at the bottom.

His mother said, "Visit us whenever you can, Gabrielle. You're one of the things that were part of him, that we can still touch." His little sister Katie sat cuddled up next to Gabrielle most of the service, even though she was sixteen, and had walked into the church in a very ladylike manner. Katie was dark-haired and tall, like Justin. Gabrielle wrapped her arms around them too, especially the sister, but it only made her sorrow worse. She felt she could stand anything right then except sympathy, because sympathy would make her cry.

The one thing she had to do was finish the documentary. It had to be good, so that she could dedicate it to Justin and make him proud. They had done orphans in Romania, Sudan, Ethiopia, and Guatemala. They had talked about doing one or two more countries after Russia, probably India and China, but they had never been certain they would need more if the tapes of these five were really good. And they were good. Thanks to Justin.

Gabrielle made a cup of coffee and sat down with the editing equipment. She wasn't a professional editor, of course, but she'd learned a lot of facets of the business, even using her precious vacations to take courses in areas she had missed. She could narrow some of this down to what she needed before she got a professional editor on the case. Her plan was to do an off-line, a longish rough cut. Then the pro could finish the on-line. Justin's photography was the heart of the project and the heart of his brilliance. Justin wasn't an editor either. His eye was so good, though, that he had a reputation of being able to "edit in the camera."

## 3

One of the saddest and best things about screening these tapes was her increasing realization of what a great photographer Justin had been. The footage had a realistic cinema verité quality that would make a viewer feel as if he had walked into the orphanage personally. But underneath the naturalness was beautiful framing. Justin led your eye subtly to the important point of the shot.

She digitized the material shot in the field into the hard drive of the editing machine, then started to do a little simple editing on the screen. Since every bit of tape had been duplicated and the dubs stored at the studio, she didn't have to worry about accidentally erasing anything. Justin had laughed when she told him she was always afraid of doing that. He claimed it was harder to do than she thought. "Harder for you," she said.

Fortunately, all their editing equipment except the little portable was here in New York. Much of it was rented. They hadn't taken it to Russia because they got by with just the portable. All they needed there was to screen what they had, log it in, and time the tape. If they had taken the big editor, it would have been smashed like all the other hardware, and it was the most expensive equipment they owned, all computer-driven now. Their smashed equipment had been fully insured. They might have been optimistic about their project, but they weren't naive. CNN had also insisted that even though Gabrielle and Justin were technically taking a leave of absence, their life insurance and medical would be kept up. So Justin's family would get something. It was money they would have done anything not to have this dreadful reason to receive.

The insurance company was taking its time to pay on the equipment they had owned, the digital camera, batteries, battery cases, tapes, tripod, all the rest of it. A couple of weeks was nothing to an insurance company, but it was a lot to a filmmaker with a deadline. Thank goodness she had saved quite a bit from her salary. She didn't need most of the equipment right now, she had to admit, but what if she had to go back and shoot something over, or go to one or two more countries?

Well, she didn't need it right now, and that was that. Thank God she'd never have to go back to Russia.

Her early ideas about the documentary had to do with orphans in general, but she soon realized it was *too* general. There were orphans all over the world. Packs of orphans ran in the street in Rio, stealing and attacking tourists. Orphans lay on sidewalks in India. In the United States orphans were farmed out to foster families, some of whom loved them and some of whom took them in only for the money.

She had decided to limit herself to babies under one year old.

There were still way too many. Too many orphaned babies.

Gabrielle had always considered herself a writer rather than a talking head. She had got into television writing news at a small station in Michigan's Upper Peninsula, and sort of backed into an on-camera role when a blizzard kept most of the reporters from getting to work for several days and she was snowed in at the studio. Most of their reporters lived farther from town, in houses near the lake. She was able to trudge from the studio to a few houses nearby. Her stories about how people coped, snowed into their houses for days on end, had been seen all over the state. A television station in Grand Rapids had picked her up. And there she'd been seen by NBC and the rest was history.

Gabrielle had spent a lot of time while she and Justin had traveled trying to decide what to call the film. *Orphans* was one simple and honest possibility. *Orphaned Infants* was too off-putting. *Help Me* stuck in her mind for a while, but it sounded like a suspense film, so eventually she dropped it. *Suffer the Children* had already been used as a book title and anyway was too specifically religious. *Babies in Peril* might work. Lately she thought the best was *Babies Without Parents*. She liked using the word "babies." Everybody loved babies, and the title was a bit intriguing. How could you have babies without parents? How did the babies lose their families? What would happen to them?

She needed the spur of a working title to draft the narration, and she needed an outline of the narration to guide the choice of taped segments. The process involved parallel work. There was a saying that "the picture always leads." And that was true. If you didn't have good visuals, you didn't have anything. She needed to know what were the best sequences on the tapes to be sure to include them. So they dictated what had to be worked into the narration. But she also needed to know where they going with the documentary in order to organize it.

She had started the project with more enthusiasm than planning. One time, in a fit of self-doubt, she had mentioned this to Justin, and he said, "Of course."

"What do you mean 'of course'? We've taken half a year off from our jobs and we may have nothing to show for it because I didn't plan ahead."

"People who look at all the problems before they start never get anything done. Or if they do, it isn't anything fresh."

Dear, sweet Justin. She surely hoped he was right. At least today his voice in her mind's ear made her feel better.

The first thing she had to do, instead of this sampling tapes here and there, jumping around through the material, was to sit down and look at everything they had, a process that would take at least ten days. There were hundreds of hours of material. It was time to screen it all.

# 4

Once a week, Gabrielle telephoned Moscow. The man from the U.S. Embassy, Henry Stover, had located a detective in the police department who spoke English. And once a week she called the detective and asked him whether they had found Justin's killers. They had not. She kept calling, as regular as the sunrise. She was not going to let them forget Justin.

# 5

## New York City
## Thanksgiving Day

On Thanksgiving Day, Gabrielle stayed home to screen tape. Her parents were both dead and she had no brothers or sisters to spend the holiday with. Justin's parents had invited her up to their place, but she just couldn't bear the idea. As kindly as she could, she leveled with Justin's mother. "It would just make me too sad," she said. "I'm sort of just staying in and working."

"Does it help?" Mrs. Craig asked.

"Um. Not too much."

"I've been trying the same thing. I reupholstered all the dining room chairs. Myself." She gave a choked sob. "Are you sure you don't want to come, Gabby?"

"Maybe later."

"Maybe Christmas?"

"Yes. That might be good."

So she sat on the floor of their "studio"—which was actually a small room, this being New York—with a bare wood floor and no furniture except a microwave, two swivel chairs, and a four-by-eight sheet of three-quarter-inch A-D plywood, the smooth side up, placed on two sawhorses. Everything else in the room was editing equipment, video equipment, and tape storage.

Next to Gabrielle on the floor was a Swanson's turkey dinner, which she had just heated in the microwave, and two bottles of Anchor Steam beer.

She was still trying to decide the basic structure of the documentary. She didn't want to do a day in the life of one particular orphan in each country, although in the first three countries they had shot a lot of film on one particular child and his or her surroundings, just in case. She had decided that was too limiting. She had decided to take each country in turn, rather than hop around. What she wanted to present first of all was scope, something that showed how big the problem was, and then serious descriptive content, exactly what happened to abandoned infants. Put another way, she thought to herself, the babies were heart-wrenching enough without getting hokey about it. Just the facts, ma'am.

Gabrielle believed that television was, if anything, too powerful a medium already. It came directly into people's homes, seemingly into their minds, with its vivid pictures. One of the reasons she had made an important name for herself as a reporter was that she really cared about the words she used; she gave abundant, accurate details without putting a curve on them. She treated the viewer like an adult, providing whatever information she could dig out, and let the viewer draw conclusions. This was harder than it sounded because you were making choices among all the pictures you could show and all the background facts you might include and the other choices, of course, were not seen by the viewer. But still, she was careful to leave out editorializing.

The babies and exactly how they lived in all the orphanages and war zones that she had filmed would be the story by themselves. What they ate. Where they slept. Who cared—or didn't care—for them. One country after another. Let the viewer think of the horror of it. She would show, not tell.

To go to China or not? she wondered. She would have to take a new photographer, maybe Gordo. Maybe Sam would be well enough by then to produce. He was getting better little by little.

She and Justin had talked about whether China was necessary. She believed they needed a taste of each of the world's major ethnic groups, and up to now they had no Asians. Justin had doubts because he thought the visuals would be limited.

"Sam says they don't let you in the orphanages at all," he said. "If you have proper papers and you're approved to adopt, you go to a room and wait there. Sometimes it's just a hotel room. And they bring you a baby."

"But we wouldn't be adopting. We'd be going to see the unadopted babies in the orphanage."

"They won't let you."

In China girls were not valued. When a girl was born friends extended condolences to the family. But the national policy of one-family-one-child had exacerbated the problem. If a couple gave birth to a female baby, they didn't want to be stuck with her. If they gave her away, they could try again for a male. So the orphanages were overflowing with girls. China had become *the* place to adopt baby girls.

Justin said, "All we'll get to see is a procession of girl babies carried into a hotel by nurses."

"It would make that segment different from all the others."

"I don't like it." He was uncharacteristically negative about this,

BARBARA D'AMATO

152

PROPERTY OF
HIGH POINT PUBLIC LIBRARY
HIGH POINT, NORTH CAROLINA

seeing the pictures in his mind as too uniform. "I guess the segment could be shorter than the others."

"You might be wrong that we can't see the orphanages. I want to try. I'll get Sam to check it out."

But he wasn't wrong. Sam Bielski reported that, if they went to China, there would be no orphanage tours. Eventually she would have to make the decision, go or don't go.

Today Gabrielle tried out a scratch-track version of her voice-over. She wanted a short background of what was happening in each of her target countries, to give an idea of the social events that had caused the orphaning of so many children.

When she spoke directly to a camera, she pictured the camera as her grandfather, a measured, judicious man, a courtly man who loved children. Now, even though she was recording only her voice on a scratch-track for time, she did the same, speaking as if she wanted to tell her grandfather something important, but being reasonable about it, not emotional.

"When Nicolae Ceaușescu came to power in 1955, at his wife's instigation he passed laws designed to increase the birth rate. Among them was Decree No. 770, passed in 1966, making abortion illegal for any woman under forty-five who had not given birth to at least four children. Birth control was unavailable except on the black market or to certain favored government officials. Unfortunately, there was no system in place to help the women care for or feed so many children. As a result, huge numbers were abandoned at state orphanages. The orphanages were given very little money, and therefore they were seriously understaffed, could provide virtually no medical care and only the poorest food. The children had little human contact or stimulation, let alone love. The effect of the lack of care was physical and mental damage to the children and a diagnosis a few years down the road of mental defect.

"After Ceauşescu's execution, a spate of news media stories on the orphans appeared in Europe and the United States, including photos of the abandoned children beating their heads against the bars of their cribs in hopelessness. The world was horrified and rushed in to help. In the uproar that followed, more than ten thousand of the children were adopted out of the country. But in 1991 Romania suddenly stopped all adoption by foreigners in order to curtail rampant baby selling. After some time passed for reappraisal, adoption resumed. Four years later, in response to public fears that children were being adopted for use by pedophile rings or as organ donors, a new set of laws was passed. Adoption was permitted only through the Romanian Committee on Adoptions in association with national organizations outside of Romania. Adoptions again dried up. Efforts are now being made to establish Romanian family home-style units in place of orphanages, but much of the orphanage system still exists and abuses are said to be widespread. A program has begun to encourage Romanian families to take orphans home for a weekend visit and to give them some experience with life outside the orphanage. Despite this, those orphans who survive the system without severe physical or mental damage will be released on their eighteenth birthday with very little knowledge of how to get along in the larger world. Many have never ridden a tram or a subway. Many have never even shopped for food in a store."

She paused.

Well, she thought, replaying the voice-over, that certainly needed work, but it was work she enjoyed. Should she try to find some stock footage of Ceauşescu, which she could easily get from any film library, or was he beside the point? No. The point, after all, was the babies. As far as her video on the Romanian babies was concerned, she was pretty much satisfied with the footage she already had. She certainly wasn't going back.

Babies—the documentary had to be the babies, with just a small amount of background.

So she started to review all the tapes again. Now she had a plan.

That was, until she made her discovery.

# 6

## Chappaqua, New York
## Thanksgiving Day

The big white house was redolent of Thanksgiving. Dooley marveled, not for the first time, that the human nose could distinguish dozens of scents at once. He smelled the tang of simmering fresh cranberry sauce, mashed potatoes, sweet potatoes, roasting turkey, of course, gravy, and under it all a rich brown-sugar sweetness he was sure was pecan pie.

His in-laws lived in Chappaqua, thirty-five miles from Manhattan. Chappaqua wasn't a posh suburb because a former president lived there; the former president lived there because it was a posh suburb. The Tarkingtons had called it home for decades and were cautiously proud that the Clintons realized how desirable it was. Even though Daniel Tarkington was a Republican.

Daniel Tarkington, Dooley's father-in-law, came toward him, holding out a glass containing three fingers of Laphroaig scotch. Dooley said, "Thanks, Daniel," and accepted it gratefully. He preferred bourbon, but Daniel preferred scotch. In the Tarkington house, you did what Daniel wanted.

Even Ruth Tarkington knew that. She said, as she always did,

"Oh, Danny! That's not an aperitif!" but she didn't expect Daniel to alter his behavior.

The women—Claudia, Ruth, Ruth's unmarried sister Evelyn, and Miss Penny, an elderly teacher from the local high school whom Ruth often invited to holidays claiming she was lonely—were all accepting sherry from a lad hired from the local junior college to serve as butler-for-the-day. Sherry, to Ruth, was an appropriate aperitif as long as it was very dry. Very dry sherry reminded Dooley of printer toner.

Teddy was given a plastic glass of apple juice. Ruth picked Teddy up and sat on the sofa with him in her lap. Teddy had always liked visiting his grandmother and sometimes stayed overnight. She said to him, "Once upon a time there were three little pigs—"

Aunt Evelyn, Claudia, and Miss Penny chatted together. Dooley heard Claudia say, "Then he said, 'If I can't, neverbody can.' "

Talking about Teddy, Dooley deduced. Miss Penny laughed the hardest. Briefly Dooley realized he didn't know whether Penny was Miss Penny's last name or whether it was short for something like Penelope.

Dooley took the opportunity to watch Claudia when she didn't know he was looking at her. He was worried about her. If there was some way to avoid the disaster that was rushing toward them, he would move the world to spare her. If there was no way to head it off, what then? When he first realized that Claudia might even take Teddy and run, he had wondered how, what would she live on? But now he suspected her parents would help her.

"Hey, Dooley," Daniel caroled, patting his shoulder too hard. A bit of a grown-up bully, Dooley thought. "Do you know what the future in marketing is, the one word that describes the future?"

Dooley, who was a fan of old movies and medium-old movies, and had loved *The Graduate*, wanted to say "plastics." But Daniel had very little sense of humor at the best of times and none whatsoever where his own pronouncements were concerned.

"What, sir?" Dooley asked, tilting his head agreeably.

"Destination malls!"

Dooley tried to look suitably impressed, but he really didn't understand. Daniel Tarkington was a mall developer, had been for decades. Malls were a new thing back in the late sixties, when Daniel's career was just taking off, and he'd made a mint in the business, building on a nice piece of change that his father, founder of a chain of bakeries, had handed on to him. Malls were not a new thing any longer.

"Dan, I thought you already built malls—"

"*Destination* malls, Dooley! Pay attention! You'll never get anywhere if you don't pay attention! There are many types of malls. Little strip malls. Local malls. Big malls. Theme malls. The mall of the future is the destination mall!"

"What is that?"

"More than a mall, that's what it is. It's a total entertainment experience. Movies, restaurants, singles bars, lots and lots of stores, fast food, barbershop quartets singing in the atrium, trams that run visitors—notice that I say visitors, not customers—from one part of the mall to another, art galleries, music clubs, light shows, indoor playgrounds for the children—" He stopped to take a gulp of his scotch.

Before he could start up again, Dooley said, "It sounds very expensive to build."

"Very! But it's the only way to go. Little strip malls are dying. Local stores only get local people. Not enough clientele. Today everything is e."

"Eee?"

"E-business. You can order toys and clothes and hardware over the Net. You don't actually have to *go* anyplace anymore. You can get food from Peapod off a long list of products and you don't have to deal with human beings. All your necessities can come to you directly. No more standing in line while the clerk waits on the person ahead of you. Slowly. No more dealing with rude clerks."

"Yes, but then why build stores?"

"I'm not building stores. I'm building *experiences.* It's entertainment. You go to a destination mall to spend the whole day. Hell, you spend the evening there too. Fine wines, your choice of restaurants, your choice of movies, dancing, shows. Horses, merry-go-rounds, petting zoos, Ferris wheels! There's even on-site baby-sitting!"

He took another sip of scotch, and Dooley, racking his brain for an intelligent response, was relieved to hear Ruth say, "Dinner is ready, everyone."

The Tarkingtons normally had a butler, who seemed to be off today, and a live-in cook/housekeeper. She was Mrs. Shaughnessy, an Irish widow. Mrs. Shaughnessy did not believe that cholesterol was bad for people, which made her mashed potatoes whipped with butter and cream a symphony. For all the difficulty of carrying on a conversation with Daniel—assuming a conversation was an event that involved two participants, not just one person talking—Dooley liked going to the Tarkingtons now and then just for the food. Claudia couldn't very well remind him that he wasn't supposed to have gravy, potatoes, stuffing, and large slabs of turkey with the skin on when it was her own parents serving the feast.

Daniel Tarkington carved the twenty-five-pound bird himself, of course, removing the two drumsticks neatly with a horn-handled knife, then severing the thighs from the carcass with game shears, cutting the meat from them into two or three pieces each, and placing them on a platter. Next he sliced slabs of white meat, laying the slabs on the platter, which Mrs. Shaughnessy carried around the table. She served each person as she went.

Unlike a lot of children, Teddy never asked for a drumstick. From a bird this big, it would have been more than he could eat anyway. He had always liked the wing, and his grandfather cut one into pieces for him with the game shears.

"Wait!" Aunt Evelyn said.

Daniel Tarkington said, "What, Evelyn?" with ponderous patience.

"We should give thanks. It's Thanksgiving, after all."

"If you like," he said in a tone of voice that meant "If you must."

"Bless this food, Lord," Evelyn said, bowing her head. "And make us thankful for what we have. There are so many who have so little. Let us all be mindful of our blessings."

Dooley squirmed mentally, wondering why people spoke in awkward ways when they said a prayer aloud. At the same time, he admitted that she had reminded him of what was important. Everyone raised their heads and began to pass potatoes and gravy. But Dooley said impulsively, "You know, Teddy, I'm grateful for you."

*And may he live with us for always.*

"Why are you grateful for me?"

"Well, you know we chose you for our little boy. We had to go halfway around the world to find you."

"Why?"

"Because you were there and we were here."

"Oh. You wanted a little boy and not a little girl?" Teddy asked.

Claudia said, "We wanted you. Exactly you."

"Adoption is a very decent thing," said Miss Penny. "A good deed in a naughty world." She giggled. "Shakespeare, you know."

"Well," Ruth said, "this certainly is lovely stuffing. I always enjoy it with giblets." She was uncomfortable with talk of adoption.

Claudia's Aunt Evelyn said, "Whose fault was the infertility exactly?"

Dead silence. Ruth, being the hostess and Evelyn's sister, must have felt the onus was on her to fix this gaffe, if possible.

"Evelyn, in matters like that, one doesn't speak of *fault.*"

"Well, you know what I mean."

"What you mean, Aunt Evelyn," Claudia said, "is that you're sorry you asked."

# 7

"My God, Aunt Evelyn can be a bitch sometimes," Claudia said. They were heading home to Manhattan in the car, with Teddy sound asleep in his car seat. He had fought valiantly to keep himself awake, entertaining his grandparents with stories about playschool, up to the moment they pulled out of the driveway, waving and calling, "Wonderful dinner." Then he'd fallen fast asleep in his car seat as if someone had flicked a switch.

"I'm not sure your mother liked the way you snapped at her."

"My mother wanted to snap at her herself. Sisters don't stand on ceremony with each other."

"Yes, I guess you're right."

"But you're right too. She didn't want me to do it. Dooley, do people really still think in terms of fault? Is my inability to get pregnant a fault?"

Dooley knew what Claudia really wanted to ask. He produced viable sperm. She did not reliably produce eggs and a hormonal problem stopped the ones she did produce from implanting even if they were fertilized, even if fertilized in vitro. Claudia was chronically worried because she knew that he could have had his "own" children if his wife had been able to conceive. She worried that he blamed her, even though they had talked about it several times and he had told her over and over again that he didn't, that the very idea was silly. It didn't seem like the time to have that discussion all over again.

Dooley answered the unspoken question elliptically. "Nobody could think that Teddy," Dooley looked back at him in his car seat, to be sure he was asleep, "was anything less than the world's greatest blessing."

"No, they couldn't, could they?"

"That's why—um—I've been thinking. The leukemia thing was a scare. It was a near miss, thank God, but—"

"But what?"

"We have almost no information about Teddy's medical heritage. We don't have any idea what diseases or conditions may be in his genes. You know, more and more diseases are showing up as inherited. Everything from heart disease to osteoporosis to high cholesterol to depression."

"Ye-es."

"That's why we need to find out about his parentage," Dooley said, lying.

"But how would we do that?"

"I have that seven-day leave that made up for my being here last vacation. I think I should go to Russia."

"You seriously think you could get answers out of a bunch of Russian officials?"

"I can try."

"Oh heavens, Dooley. They'll block you every which way."

"You have contacts through the U.N."

"Well, that's true."

"I should be able to find a friend of a friend through the medical grapevine. Plus, why should they block me? I have to try. As he gets older, he'll need the information more than he does now. Heart disease, certain types of cancer, all the diseases that start in middle age— by the time he's in his late forties, he'll wonder why we didn't find out when we still could."

"I don't like the thought of you going there. Russia isn't all that safe."

"Oh, it's safe enough if I'm cautious. Look, as time goes on it's going to be harder and harder to find his parents. Who knows where the father is? All we ever had on him was a name. He could be dying of vodka poisoning. And the mother could lose herself forever. It's a huge country. If I'm going to do it, I'd better do it now."

"They didn't tell us much of anything about the parents when we were there in the first place."

"We didn't ask. We were too excited about getting Teddy."

Claudia was quiet for half a minute. "Well, I suppose if you were careful, it couldn't hurt. And I can think of one or two people who have contacts over there."

"I think I should go sometime next week, if I can make arrangements fast enough."

"They can make it take weeks."

"But why should they? If I can get the letter of invitation expedited, the visa shouldn't be any trouble. We've been there before and they know I'm not indigent. All they really want to know is that you're not going to live on their so-called welfare. The Russian Embassy is practically next door to us here. I can go ask them. I want to do it before the Russians get all involved in Christmas."

# CHAPTER TWELVE

My baby girl was born August forteenth.
She is beautiful, but I cant afford to keep
her. Maby you will be the family she
needs. Her pictur is here. One in her little
jungle jim and one in the bathtub. Write to
me at Box 233. I have just so many bills
and no income.

**CLICK FOR PHOTO >**

## 1

Gabrielle had frozen several images, moved them forward and back, snipping on the editor, a process that took a long time and exhausted her patience. Finally she had them in two rows on the monitor, just as if they were from a series of home photos she had made and was looking over to pick the best one. She isolated, ADO'd in, and enhanced them. They were from two different tapes out of the dozens and dozens Justin had shot, one tape made weeks earlier in Romania and one from the three they'd shot in Russia.

Gabrielle stared at them, soon becoming aware that her mouth was slightly open in surprise. When she first saw this, she assumed once she got the pictures up on the monitor she'd see real differences between the men, but in fact it was quite the opposite. She saw no differences whatsoever.

The clothing was different, but that didn't matter. In the three frames from the Russian tape, the men were wearing very "Russian" suits and topcoats, made of some kind of wool that had all the play and softness of corrugated cardboard. The four shots from Romania showed men wearing clothes of a more Western cut and fabric, but the fabrics themselves appeared more worn. Now that she looked at the images closely, the somewhat shabby clothing mimicked that of the other figures in the Romanian pictures, and she suspected that the intent of the men was to blend in.

Here was a perfectly obvious fact that she had not noticed until she had viewed the tapes twice, and even then she had not been really sure until she went back and checked a third time. Justin had picked up on it at once. As far as she could remember, it had been vague the way he told her about it. "Couple things I want to show you in today's tapes," he had said, "when we get a chance?" Yes. She would have understood if he'd been clearer. He had come to her room that night in Moscow. He had told her he had dubbed the tapes and he had given her copies for herself, the ones she had put in her bag. She and Justin always duplicated everything important. Who knew what might happen?—fire, flood, automobile accident, civil insurrection?

Or murder?

Later he mentioned looking at the tapes and that was all. They had gone to bed and the next morning he was dead. Dead before breakfast.

She searched the short segments of tape and isolated a left-side profile of the first man, the one she thought of as the Thug, from the Romanian tape, and a left-side profile of him from the Russian tape. She couldn't get a right-side profile of him and the full-face of him in the Romanian tape was looking down, with his arms folded as if he were thinking. In the Russian tape he was looking up a bit, with his arms behind his back. The Thug was square-faced, with a wide nose and five o'clock shadow on sturdy jowls. The other man, the one she called the Wine Taster, was full-face and looking sour in two shots from Romania and one from Russia. He showed clearly in a three-quarters face in one shot from each country. He was leaner, with a thin nose, arched eyebrows, long ears, and a forehead that went far up into a receding hairline.

After hours of work with the editing board and special effects unit, Gabrielle had got the corresponding poses of each man to approximately the same size and now juxtaposed them.

They were the same two men.

It had been over two months since she had been introduced to these two men in Romania. She had seen them merely in passing, just because they had practically bumped into each other, the men inside a small anteroom that she and Justin and the medical director of the orphanage were entering. The director spoke serviceable English and had mumbled something like "Mr. Anatole, Mr. Bassable, state inspectors. Good day, gentlemen. Here are visitors from the U.S., Ms. Coulter, Mr. Craig." Justin's camera had been running, as usual, but the medical director had pushed her and Justin back out the doors quickly. "We'll not intrude," he had said.

She knew that the names Anatole and Bassable were not exactly what he had said, but they certainly sounded like that. That fact was clear enough for Gabrielle to know that the names had *not* sounded like the ones given to them in Russia.

That visit was more recent and she could remember it quite clearly. Vlasta had made the introductions. "Miss Coulter and Mr. Craig. May I present Mr. Krysigin and Mr. Lupov." This was also a phonetic memory, of course, but Gabrielle thought it was very close to the actual names. Then Vlasta had added, "From our Ministry of Education." One of the multiplying Russian ministries? Indeed.

Here, too, the director had hurried them along.

A new thought hit her. In Russia, had Justin suspected these were the same men they had seen in Romania, and had he photographed them intentionally?

Of course. The moment he had seen the men in Moscow he had known he had seen them somewhere before. He'd made a specific effort to photograph them. They had no relevance to the babies in her story. He'd wanted *their faces.*

Gabrielle threw the tray from her Swanson turkey dinner into the trash with much of the food still in it. She was too impacted by the implications of all this to finish.

2

For several minutes, Gabrielle was hot with anger. Her body was aware of the implications of the videos before her mind. Even now, it didn't make sense. But she knew now there wasn't any simple explanation for Justin's death after all.

It had seemed to be a simple thing, hadn't it? However horrible and unutterably stupid, an act of plain dumb national chauvinism was pretty straightforward. Stupid but commonplace. You're going to show the world something negative about our country? No, you won't. We'll make you dead first.

That was only what it had been made to look like. The slogans on the backs of the doors were for show.

Justin had videotaped people who were not what they claimed to be. Then Justin had been murdered. B follows A, does it not?

And the video equipment had been smashed and all their tapes ruined, except the ones in Gabrielle's bag, the ones they didn't know she had.

So the government had done it, killed Justin and covered up. Sent in the police as if they wanted to solve the crime, but just went through the motions, gave her a bit of a hard time, then fobbed her off with promises and let her go.

No, wait. That wasn't right. Not the Russian government. The police had gone through her shoulder bag while she was held at the station. The man from the embassy said so, and knowing state police officers the world over, she was sure he was right. If the government had been to blame, they would have confiscated the copies of the tapes in the bag. Easy as anything; they could even call it evidence.

So who then?

What did the two wrecked rooms tell about the killers? They had not taken money. If anything, they'd made a point of not taking valuables, like cameras and video equipment, smashing it almost defiantly, when some of it could easily have been carried away and sold. They were saying they weren't thieves. In fact, they'd made a point of warning her off showing the Russian orphanage system in a bad light. Of turning any light at all on it, actually.

So—somebody from the orphanage? An administrator? The director? The medical establishment? The Russian adoption system?

But weren't they all government-connected? Certainly. They were all arms of the state. If so, couldn't they have prevailed on the police to seize her tapes?

Well, not necessarily. Maybe they didn't think the duplicate tapes existed. The obvious tapes and duplicating equipment were in Justin's room and they searched her room thoroughly after they killed Justin. Anyway, one big thing you learned about Russia was that the right hand didn't know what the left hand was doing. Even inside the police hierarchy, one sergeant might be in favor of a particular public policy and another sergeant in favor of another, and both could be actively throwing cases or making arrests based on their political persuasion. One could even be spying on another.

What about killing Justin? Had they meant to kill Justin, or was he only in the way? Was his death a more powerful warning than just breaking up their cameras would have been? If she had been in the room too, would she have been killed?

Well, Justin had fought back. And that made it difficult to be sure. If he hadn't, they might have just pushed him around, trashed the place, written their warning, and left. After all, with those ski masks on, he could hardly identify them. The video they made of the murder told as much about them as Justin could have.

And what about that video? Since they brought the camera with them, they intended to make a record. But did it follow that they were planning to make a record of murder? Not necessarily. Again, if Justin fought back, they may have had to kill him. Given a few minutes he could have roused the whole hotel.

Why make the video at all? Sheer hubris? Or to have their own record of what had happened in case the Russian government claimed different? But that would mean two copies and she doubted they had the time to make any copy while they were there.

Everything in Russia was so complicated and so tortuous. You never knew whose side anybody was on, or when you were supposed to slip an official extra bribe money, or which cab driver might take you someplace where you could be mugged in private, or which concierge was taking kickbacks to direct you to a certain restaurant.

*Well, be fair. They did that in New York too.*

Her head was swimming.

But not swimming so much that she felt totally stupid. Having gotten to this point, she decided she'd have to think this through a lot more carefully, and maybe get some advice. But one thing was sure. If people were willing to kill to destroy the tapes, the tapes meant something to somebody. Immediately, she duplicated both tapes, the Romanian and the Russian, for the second time, but now she put the new copies in a padded envelope and mailed them to Lilliana Sanchez. Lilliana was a friend from college. They saw each other at most once every couple of years, since Lilliana had gone back to her hometown, L.A., after college, to work in TV. But they had made a secret pact that if ever sensitive material came into the hands of either one, a copy would go to the other for safe keeping. Nobody in the world would guess that Lilliana held the extra tapes.

Having dubbed them, Gabrielle went out to a mailbox and mailed them. Done. Out of here.

Then she went back, washed out her bitter-tasting mouth by drinking more bitter coffee, and tried to think.

On the whole, it made the most sense that since the attackers came equipped with the video camera, the tape, spray paint, and the box cutter, they were ready to kill Justin. They went to Justin's room first, assuming that was where his tapes were most likely to be. And they were, several of them, but they certainly couldn't take the time to view all those tapes and couldn't be sure the important one wasn't in her room. They may have intended to trash the equipment and tapes and give Justin a beating, spray the warnings on the door, leave their own tape of the beating as a visual exclamation point, and leave. By destroying all the equipment they hid the fact that would otherwise have been obvious—that they were really intent only on destroying the tape with the men's pictures on it. The whole incident would look like patriotic hooliganism, and with the number of weird gangs running around Russia these days, the police might buy that. They could easily write it off as unsolvable.

In other words, the gang could achieve their goal of destroying the tape without anybody knowing that was the object.

Why hadn't they killed her? Well, they may have intended to. Had she left for the bakery ten minutes later, they might have caught her in the room. Why hadn't they waited there to kill her? Probably because she took so long at the bakery. Russian inefficiency might have saved her life. Certainly she could see why they didn't want to wait around for long with a dead body.

Why hadn't they found and killed her later? They may have wanted to, but she changed hotels and the new one was very secure. She had taken friends with her when she went out to jog.

Were they tracking her even now to kill her?

For a few seconds she was bathed in fear. She checked the lock on the door and sat back down to think. With the tapes destroyed—they thought—and Justin unable to give evidence against them, maybe they thought she wasn't a threat. Many days had gone by and there was no hue and cry out for them. They had every reason to assume she didn't know anything.

Gabrielle was assailed by doubts. For all she really knew, crazy patriots *might* have killed Justin. It was possible. The guys in suits, whether they were up to no good or just giving out false names and titles, might never have noticed Justin or cared what he was taping.

But what if she were reporting on this incident? she asked herself. In her professional mode would she overlook this strange coincidence of two men giving two different names being taped right before the crime of murder in which the tapes were destroyed? Absolutely not.

Not in a million years! If she were actually reporting on this crime, she would sure as hell find out who they were.

And what they were really doing.

Gabrielle realized that she was still filled with fury at Justin's sad death, so much before his time.

She would have to go back to Russia, find out who those men were, and if they had killed Justin make them pay.

# 3

## Chicago, Illinois
## Two days after Thanksgiving

In downtown Chicago, a block south of the ninety-five-story John Hancock Building and two blocks west of Lake Michigan, is a small park. Seneca Park is a city block wide and long, and is divided into two parts. One side is a playground for children, surrounded by fences, and guarded by a heavy gate that parents and children's caretakers open and close, but which is too heavy for little ones to open. Across from this children's park is a large area, grassy in summer, in which stands a life-size deconstructed iron horse. The horse looks very much as if it had been patched together from pieces of bark.

In the winter, larger children, the six-year-olds and up, liked to hide behind the horse in the snow and throw snowballs at each other.

On Saturday morning about a dozen six-, seven-, and eight-year-olds were throwing snowballs while their parents stood around stamping their feet and trying to keep warm. A few older children who weren't too grand to come to the park were wrestling in the snow. Younger children watched, some of them frightened enough of the snowballs to hang on to their mothers. One was crying. A few strollers and carriages held babies.

The old woman approached this merriment from the Michigan Avenue side. She dragged along two shopping bags filled with tattered clothing. In her pocket was fifty dollars in wrinkled fives, tens, and ones.

The old woman was homeless but not stupid. She knew the man had given her wrinkled bills so that if she were searched by the police, she would appear to have just collected handouts.

As instructed, she approached the group around the horse and slowly sank to her knees. Then, setting aside her bags so that the clothing wouldn't spill out, she let herself fall all the way forward, cradling her face in her left arm and splaying the right arm sideways and, she thought, pathetically.

Several of the parents ran to her. They crowded around, asking her if she was all right.

She thought they were stupid. Would somebody fall facedown in the snow if she was all right?

She held her position for a full minute, listening to the parents argue about whether they should dial 911. When she heard one of the mothers say, "I'm going to call," the old woman sat up.

"I was dizzy," she said.

"I'm going to call 911."

"No, please don't."

"You're sick."

"Please don't. I was just dizzy. They'll put me in a shelter and the shelters are dangerous."

"I've heard that," one of the men said to one of the women.

The old woman reached out a hand and the man helped her to her feet. "Thank you. I feel better. I do. Really," she said.

"Well—" the man said.

"If you're *sure*—" one of the women said.

Another said, "Do you need some money? Have you eaten?"

"I'm fine."

"Just let me give you this." She held out a five-dollar bill.

The old woman thought a little extra money wouldn't hurt. They wanted to give it to her, didn't they? "Well, thanks." The old woman walked slowly away.

Meanwhile, a man with a baby carriage had approached a similar baby carriage. While the adults fussed over the old woman, he picked the baby out of the second carriage quickly and placed it in his, under a lump of blankets that by itself had looked quite a bit like a sleeping baby. Then he bunched up the blue plaid blankets in the now-empty carriage so that at a casual glance it looked as if the baby was still there. He pushed his carriage away, out onto Pearson Street.

A car pulled next to the curb. The man placed the baby in the car seat, collapsed the carriage, and shoved it into the other side of the back seat. He slammed the door and watched as the car accelerated away toward the west.

He was quite sure that the license plate was either doctored, with an "O" maybe being touched up with white paint to make that "C," and the "F" made from an "E," or maybe the plate had simply been stolen.

In any case, it didn't make sense for him to remember any of it. Maybe it would even be dangerous to try.

For his part, he had been paid $500 on the investment of ten minutes' work, and that was a very good bargain, he thought.

He walked over to Michigan Avenue and strolled south. He was a few blocks away, past Brooks Brothers, before the mother realized that her baby was missing.

# 4

A little more than an hour later, a woman with a small baby prepared to board a flight out of the international terminal at O'Hare. Her baby, who lay sleeping in a blue carrier, was dressed in a blue, footed suit. She carried a diaper bag.

"Going to Berlin?" the customs man asked her.

"My husband works for Daimler there." She didn't like so many questions. After the attacks on the World Trade Center, flying had become much more difficult. She wanted to put an end to all these questions.

"And who's this little gentleman?"

"His name is Kurt. He's just four months," she said, sliding her hand under the little boy and pretending to cuddle him. The baby was traveling on her passport. She had a birth certificate in her purse, just in case.

At the right moment, the baby woke up and started to cry. She said, "Oh, heavens! What if he's like that the whole flight?"

"Most of them fall asleep. It's the motion. Or the droning sound, maybe," the man said. "I have two and they both sleep the whole way."

"Well, I sure hope so."

"Go ahead, Mrs. uh—Bergen."

"Thanks."

She stopped pinching the baby. She put her papers away, gathered the baby and the baby's bag, and boarded the plane. Her passport was forged, but in the name of a real Mrs. Bergen, whose husband did not work in Germany. Mrs. Bergen was a German who hardly ever traveled. The birth certificate was also forged, not quite as expensively as the passport. Nobody ever more than glanced at them. The name wouldn't flag on any INS lists.

When she got to Berlin, she would switch passports and go on to Moscow as Mrs. Ulrique Lake, a Swiss citizen. When she returned to the United States late tomorrow, it would be as Ella Romano, an Italian citizen visiting the U.S. She might leave as Ella Romano next weekend, taking home her small child who had been in the United States for medical tests, being cared for by his paternal grandmother while there. She would come back by way of Berlin as Mrs. Bergen again, and if passport control thought to ask, which was extremely unlikely as she wasn't on any watch list, baby Kurt was staying with his father for a few weeks until she could get time off from her job.

But she didn't think they'd ask.

For this she was paid $2,000 for two days. She made these trips about eight to ten times a year, either when she had a vacation from her regular job or on weekends. Her regular job was as a dental technician.

She had no idea who paid her. Each time, she just got a message, where and at which airport to meet the man with the baby. The tickets and documentation were provided. The payment was always in cash and anyway she didn't want to know where it came from. She was frightened and deeply excited too by the trips. She knew she was putting herself in harm's way. But the money paid for wonderful extras, especially clothing. And there was something about risk that excited her.

What troubled her a lot more was how her employers had found her. Maybe they knew something about her earlier history, including the events she called her "scrapes." She had never done anything violent and never got involved in substance abuse, even though she knew a lot of people in the medical field did. But she had a few unfortunate run-ins with the law over shoplifting and check-kiting. Three of these had been dismissed in court for lack of evidence and two pleaded down to misdemeanors, but there was a paper trail somebody could have found. Or maybe her illicit employer was actually somebody she knew, somebody she saw every day even. That thought was downright eerie.

Whatever, somebody out there was a very good psychologist.

Now that they were comfortably on the plane, she took out a bottle of baby formula, lightly laced with a sedative.

# CHAPTER THIRTEEN

To whom it may concern: My husband is 47. I am 41. We have tried for years and years to have a baby, and had every treatment there is. Now that we know we can't get pregnant, the agencies are telling us we're not prime candidates to adopt because we're too old. **It's just not fair!** We're solidly established in our jobs as younger people wouldn't be. We have more time to give a baby than younger people would. We have a lovely country home in upstate New York. If you are looking for a loving family for your baby, please think of us.

**UTYR-NY@AOL.COM**

## 1

### Madison, Wisconsin
### Early December

"I'll put it in the overhead rack, dear."

"Thank you, darling."

"Don't mention it, sweet'ums."

With a cheery smile, Walter hefted Pepper's carry-on into the luggage rack and slammed the cover down, maybe a little harder than absolutely necessary. They were flying out of Madison, Wisconsin, to

Chicago. They'd pick up a flight at O'Hare for New York. The real George and Sylvia Carroll had left Madison by car the day before to be driven to Milwaukee, where, as Tina and Sam Bronson, they would board a flight from Billy Mitchell Field for Raleigh-Durham. They would go on to Central America.

"This is stupid," Walter said. He had made sure that the seats in front of them were unoccupied before he said anything unguarded.

"Well, at least you don't have to wear these godawful flowered dresses."

"I think you look very nice, dear."

She wore one of Sylvia Carroll's favorite dresses, a print of big yellow cabbage roses on a blue background.

"I feel like a freak," Pepper said. "Plus these damned high heels. I'm going to ruin my feet and I won't get work-related injury pay."

"What a pity."

"Plus having to live on deep-fried lard for the last three weeks. Who's going to fix my arteries? And this weight is going to be a lot harder to lose than it was to gain!"

She was chubby, but pleasingly so, Walter thought. He certainly wouldn't tell her that. Actually, if she'd put on a few pounds for this assignment, and he could hardly doubt that she had, she must have been one of those whip-thin, steel-muscled women agents that made him feel like an 1880s man, happy for a little flesh on his woman.

Oh well.

Two women came down the aisle and sat in the seats ahead of Walter and Pepper. He held up his finger to caution her, but she knew. She had already sat back in her seat and closed her eyes.

## 2

Three rows behind them, on the other side of the aisle, a middle-aged man said to the slightly younger man next to him, "They don't look very affectionate."

"They've been married a long time, Ron."

"They look tense. And they didn't drive their car to the airport."

"Didn't want to leave it there, because they don't know how long they'll be gone."

"Yeah, I guess they're okay."

"Keep watching. That's why they pay us the big bucks."

"Matter of fact, I think I'll stroll past them, just eyeball the situation."

## 3

Deplaning at O'Hare, Walter and Pepper had an hour and a half to kill. Pepper said, "Let's get coffee. There's a place—"

"Designer coffee! It's all flavorings. You can't tell me companies use the finest coffee when they know you're going to tart it up with hazelnut or chocolate."

"I'm not trying to tell you that. I'm trying to tell you I want a cup. If you want to just sit here, you can watch the bags."

"I'll watch the bags."

Walter knew he was being surly. Fine! He didn't mind that. He felt surly. What was more of a problem, he believed they were under observation. The idea seemed paranoid. It was unrealistic to think that a simple adoption agency would follow prospective adoptive parents around just to make sure they were the real thing. Most background checks could be done in cyberspace these days. Did Sylvia and George Carroll really exist? You could find that out in two minutes with only a touch of expertise. Had they existed for a long time, so they weren't plants? Did they have money? Even photos could be obtained on the Net. But to think that their behavior would be monitored—that was going too far.

Except that this wasn't a simple adoption agency. He was sure of that, at least. And for a couple hundred thousand dollars in fees, they could certainly invest a few thousand to make sure they were selling to a safe buyer. They could do a couple of spot-checks, without having to follow a target the whole way.

"Brought you one anyway," Pepper said coming back. She handed him a cup. "Regular. Want sugar?" There were a couple of packets of sugar held against the cup by her thumb. "Or would that be tarting it up?"

"No sugar." Walter sighed. "But thanks for the coffee."

Suddenly Pepper threw her arms around Walter's neck and snuggled up to him. His back stiffened. She whispered in his ear, "If you think somebody's watching, we shouldn't look like we're fighting."

"Married people do fight. But I suppose you're right."

She murmured into his cheek, "I don't think anybody's watching."

"Neither do I. But what if they are?"

"An adoption agency? The way everybody's carrying on you'd think they were the secret police. With informants behind every potted plant."

Walter turned his face so that he spoke into her ear on the hidden side, the side that faced the wall. "Every time somebody says they're only an adoption agency, I get more uneasy."

Walter snaked his arm around her shoulders, the very gesture a supportive husband would make when he and his wife were facing a stressful and uncertain future. He gave a little pull, cuddling her to him.

# 4

"Thirteen minutes in New York and already I'm feeling hostile," Pepper said, her fists on her hips as she saw the huge line waiting for cabs at Kennedy Airport. Wind from the Atlantic Ocean blew cold damp washes of air across their faces. It was dark, almost dinner time. They would meet the adoption agency people tomorrow morning.

Walter laughed at her remark, then he remembered he hadn't wanted a partner on this case, and wiped the laugh off his face. Pepper and Walter were flanked front and rear by families with tired, screaming children. When one young lad expressed his frustration by placing a wet lollipop against the silky ends of his sister's long hair and rolling her hair up over the sticky pop, Walter sympathized. He certainly didn't blame the kids. He would have liked to pull the braids of the man in uniform who stood impassively accepting tips and putting people into cabs.

"Do we really want a baby, dear?" Pepper asked.

After nearly half an hour, the family in front of Walter and Pepper were loaded into a cab, reducing the decibel level somewhat. A nice, shiny cab pulled up for Walter and Pepper. Not only was it one of the few clean ones they had seen, but also the doors were undented.

"Ma'am," Walter said to the family behind him. "You have tired little ones. Please accept our cab."

The woman goggled at him, but she was alert enough to move her brood forward quickly. Then she recalled her social obligations and said, "Thank you, mister." She cocked her head. "Who says New York is an unfriendly place!"

Waving, the family drove off.

"You think Windsor House is sending bugged cabs?" Pepper said scornfully.

"No. I don't see how they could." The taxi lines were chaotic, with cabs jockeying for position, and it would not even have been apparent that the group ahead of them had been one family or a man with a son and a woman with two daughters unless you waited and watched the interchange for a while. Although the dispatcher with the braids would know.

Pepper said, "Here's our cab."

# 5

Windsor House had advised them on hotels and had suggested the Holmes Inn very forcefully. "Reasonable rates. For New York, that is," the agency secretary had told Walter with a charming laugh. "Good location right near our office. It's up to you, of course, but this is a very, very clean hotel."

And Walter wanted to appear cooperative. Unsuspicious.

# 6

Walter and Pepper ate dinner in the hotel dining room, conversing awkwardly. Then, suddenly back in their room, they were alone together for the first time. The room was clean, as Windsor House had told them, but very small. There was a table, one straight chair, and one easy chair covered in a beige nubby fabric. The walls were smooth, papered in a pattern of vertical stripes; the ceiling was roughly plastered in a material that looked like cottage cheese. A molding ran around the top of the walls. Walter could not tell whether there were fiberoptics in the holes in the rough ceiling or the crevices of the molding. Or microphones in the lamps, television, or telephone. And he couldn't look closely, because if there were cameras he couldn't be seen looking for them. And even if he found them, he couldn't remove them because that would give away his suspicions and his expertise.

A table, two chairs, two nightstands, a dresser with the television on it—and one king-size bed. They'd expected this, of course. Both Walter and Pepper looked at it a beat too long, but Pepper recovered first. "Lovely room!" she trilled.

"For a small fortune," Walter said, relieved that she'd come up with a remark.

"I'll wash first," Pepper said, going into the bathroom and closing the door. Walter sighed.

Walter lay back on the bed, trying to look like a man eager to adopt. Slightly worried, but with serious purpose. How did you do that lying on your back? Just in case there was a peeper cable, he turned over a couple of times, sat up, then lay back down. No smiling. An unfocused gaze as if looking toward the future. There was no point in turning the lights out at this stage; most spy devices were video and could be enhanced to give decent pictures in very low light anyway.

Pepper seemed to be showering three times over. Then he heard the hair dryer. Then there was a long period with no sounds at all, during which Walter wondered whether a real husband would ask whether she was all right. Finally the bathroom door opened.

Pepper emerged wearing flannel Winnie the Pooh pajamas. The top had long sleeves with elastic cuffs. The pants were long too, also with elastic cuffs.

Walter started to say, "What were you thinking?" but instead said, "What—are you cold?"

Pepper smiled sweetly and replied, "Not yet, dear. But I was afraid the hotels in Romania and Russia wouldn't have heat."

# CHAPTER FOURTEEN

Hailey was born August 19, 2002.
She has brown hair and brown eyes.
Hailey is a special needs child,
born with a clubfoot that can be
remedied with adequate medical
attention. She is ready to give all her
love to a family that is ready to do the
same for her. Video upon request.

**RACE: NATIVE AMERICAN**
**DISABILITIES: MILD MEDICAL**

## 1

### New York City
### Early December

A small brass plaque on a paneled door painted with dark green glossy enamel read WINDSOR HOUSE ADOPTIONS. The offices inside were just as tasteful. Walter took note of the moss-green rug, the walls paneled in dark oak, the small but impeccably framed charcoal sketch of a sleeping infant, the oak desk, and the very attractive woman receptionist behind the desk. Her chair was green leather with brass studs and her dark green desk blotter was framed in moss-green leather. She herself did not wear green, but a dusty rose-colored suit that enhanced the green beautifully.

"May I help you?" she said in a British accent.

"Mr. and Mrs. Carroll. Mr. Blandford is expecting us."

"Indeed he is. I am Ms. Porter. Let me see whether Mr. Blandford is free."

She touched a button. Apparently he was free, and not given to showing his importance by keeping them waiting. A nice note, Walter thought. Just right.

Mr. Blandford appeared in a doorway recessed into the wall to the right of Ms. Porter's desk. He repeated their names as a question; they agreed that was who they were and he escorted them into his office.

In color scheme it was exactly like the anteroom. The desk, though, was much larger, and a side table held a terra-cotta sculpture of the head and shoulders of a young child.

Oh, well done, Walter thought to himself.

"I must tell you, Mr. and Mrs. Carroll, how pleased we are at Windsor House that you would entrust us with possibly the most important decision you will make in your life."

Pepper reached over and took hold of Walter's hand. He thought that was a nice touch too, then he thought, no pun. He glanced around the office, as if admiring the decor, noticing the egg-and-dart molding where the wall met the ceiling. Quite appropriate for concealing a video camera lens. He had absolutely no doubt all the "customers" in the office were taped.

"We have your paperwork, of course," said Mr. Blandford, "and I thank you for sending it ahead. We want to expedite this for you. We're familiar with the Wisconsin home visit and other state requirements, of course. It's part of our service. We have had many clients in your state."

"Yes, we saw the responses of several on the Net."

"The Net. Yes, Internet communication has made everything about adoption much easier. It used to be that a couple wishing to adopt wouldn't know if there was an appropriate baby just a few miles away over the state line. It was quite unfair. And now we can find them all across the world. Of course, relying on the Net alone can be risky."

"Yes, so I understand."

"The help of an established agency such as this is really a must."

"It's a godsend," Pepper said.

*Maybe she is useful for something. I couldn't have said that to this guy without gagging.*

"You know thirty percent of U.S. adoptions fail. There are six people looking for a child for every one who succeeds."

"That's horrible."

"And of course the international aspect is one of the reasons we are so anxious to expedite our work here. You need to be forewarned that events abroad can take quite some time."

"We understand that," Walter said. He took out a pad of Post-it notes and a pen. "How long do you think?" he asked.

"We've heard of people having to stay in Romania as much as three months. Russia sometimes two months."

Walter wrote "Rom: 3 mo. Russia: 2 mo." on the top sheet. He stuck it on the arm of his chair. Then he shook his head, frustrated, took back the Post-it note, and faked losing his grip on it. It dropped to the floor, garnering lint. He picked it up, crumpling it, shoved it in his pocket.

"Sorry," he said. He took his Palm Pilot out of his pocket. "Gadgetry," he said. "I'm too old to get used to this cyber stuff."

Now that he had trace evidence on the Post-it note, which was treated with a substance similar to the coating on gel-lifters used for fingerprints in dusty environments, he switched to the perfectly genuine Palm Pilot, into which was built an Ultra-Pocket by SMaL Camera Technologies. His job was only to gather information, on both people and places, not necessarily to accumulate documented evidence for trial.

"Two or three months!" Pepper said.

"But that's another of our services, of course." Blandford was going on talking to Pepper, ignoring Walter's fumbling. "Knowing how to expedite."

Pepper said, "Three months! I'm not sure I can take that long off work."

"And it's not just the time. You may not fully appreciate how frustrating it is for most people until you get there. The adopting parents' hopes are high, you see. First there will be the search for a baby that suits you. One day you will look at a child—ah, you say you are looking for a boy, as you mentioned—and he will look at you, and you will know that you are a family. It doesn't happen with every baby. Then there will be the process of getting his papers in order and then the exit visas and so on. It is in these two areas that we produce our most valuable service. In locating the child and in facilitating your exit with the child. Persons who have made the effort without the help of experienced agencies such as ourselves have indeed spent months in the country of the child, waiting for papers that affirmed the birth parents either were deceased or had abandoned the child. Some unfortunate people have gone back and forth to Europe several times and still have not succeeded in adopting."

"That's horrible," Pepper said.

"But that won't happen with us on the job. Now—the first detail we must talk about is our fee."

# 2

Twenty-five thousand dollars U.S. was strapped around Walter's waist, held flat by a device called a male corset. Another thirty thousand U.S.C. was strapped around Pepper's thighs, fifteen on each thigh. Mr. Blandford had said that was how it was always done. Customs agents would not search her thighs. Ms. Porter had taken her to the women's rest room and showed her how to place the bindings.

"You won't be searched on leaving the country in any case if you don't set off the metal detector," Blandford said. "Nor when you get to Paris. They search certain people for drugs when they enter the United States." He smiled tightly. "Nobody expects drugs to be taken *out* of the United States."

We're just that sort of folks in this country, Walter thought.

Thirty thousand had gone to Mr. Blandford as attorney's fees. Another twenty to Windsor House for "preparation of documents" and "search fees."

"I'm uneasy about this money, anyway," Walter had said to Blandford. Walter nervously scratched his new beard. "It's illegal, isn't it?"

"Don't worry. We do it all the time." Pepper's microphone picked this up very nicely.

Hours later, waiting to get on the flight that would take them to Bucharest, Pepper gave Walter the so-we-can't-be-heard hug and said, "Whatdya bet the agency put us in coach?"

"I wouldn't bet against it."

"I mean, the government buys nine-hundred-dollar socket wrenches. They give us forty-five thousand cash for payoffs and bribes and fifty thousand for fees. But they're gonna save three-ninety on the airfare. Because it's only us."

"Pepper, you're preaching to the choir."

# 3

Charles de Gaulle Airport was partly French and partly every airport in the world. Pepper said, "We have two hours. Should we go out and walk around Paris?"

"Paris is thirty kilometers away."

"Oh. Better not. We don't want to miss the flight."

No problem if any listeners heard that exchange. Then Pepper said, "Oh!"

Walter looked at her.

She leaned in and did the hug thing again. "I forgot to call Howie."

"Who's Howie?"

"My semisignificant, formerly-significant, insignificant other. Might have been significant if I stayed in one place more than six months." She pulled out her cellphone. Then she put it back. More loudly she said, "Darn! Low battery." She leaned close and whispered, "Better not use a cell. I'll find a random pay phone."

Walter nodded.

# 4

Pepper found a phone that took a charge card and allowed you to dial for yourself. Since her French was nonexistent, she was pleased. The number she called was not answered by a human being, but by a series of tones. This confirmed to her that it was the right place.

She said, "All multigrain bread." She waited. Her code should have activated the scrambler.

"Pepper?"

"Yes, Mr. Bettenhausen."

"What's happening?"

"Well, we're in Paris as you'll see from your CLI, sir. We leave for Romania in forty-five minutes."

"How is he?"

"He's behaving perfectly normally as far as I can tell. Of course, I've only known him three weeks."

"No nervous tics? Hyper talk about adoption?"

"No."

"He's not carrying any weapons?"

"Nothing but the—the research materials you gave us."

"Okay, okay. Keep watching."

# CHAPTER FIFTEEN

Confidential! Legal! Safe! Reliable!
Efficient adoption! We are happy to
consult with your attorney. We have a
twenty-four-hour hotline for your
convenience.

**OR CONTACT US ON-LINE AT
SOLVEYOURPROBLEMS.COM**

## 1

### New York City
### Early December

With Teddy between them holding their hands, Claudia and her
mother made a wide circle on the ice, sweeping past Dooley at the end
of their glide. He had the camera set for several shots in automatic
succession one-half second apart. "That's great, ladies and big guy!"
he yelled. "Now one more time."

When they swooped to a stop next to him, each woman still
holding one of Teddy's hands, Dooley said, "Ted, my man! What a
skater you are."

"I'm a greatest skater!" Teddy said.

The rink was crowded. It was almost impossible to get a turn on
the ice at Rockefeller Center in December. You had to get tickets

ahead of time. Claudia's mother, Ruth, had skated there as a child, and claimed that early in the day would work, and she was right. Not an especially athletic person, she had done enough skating to look quite expert, and was obviously proud of it. Her face was glowing with the cold and pride.

Claudia was happy too. Dooley watched them both with sickness in his heart. He covered his face with the camera again, crouched down, to take a close-up of Teddy.

Teddy, released by the two women, promptly fell down. "I fall down!" he said, delighted. His feet were up in the air when Dooley clicked the camera. He knew it was a really great shot.

Next year, would pictures be all they had left of Teddy?

Ruth said, "Would Teddy like to come visit us again sometime?"

Teddy said, "Visit Gramma!"

"We have an ice rink in the village park, Teddy, and a little sledding hill."

Dooley thought, not for the first time, how much better Ruth got along with children than she did with adults. She was very formal with adults. There was something sad about that, but charming in a way too. Possibly she had been forced to grow up too soon and needed to live what she missed.

"He'd love that," Claudia said.

They went to a deli nearby that served cocoa. Teddy was delighted again.

"What a good little guy you are," Claudia said.

Daniel was to join them at the deli after some meeting he had to attend, and just before going to another meeting. "Grampa's coming," Dooley told Teddy.

"Grampa," Teddy said, with less enthusiasm.

The three of them chatted while Teddy fished marshmallows out of his cocoa and asked for more. A waiter, charmed by the little boy, overheard and brought him four in a little cup.

Daniel arrived just as Teddy was dunking a marshmallow fixed on the prongs of a fork. A couple drops of cocoa fell on the table.

"Why'd you let him do that?" he demanded, even before sitting down.

"Why not?" Dooley asked.

"He's making a mess. And it'll spoil his lunch."

"He'll nap first, and when he wakes up he'll be hungry all over again."

"How was the meeting?" Ruth asked.

"Ordinary. I have to explain everything to them twice. I have another meeting in thirty minutes."

Daniel had a cup of tea, claiming that delis never made good coffee.

"Will you be coming to our house for Christmas dinner?" Ruth asked.

"Oh, Mom, you know we promised to go to Dooley's parents for Christmas day if we went to your house for Thanksgiving."

"Christmas Eve, then?"

"Depending on how much time we need to allow to get to Burlington. I'll come up some weekend between now and then, while Dooley's away, and bring old Tedder here, of course."

"You're going on a trip, Dooley?" Ruth asked.

"Well, yes." He would have preferred Claudia not to bring it up, but he supposed it would have come out soon anyway. "I'm going to Russia for a few days."

"What on earth for?" Daniel demanded.

"Uh, Teddy was sick a couple of weeks ago. Fortunately, it wasn't anything horrible." He glanced at the boy, but Teddy was playing with his marshmallows and didn't appear to be listening. "But it made me think I should try to find out whatever I can about his health history."

"That's about the dumbest thing I've ever heard!" Daniel said.

Claudia said, "Daddy, a lot of diseases are hereditary. Teddy may want to know some day."

"That's true, dear," Ruth said. "He may need to know. God forbid, of course."

Daniel said, "Ruth, you don't know the first thing about it. Dooley, I hope you give up this fool idea. They won't tell you anything anyhow."

"I told him that, Daddy," Claudia said.

"Send for the info."

"I don't think I can trust what they might send." To keep the peace, Dooley added, "But I'll think seriously about what you say, Daniel."

Then Claudia said, "Look."

Teddy was getting droopy after all the exercise. His eyes were closed, his head was on his arm, and he held a marshmallow in his mouth with the aid of two fingers. His hand was propped under his chin.

"We'd better get him home."

Claudia slid him into his stroller and strapped him in. His snowsuit made his arms stick out. Dooley wiped Teddy's sticky hands with a paper napkin dipped in water.

They said good-bye to Daniel and Ruth, letting Daniel get the check as he insisted. Ruth would Christmas shop while Daniel was in his meeting. Then the two would take a commuter train back to Chappaqua. Dooley and Claudia would walk home, pushing the stroller. It was only nine blocks.

"That was really fun," Claudia said.

"It's nice that your mother gets to play with Teddy," Dooley said.

"And gets time away from Daddy, you mean?" She had heard an odd note in Dooley's voice.

That wasn't what he had been thinking about, but he answered, "I guess. Daniel isn't very good with kids, is he?"

"He doesn't like kids at all. I've told you he was an impossible father. Totally remote. Although he's worse with little kids. To be fair, when I got old enough to talk like a grown-up, he was better."

"Mm."

"I don't think he's doing too well."

"Your father? What do you mean? He looked healthy enough to me."

"I don't mean sick. I mean I don't think he's doing too well financially."

"Claudia, he's rich!"

"He's not *rich* rich. He's not Bill Gates rich."

"Nobody is. Not even Canada."

"Well, but he's not Rockefeller rich. Or even Tom Hanks rich. He's always been well off, but that's not the same thing."

"It is to me."

"Dooley, you're so naive about money. My grandfather left me some money, but not millions. He left more to Daddy, but not millions and millions. And Daddy looks like he may have made some bad investments lately."

"Did he tell you that?"

"Oh heavens, no! He never would. He's the strong silent type, he thinks. No, he's been cutting corners. They got rid of Charlie."

"Charlie the master butler and man of all work? Was that why that college kid was passing drinks at Thanksgiving? I thought Charlie had just retired or something."

"I don't think so. Charlie has been gone more than a year."

"He told me he was doing destination malls and they were a gold mine."

"Listen, Dooley. Destination malls probably are a gold mine, but he didn't invent them and as far as I know he hasn't built any yet, either. Creating a trendy destination mall is a young person's game. They're more like entertainment than sales. They're kind of deceptive. You know, lots of well-advertised products at bargain prices at certain stores, and then you pay a whole lot for the entertainment elements but you don't notice that was part of your costs."

"The entertainment *is* voluntary, of course."

"Of course. Anyway, Daddy was mostly in strip malls, and strip malls are *not* doing well."

"How do you know that?"

"I still hear things from my old firm, and I'm telling you this is true. They were one of the first things hit by on-line shopping and the e-marketing boom."

"Oh."

"I think Daddy's in trouble."

"Amazing. Who would've thought it?"

"Although less so. A couple of years ago he seemed much more worried."

## 2

Gordon Ridley said, "Take, for example, currency. Ordinary cash. Twenty-dollar bills."

"I get the idea, Ridley," the Boss said. "Get on with it."

"A majority of the counterfeit money out there is produced on ink-jet printers. I mean, what a change from the days of gangs of crooks with a printing press in the basement, huh?"

"Get on with it, Ridley."

"Certainly. Now, the new currency is made to be difficult to ink-jet copy. There's a watermark that you can see when you hold it up to light. That green-black ink on it varies in color as you turn the bill. Here, take a look at this one. Also, there are threads in the paper and part of it is made to glow in UV light."

"Devilishly clever. Makes it expensive to forge."

"Exactly. Genuine bills have a magnetic signature, also, that can be discerned with a color analyzer and watermark reader. When a counterfeit bill is discovered, it is examined by a document examiner from the U.S. Treasury."

"But that's only when it's suspected of being counterfeit."

"Exactly. And most of them are so good they don't make anybody suspicious. Half of forged currency today is produced by computer. Desktop publishing software and ink-jet printers. Offset printers are going the way of the dodo. The point is, I.D.'s are forged with the same tools. Our man is a master."

"We pay him well. Possibly too well?"

"You know how firm I am about keeping costs down, but he's worth it."

The Boss said, "Really? Anybody can make I.D. Fake I.D. is sold on the Internet."

"Indeed it is. Openly. Vendors are legally required to call the I.D. 'novelty items.' The so-called forge-proof driver's licenses are easy to forge, as you say. But this is the heart of our most lucrative line. No question must *ever* be raised. We get *very* good passports from our man."

"I should hope so."

"The U.S. Treasury tries to stay one jump ahead of the counter-feiters, but that's about as far ahead as they can manage. All of these validating documents are like the lion jumping after the gazelle. The forgers catch up to the legit method and the government puts in another 'safety feature.' Passports too, of course. Besides which, even after September eleventh, most people who examine visas and passports at checkpoints and so on are seriously rushed and not very careful. They're usually two steps behind. If it looks good and there's nothing to excite their suspicions, nothing on their watch list, it works. But our material is even better than that."

"Good."

"And that's why he's expensive."

"Oh, very well."

# Chapter Sixteen

Children here are filthy and unattended. They lie in
their own waste, covered with flies. Young girls, their
heads shaven, were kept in a giant cage like animals:
wild-eyed, screaming, half-naked.
— Ted Koppel, *20/20*, October 1990

## 1

### Bucharest
### Early December

Nicolae Ceauşescu had ruled Romania for thirty-four years. His
regime was one of the most despotic on earth. In December 1989 a
popular uprising deposed the dictator. When he was executed by firing
squad, Romanian national radio announced, "The antichrist is dead."

During the years of harsh rule, Ceauşescu's wife Elana had pro-
moted childbirth, had forbade abortion and contraception, and put
heavy financial burdens on people who didn't have children. She
believed that a larger population would help the nation's financial picture. It didn't, and many of the children, unwanted before their birth
and a burden afterward, were abandoned.

After Ceauçescu and his wife were executed the world press
flooded into Romania. They publicized neglected and dying children
with horrifying pictures, and people from the West flocked in to

adopt. Most of the fees the adopting parents paid went to orphanage officials, not to improvement of the orphanages. By 1991 there were baby brokers, and baby spotters, and under-the-table payments. An enormous black market in babies developed almost overnight. Romania placed a moratorium on adoption to try to clean up the mess. After a second moratorium, some progress was made. Adoptions began again.

# 2

Bucharest-Otopeni International Airport was jammed with people. Pepper and Walter were confused by unreadable signs and the crush of bodies around them, pushing and shoving. As they came through Romanian customs, Pepper spotted a hand-lettered sign saying, "Mr. and Mrs. Carroll."

Pepper pointed to it in relief. The man holding the sign was about the size of a thirteen-year-old boy, wizened and amber-skinned. As they drew close to him, Walter realized from the smell that the little man was pickled in nicotine.

"Mr. Tapp?" Walter said.

"Yes, indeed I am, sir. Come this way, sir and ma'am."

He reached for their bags, but Walter gestured toward Pepper's, and continued wheeling his own.

"Here, sir and ma'am, we must take a cab. Otopeni International Airport is sixteen kilometers from the city."

"How much is the cab?"

"About twenty-five thousand leu."

Pepper gasped, but Walter said to her, "The exchange rate is about twenty thousand leu to a dollar."

"Oh."

"Yes, indeed, sir and ma'am. You will find all things in Bucharest very payable. Good food, good hotel."

"How much is the bus?"

The little man looked crestfallen. "About one thousand five hundred leu, but it comes sometimes only once an hour. No! No! Not that one!"

Pepper had started toward a man with a car who had opened the car's back door and gestured.

"Real taxi!" the little man said, waving them away from that car, leading them to a taxi line. "Those persons are *hustlers.*"

# 3

Things were better in Romania these days, everybody said, but it is not a happy country. Surrounded by Serbia, Hungary, Ukraine, Moldova, and Bulgaria, it has been invaded and attacked since the Stone Age. Romans conquered the Dacians, Goths threw out the Romans, Bulgars and Mongols and proto-Germans and Turks all occupied chunks of Romania in their turn. Vlad the Impaler ruled the southern chunk for a while, declared war against the Turkish garrisons, and impaled 20,000 Turkish and Bulgarian captives on stakes in a forest of death said to have been a half-mile wide and two miles long. Two world wars flamed across Romania. The arrest, trial, and death of Nicolae Ceauşescu put an end to decades of iron rule, but the country's economy is recovering very slowly. Romanians have survived by sheer endurance. They adapt. One of the recent adaptations has been as a source of babies for Europe and America.

When the influx of people wanting to adopt babies from Ceauşescu's orphanages began, Romanians were embarrassed. After the first reforms were put in place, however, and foreigners wanting to adopt babies found it more difficult, a black market grew up. Walter and Pepper's guide, Mr. Tapp, and their driver slowed to a stop at a corner and Tapp rolled down the car window, much to Pepper's relief. The car smelled like tobacco tar. Despite the snow, there were clumps of men on the street corner. It was late afternoon.

"I will ask them about babies," Mr. Tapp said.

"Wait! Don't!" Pepper said, but it had already been done. The men on the corner shouted out several sentences, and two of them hurried away. They returned in less than a minute with two women and four children, one a baby in arms. The men pointed at the baby.

"Two hundred dollars American," one said, in heavily accented English. The other pointed to the swollen belly of the younger woman.

"Soon, soon," he said. "Four hundred dollar."

"Please drive on," Walter told Tapp.

"I show you for comparison sake," the wizened guide said, pulling away from the shouting men.

The streets were cobbled. Snow had just begun to fall on Bucharest when the Windsor House representative had come back to pick Walter and Pepper up at the Dorobonati Hotel. They had not even had time to unpack their bags. It was late afternoon here, and the guide said they must see one orphanage before the day ended.

Now they passed tram cars carrying tired workers home from jobs around the city.

"It's very dark," Pepper said.

Their guide waved his arms. "Lighting in city very bad."

They drove thirty minutes through the gathering twilight. Finally Tapp pulled into a large cobbled courtyard in the center of a U-shaped old building. The lighting in the courtyard was dim. Walter thought the staff lighted the whole parking area with two fifteen-watt bulbs.

The interior of the baby house was Gothic. The halls were formed of cut stone and had barrel ceilings. Pepper and Walter were shown into a medium-sized room that resembled a chapel. A thin man in skirted priest's garments held out a long limp hand and said, "Welcome," in deep tones. Walter felt he was in the middle of a bad production of *Dracula*. But it got crossed with *The Sound of Music* when a young nun or novice entered, carrying a baby in each arm. The infants were wrapped in thin flannel blankets. Both had dark hair and the one who was awake also had dark eyes. The baby cried, then blew a bubble.

"Each is four months," their guide said. They handed one to Walter and one to Pepper. Unobtrusively, Walter cuddled the baby's head and in the process obtained a few hairs. He had palmed a small piece of double-sided tape. He patted it on the back of the blanket, picking up shed skin cells. He assumed Pepper was doing the same. The child made no sound. At the same moment, Pepper's baby shrieked.

Before Walter or Pepper could respond, another slightly older nun arrived, also bearing two infants. One had brown hair and one had black hair. Walter handed his baby back to the young nun.

Now everything stopped, the nuns standing as if for inspection and the babies all quiet also. The guide looked at Pepper and Walter.

"Uh—" Pepper said.

"Well," Walter said, placing his hands together. "I don't know quite how to say this, and they are wonderful babies, I'm sure, but we did really say blond. And a boy. Are they—"

"Is girl," said the younger nun, cocking her head at the wide-awake baby. As if to prove it, she unwrapped her. In the cold air, the child immediately began to scream.

## 4

"I feel awful," Pepper said in the car. "I mean, how can I live with myself if I actually *reject* a baby? What kind of person does that make me?"

Walter thought this comment was in character for Sylvia Carroll. But he wondered whether it also represented Pepper's real feelings.

It did his.

## 5

The next stop was nearly half an hour in the other direction. A sign on the road pointed to Balotesti.

It was now fully dark, even though it was only six o'clock local time. The streetlights glowed feebly and were placed very far apart, more like distant beacons the car steered toward as it tacked and bumped over cobbles and holes than like anything designed to actually light up the road surface.

The next orphanage turned out to be a tall, narrow-fronted building shouldered into insignificance between two larger elderly apartment houses. Their guide parked directly in front. There were no other cars on the block.

Inside, a gray-haired woman in a steel-gray dress spoke incomprehensibly to Mr. Tapp. "We shall follow her," Tapp said, unnecessarily. She had already turned away.

The first room was long and very narrow, running, Walter guessed, along the side of the apartment building next door. This left it with only two narrow windows at the far end. Since it was dark outdoors, the window did nothing to lighten the room. Four low-wattage bulbs emphasized the shadows. The room stank of wet diapers. A matronly woman pushed a rattling cart topped by a tray on which were several dozen baby bottles. The woman in gray snapped words at her and she slipped out the door.

Mr. Tapp waved his hand at the babies. "All under six months!" he said with apparent pride.

Pepper walked to the nearest crib. A little black-haired child lay on his back, lips pushing in and out. "May I pick him up?" she asked, but she was already doing so.

The woman gasped and uttered a spate of indignant words.

"Did I do wrong?" Pepper asked Mr. Tapp. She still held the baby.

"No. Ah, no."

Walter said, "What's the trouble?"

Mr. Tapp, usually voluble, hesitated. "She says you don't want that baby."

"Why not?" Pepper asked. "He seems alert and well. Is his mother coming back for him?"

"No."

"What is it?" Walter said again.

"It's a gypsy."

The woman spoke again. This time Tapp translated. "You can't want gypsy children," he said.

"Why not?"

The woman replied to Pepper's tone, not her words, but she was right on target.

"Gypsies are thieves!" Tapp translated. The woman went on angrily and Tapp translated. " 'I have heard Americans will take gypsies,' she says. She says it is so foolish. Inheritance is everything. Would you buy a dog from a long line of vicious dogs?"

# 6

They said goodnight to Tapp at the curb. Smoke followed them from the car as they stepped into the street.

"Tomorrow at the first thing. Nine A.M.," Tapp said.

On the way to the hotel door, Pepper muttered, "I think they're exhausting us intentionally. I mean, we've just arrived after three flights and thirty hours' travel, and they take us out right away."

Walter thought the real Sylvia Carroll might say something like that but he still made a discouraging growl in his throat. Personally, he believed they had just been treated to a great piece of theater, and would probably get more tomorrow.

They bought sandwiches to take to their room, too tired to sit through dinner in the restaurant. They were almost too tired to eat.

Pepper threw herself into the narrow double bed without ceremony. In New York they'd had a room with a king-size bed, which had at least given them room to ignore each other. They would probably both have slept in one bed anyway, to make the illusion that they were George and Sylvia more believable. Even so it had been a very uncomfortable night.

Now they were both so tired it didn't matter. Pepper turned over and appeared to be asleep in seconds. Walter washed up in the bathroom, turned off the two lights, and crawled into bed only fifteen minutes later.

But in the dark, he heard Pepper sniffling. She had shown no signs of a cold. She was crying over the babies.

He considered that for a few minutes. For all he knew, the room was bugged. But after he thought about it, he decided that crying was something Sylvia Carroll might perfectly well do tonight.

# 7

Walter was deeply asleep when he heard knocking at the door. He got up, put his coat over his pajamas because it was the handiest thing, and went to the door.

"Who is it?"

"Sir. Sir?"

"Who is it?"

Cautiously, he opened the door. Pepper rustled the sheets behind him. He thought she had sat up. Probably frightened.

A woman stood in the door with a baby wrapped in a red-and-brown cloth.

"Sir? Missus?"

Pepper had reached his side. She said, "What do you want?"

The woman obviously did not understand her, but she unwrapped the baby. It was a girl. The child was seriously impaired. The forehead receded and was unusually shallow. The tongue was very large.

"Good baby," the woman said. "One hundred dollar." She paused. "Fifty dollar?"

# Chapter Seventeen

Pregnant? Worried? Feel you can't raise a child?
Scared for the baby? Don't consider abortion. We can
find a good home for your baby. We pay all medical
expenses and may be able to offer you free housing
while you await the birth. Call us today, or come to
the office. Call . . .

## 1

### Shannon, Ireland
### Early December

The Aeroflot plane came in over the sea, gliding down to Shannon Airport in Ireland. Dooley was jet-lagged and cramped from sitting in an airline seat, but most of all he was frightened.

He allowed himself six hours in Ireland. Then he would go on to Moscow. If Claudia looked at his ticket she might think New York to Moscow via Shannon made sense, but not if he stayed a whole day or more. He shouldn't have to, in any case. Limerick was just twenty-four kilometers away.

The rental car was waiting. Its steering wheel was on the right, not the left, of course. Maybe that would remind him to drive on the left side of the street.

He made sure to pay for the extra insurance. Then he stopped a minute at the airport shop, bought a box of chocolates, and got into the car.

In thirty minutes he was on his way to Limerick.

Dooley's Internet investigator had assembled a long list of possible names from lists of missing children around the world. Once the investigator had a list of infants whose gender, ethnicity, age, and physical characteristics matched Teddy's, and selecting, of course, only those who disappeared in the target period, he then double-checked by invading driver's license records and correlated the parents' physical descriptions with the child's data. Dooley told him not to eliminate any child from the list solely on the basis of the parents' physical data. After all, the parents might have adopted the child in the first place, or only one custodial parent might be the biological parent. He used info about the parents to flag possible errors in the reports about the child. Double-checking never hurt. He was a finicky, detail-oriented cyber wizard, and he knew people made incomprehensible-to-him errors all the time. When there was a seemingly impossible discrepancy, he went into hospital records to check. "You can't hack into hospital records," Dooley said. As a doctor, he found the idea revolting. "They're confidential." The investigator smiled patronizingly. He found several egregious errors in the missing-children reports. In one case an abducted child had been described by the police files as having blond hair. But news photos, made from pictures the parents had taken earlier and supplied to the media, showed the baby had straight, dark brown hair at birth and it stayed straight and brown all the way up to five months, when he was abducted. The investigator checked the hospital birth records, just in case the parents were pulling a fast one. The police reports were wrong.

Very quickly, the investigator provided Dooley with sixteen most likely. There were forty-five he considered the next most likely.

Dooley had decided it was safe to send investigators to get DNA samples surreptitiously from the parents of the most likely children. He hired three reliable people, one woman and two men. Unlike asking a detective to find cases of missing children of a certain type, with these investigators he could just hand out a list of people, in fact parents of missing children, and ask for materials that would contain DNA. He discussed carefully with the investigators what kinds of samples would be suitable. It was now possible, for instance, to get mitochondrial DNA from a hair shaft, not just the root. But the shaft was prone to contamination, the process was very expensive, and often the amount of DNA wasn't sufficient. Still, the important thing was, it could be done. Even fingerprints, in some cases, yielded DNA. But he wanted to be sure. Whenever possible, he wanted blood, skin cells, hair roots, or saliva. Although most detectives already had some familiarity with it, he explained in detail the handling of DNA evidence.

He said absolutely nothing about why he was doing this. He did not even mention that the targets had ever had a child. He was careful to use several investigators and give each only a few cases. They might suspect these were possibly parents or relatives involved in a paternity case, but they wouldn't know for sure. No one detective would know too much about what was going on. In most cases, the targets were male-female pairs. Get either, but on the whole, he told them, he would prefer samples from the women. They might assume that was true because you could be sure who the mother of a child was, but not so sure of the father. In fact, that was part of Dooley's reason. But Dooley also knew maternal DNA was easier to prove. Every body cell has two kinds of DNA. The DNA in the nucleus of the cell contains all the chromosomes that determine the person's appearance, half from his mother and half from his father. But the second kind of DNA, mitochondrial DNA, comes from the outer part of the cell, the cytoplasm. It is sometimes called the powerhouse of the cell. All of a person's mitochondrial DNA comes from his or her mother. When the sperm from the father meets the egg from the mother, it burrows in, its motor power, the wiggling tail, dropping off as it does so. The head of the sperm carries the father's half of the nucleus DNA for the blueprint of the child, and the egg carries the mother's half. But the sperm's mitochondrial DNA is all in the tail. As a result, every human being has mitochondrial DNA from only the maternal line, his mother, grandmother, great-grandmother—none from any male ancestor. Teddy's mitochondrial DNA would be identical to his birth mother's, whoever she was.

Dooley took for himself the two most likely cases of all the missing children. One was a child from Teaneck, New Jersey, who disappeared from a day-care center, where his mother, young and poor, left him while she worked as an assistant to a dog groomer. Dooley, feeling like a monster, interviewed the mother, a sweet young woman named Sunny Bakeley, for a "housekeeper's job," which he told her would be at twice her present salary. He met her at a neighborhood delicatessen. She was a thin, milk-white little person, with curly red hair and green eyes. She had thin little wrists and slender fingers; he had trouble picturing her restraining a Great Dane for grooming, but he assumed she must. She looked undernourished. When he told her to order whatever she wanted, she said, "Really?" and decided on a tuna melt with a side of cole slaw and a side of cottage cheese. When he ordered only coffee and a green salad, she said, "Won't you be hungry?"

She was a sweet child, he thought, but a child. If her son was abducted nearly four years ago, she couldn't have been more than seventeen when he was born.

Steeling himself, he described the job he had in mind for her and quailed when her eyes brightened with enthusiasm.

She had arrived at the restaurant chewing gum and dressed in a lavender grooming smock. She wrapped the gum in a gum wrapper and deposited it in the thin metal ashtray. Dooley spent the entire meal on tenterhooks, fearful that the waitress might empty that ashtray. It had a couple of cigarette butts in it and needed cleaning. Fortunately, the waitress was blowsy and casual. When Dooley and Sunny Bakeley got up to go, he palmed the gum.

Even with present DNA methods, turnaround time in the lab was ten days, more or less, depending on the type of analysis appropriate to the particular sample, days if they had enough for a PCR, longer if they had a tiny sample and had to amplify with RFLP. He couldn't put other investigations on hold to hang around waiting for results. He had to go on to the next case.

Adding to the difficulty was the fact that there were restrictions on the analysis of DNA. Dooley was using a lab mostly employed by doctors, and he had represented the samples he was sending as part of medical research. Given that explanation, he could hardly ask them to rush it. DNA analysis itself couldn't be rushed, but the paperwork could have. Dooley didn't want to call any special attention to it.

The second case sounded even more promising but was much farther away, an infant who went missing just two weeks before he and Claudia first saw Teddy in Russia, and who matched Teddy physically in every respect. The child had lived in Limerick.

The hired investigators, meanwhile, were trekking all over the country, including to Texas, Nevada, Nebraska, and Oklahoma. They got their DNA samples several ways. In two cases, the first investigator was able to bribe the mother's hairdresser to give him hair from her session. A few of the hairs had roots still attached. The second investigator, in one of his cases, bribed an assistant in a dental office to save some slightly bloody gauze packing. The father in one of his cases was known to frequent a particular bar and to be a philanderer. Overeager to get this last case finished, the investigator sent in a prostitute who seduced the father—not at all difficult, she said—and she brought back a semen sample. Dooley never knew exactly how the investigator had got the sample. The woman's fee came in under "general expenses."

The third investigator struck it lucky. She was chatting with one of her targets, a female, in Pearl, Mississippi, when a mosquito landed on the woman's arm and bit her. The woman swatted it, but the investigator was swift enough to pull a tissue from her purse, say, "Let me get that," and blot the blood smear.

In a week, Dooley had DNA material from at least one parent of each missing child.

Then Dooley had left for Ireland.

Dooley drove cautiously away from Shannon Airport down the N19 access road and onto the N18 to Limerick. Driving on the left-hand side gave him an odd feeling of abandon, of doing something forbidden. Briefly, he almost felt good.

The Irish countryside would have been green in the summer. Now it was mostly browns and grays, although a lot warmer than New York. Ireland was nearly as far north as Moscow but was much warmer because of the Gulf Stream that flowed past it.

He admired the stone fences and the small cottages. There were sheep huddling in the lee of wooden pens.

Dooley passed through Limerick, heading for Ballyneety on a road called R514. While the N18 from the airport had been a four-lane highway, the road to Ballyneety was narrow, two bumpy lanes. He watched the crossings to see whether he was heading in the right direction. Some weren't labeled. Dooley had a good map, he hoped, which he had downloaded from the Net. But sometimes the roads didn't exactly agree with the map. It shouldn't be far, just past Bohereen. He passed people working in the fields, caring for livestock, and every time he saw a red-haired, pale-skinned child, he sighed.

As he drove, he worried that the Keenan house might come up too soon, without enough lead time. He needed to know before he got too close; it would certainly look suspicious to drive back and forth in front of the place. Then in revulsion he hoped he would never find it and would have to go home without completing his horrible errand.

He passed through Ballyneety all too soon. But as if to give him exactly what he wanted, the road rose, then curved down into a large flat meadow area. There was the house, set back from the road. He knew it immediately, at a hundred yards' distance. He'd seen a picture of it in a newspaper he'd downloaded. Kidnappings are rare in Ireland, and this one got quite a bit of coverage, even though the parents were not prominent. In fact, they were rather impoverished.

He braked sharply. The car slewed sideways; then the fender bumped into a tree. The car stopped with a shock and Dooley threw his head at the driver's side door post. Hard.

He sat there stunned for half a minute. He had managed to cut his eyebrow and blood was running down into his eye.

Perfect.

He got out of the car, staggered just a couple of steps, then walked toward the house. He was halfway there when a man came from the outbuilding in the yard.

"You're in the soup, right enough," the man said. His hands were laced behind his back, his head cocked to one side.

"I kind of lost control of it."

"American, then, are you?" He spoke with a lilting accent. They spoke Gaelic around here, when not talking to visitors, Dooley knew.

Now two children came out of the door of the house, followed by their mother. All redheads, the whole family, with curly hair, skin like skimmed milk, and green eyes. Dooley's eyes teared up for a few seconds. There were a lot of different physical types in Ireland. Some had that orangey hair and some were so-called black Irish. But this family all looked like Teddy.

"I'm very sorry," he said. "I wonder if I could just wash my face? Get the blood out of my eye."

The wife said, "Surely. Step in for a moment."

"I guess I forgot that I was supposed to drive on the left. I drifted over to the wrong side and then I overcorrected."

"I've seen worse," the man said. "Been some nasty accidents. Bad collisions." He scratched at a long cut on his arm, dried and starting to heal.

"You Americans shouldn't try to drive over here," the wife said, but she was smiling.

"My name's Dooley McSweeney," Dooley said, holding out his hand.

"Ah. I thought as much. Always can tell when a person is Irish, can't you?" She shook his hand. "Anne Keenan." She was about seven months pregnant.

The older boy carried a whetstone and an oily rag. His hands were orange-brown with rust. He'd been sharpening and oiling tools, a winter occupation in farming country. There were two rows of cabbages still in the field next to the cottage. The father had a few stalks of straw clinging to his boots. His hands looked oily too. The man smelled strange but strangely familiar. It's natural lanolin from sheep's wool, Dooley thought. It smells like those raw wool sweaters that are supposed to repel water.

Inside the cubby entrance of the house, Dooley suddenly wondered whether they had running water. If they were too far out in the country, they might have an outhouse, and indoors just a hand pump for water. Then what would he do? But he was scarcely over the threshold when the wife said, "The loo's right in there," and pointed at a door down a short hall.

He went in and closed the door. It was certainly not an American bathroom. Very small, with a high window, it had a round, deep bathtub, a pedestal sink, and a lidless toilet. From outside he heard the wife call, "Use any towel you want. I laid them out fresh today."

"Thank you."

He turned on the water, and with its covering noise rummaged through the wastebasket. He found two clumps of hair, wadded as if pulled from a comb. One of the clumps looked like a child's, pale red, soft and fine. As near as he could tell, both contained a few hairs with roots. The hairs were long, which he hoped meant they were not from the father. Next to some tissues and a discarded soggy biscuit was something even better. A European sort of Band-Aid, which they called sticking-plaster here, with a bit of blood on it. Then he remembered that it was the father who had a cut. That was not quite as good, but he took it anyway.

He pocketed half of both clumps of hair, leaving the rest so that the family would not notice they were gone—although people rarely paid attention to things that they had thrown out. The missing Band-Aid would just have to be a mystery if they ever noticed its absence at all.

After wiping his forehead, he rinsed the towel as best he could and hung it on the rack.

"Thank you very much, Mrs. Keenan," he said, coming out. "I'm sorry to have troubled you."

" 'Tis nothing."

"And who are you?" Dooley said to a small girl who stared straight up at him, her thumb in her mouth.

"Maud," she said.

"Hello, Maud."

"You talk funny."

"Maud!" said her mother.

"It's all right." There were four children in the central room. They wore clean, mended clothing, most of which was wool and looked itchy. The boys, even the toddler, wore sweaters, out at the elbows. The girls wore blue dresses. Maud's was probably handed down from the older girl, since it hung almost to the floor.

"Stair steps," Dooley said. Anne Keenan raised her eyebrows. "In height," Dooley said, hating himself.

"Line up, the lot of yeh," said the mother. The children giggled and arranged themselves by height. They must have done this before. The children were possibly six, five, three, and two. There was a height gap, just about where Teddy might fit.

"What are your names?" Dooley asked.

"Sean," said the tallest.

Dooley shook his hand. "Bet you're in school at your age."

"Most of the time, sir."

"Mary," said the next.

"Maud," said Maud.

"And you, little guy?" he asked the small one.

The little boy mumbled a word.

"Eddy?" said Dooley.

"No," his mother said. "Teddy."

## 2

Sick at heart, Dooley leaned his hand on his car and covered his feelings with a big smile. "Well, thank you all so much."

"You're sure no tea?" Anne Keenan said.

"Or a jar?" said the husband, possibly wanting an excuse to start drinking early in the day.

"I'm sure. Thank you."

"You should see Ireland when it's not winter," Anne said, looking around her at the brown grass, like a house-proud woman whose house is a bit disheveled. "Fuchsias everywhere, blooming like weeds."

"I should come back again. Well, I've gotta get moving. Can you tell me the time?"

"Half four."

All six Keenans had trooped back outdoors, where the father was studying Dooley's car. "Left your key in the switch," he said.

Dooley looked back at the cottage. Did he want Teddy to come here to live? To live on a working farm and work in the sheep barn? The house was chilly. The children's grammar wasn't good. The parents seemed kind but the father was possibly somewhat stern. Teddy would sleep in a small room with the other three boys. Would he get to be a doctor or an astronaut or go skating at Rockefeller Center if he lived here?—or was Dooley just being a snob? This was a beautiful country, but not affluent. He'd read somewhere that half the young people emigrated. The EU had designated most of western Ireland "severely disadvantaged" and encouraged "traditional farming practices" including raising sheep.

"Are you sure you're all right?" Anne Keenan asked.

He'd been spacing out. Probably he acted dazed, like he had a head injury. "I'm fine. And I think the car's drivable," Dooley said, perfectly certain that it was and now anxious to leave. "I'll be going."

"Back to work, boys," said the father.

Dooley said, "Oh, wait!"

He reached into the car and took a box from the back seat. "I was taking this to my friend in Kilmallock," which was a town far enough away so that the Keenans might not know it well and ask questions, but close enough to make sense to try to reach it on these small roads. "May I give it to the children instead?"

"Chocolates!" said the oldest boy.

"Thank the gentleman, yeh all," said the father.

A chorus of thank-yous.

"It's nothing. Goodbye."

The father nodded. "Be well, Mr. McSweeney."

"Thank you, Mr. Keenan."

## 3

At the airport in Shannon, Dooley separated the two bunches of hair into four, and placed one bunch from each sample in a FedEx envelope. Then he tore the Band-Aid in two, and put one of the halves in the envelope. This package he addressed to the lab in the U.S. that did DNA testing for him. The remaining samples he put in a labeled paper envelope in a pocket of his suitcase. He was taking no chances that he would lose the material and have to come back.

Dropping the FedEx envelope in the airport pickup box, he went immediately to the bar and drank three Irish whiskies in quick succession. The bartender was not talkative, except to remark, "Ye don't like flyin', hey?"

She's pregnant again. Maybe they don't need Teddy, he thought. Then he went cold in the pit of his stomach. *Oh, my God! What kind of person am I turning into?*

The strain had gone on too long. Every minute of the day he was torn. They had to keep Teddy; they had to find out who had lost Teddy. He had to protect Claudia. He had to protect himself against what he believed Claudia would do when she found out. But still, they had to return Teddy.

Did Teddy belong to the Keenans? It would be ten days more or less before he would know. Just a little bit before Christmas.

Once he was on the Aeroflot plane and airborne, he ordered another Irish whiskey, being careful not to breathe whiskey fumes on the flight attendant. He didn't want her to cut him off until he got good and numb. But she figured it out by the third drink—his sixth counting the airport—and handed him a pillow and wished him a good nap.

When he landed and deplaned into Sheremetevo 2, Dooley was in no shape to negotiate an airport, even if it had been much more convenient than this one. Getting through Sheremetevo had been nightmarish last time, although he and Claudia had help from Windsor House and it wasn't in wintertime either. All the entry formalities were at least a one-hour gauntlet to run. He had been sitting in the middle of his plane, and this put him in the middle of the slow passport control line.

Sheremetevo is dark, with low ceilings. The airport in Moscow could have been designed to terrify people with claustrophobia. The Russians themselves jostle and bump each other and everybody else. Dooley was already feeling bruised and confused and the body contact made it worse. He couldn't tell which passport control line was for foreigners.

When he had come here before, with Claudia, Windsor House had bribed somebody to let them cut ahead in the line. He remembered being embarrassed about this, but was told it was understood. Everybody who could afford to do it did it.

He also remembered there were no luggage carts when he arrived the last time. It didn't matter now; he had brought only enough clothes for a single carry-on. Blearily, he noticed three women from his flight telling a guard that their flight number was posted over *that* luggage conveyor but their bags weren't on it, and the guard pointed to a different conveyor. The women seemed to be saying that even though they could see their bags on the second conveyor, they didn't think they should pick them up, because it was posted to a different airline and different flight number. Weaving and unfocused, Dooley nevertheless had enough sense to decide the women must be nuts.

He had no tape recorders, jewelry, or excess cash to declare, but he still was required to declare that he did not have them. The airline was supposed to have passed out declaration slips during the flight. But it hadn't, so everybody was forced to stand in line and fill them out now.

He saw a man selling no-longer-circulated USSR coins, in one-, two-, three-, five-, and ten-kopeck denominations, in plastic cases as souvenirs, and blearily wondered about whether the sale was legal. An elderly woman was selling fried cakes that smelled good and made him feel nauseated at the same time. He got two vodkas at a bar there, somewhere. Then, still clutching his stamped customs form, he slouched his way to the taxi rank. He knew enough to take a standard taxi. The others occasionally robbed their customers.

Moscow cabbies were used to sozzled tourists, and to sozzled Russians, for that matter. The elderly cabbie, who looked like a transplant from the eastern part of the old Soviet Union, said something that sounded like *"Poyekhali!"* and then asked him where he was going in passable English. It would be twenty miles, or thirty kilometers, and about forty dollars American to Moscow.

Dooley gave him a street address and added, "The Metropole Hotel."

# 4

## Moscow
## Early December

After spending most of another hour checking in at the hotel, a process that included surrendering his passport and signing a book as well, Dooley fell into bed with the hotel room making slow circles in front of his eyes. Between the alcohol and the jet lag, Dooley had no idea whether it was eight A.M. or eight P.M., since both were dark at this time of year in Moscow, and for that matter, he was quite sure he had forgotten to turn his watch ahead as he crossed time zones, so he was pretty sure it wasn't eight anything here, although it was probably eight something in—what?—New York? Shannon? Or maybe he *had* turned it ahead. Now he thought he remembered doing so. But had he done it in the air or on the ground? That would give him an idea of whether he had really brought it up to the minute—

His last thought before he slipped gratefully into sleep was that he and Claudia had been very happy when they stayed here before.

They'd been scared that they might not get the baby. They'd been exhausted from being dragged through Romania for four fruitless days. But they had seen the baby in the orphanage, had been told that the mother had definitely signed off on him, that the required waiting period had gone by, and with just a few bribes and a little patience, he could be theirs. Teddy was thin, like all the babies, but the doctor said he was in good heath. As a doctor, Dooley certainly could confirm that everything that could be seen or felt, plus any responses he elicited, all suggested the boy was perfect. And he had curly red hair and deep green eyes. Irish eyes. Here in Russia, Irish eyes.

The room swirled around him. Dooley was reading Teddy a bedtime story. He began to speak aloud, "Dorothy lived in the midst of the great Kansas prairies, with Uncle Henry, who was a farmer, and Aunt Em, who was the farmer's wife." Teddy was nestled into his chest, listening raptly. "Their house was small, for the lumber to build it had to be carried by wagon for many miles—"

Dooley fell asleep.

# 5

Dooley woke up feeling chilled and vaguely worried, until he realized where he was and why and then he felt very worried. He also had a hideous headache, nausea, and throbbing in his eyeballs. He dressed, then lurched down the hall to the bathroom, splashed his face with cold water, and found it made his headache worse. He was logy, but he didn't feel rested.

Back in his room, he saw that his watch said five, which probably meant it was actually seven A.M. here, assuming he had set it in Ireland before he behaved so foolishly. And he must have set it—now he was

BARBARA D'AMATO

226

quite sure—because he remembered not wanting to get to the Keenans' house too early. He had set it on the plane. Yes, that's right, he thought, on the plane before landing in Shannon.

So now the thing to do was to go down to the lobby and get coffee. Or tea if they didn't have coffee. Lots and lots of strong tea.

In the cavernous lobby, Dooley looked around for the samovar he remembered. Not much different from a steel multicup coffee machine, the samovar was sputtering on a table against the far wall. He hadn't brought his own mug, so he'd have to drink his tea here; the hotel staff wouldn't let you carry their mugs back to your room. That was all right. He'd either stand here and drink it or go to the dining room for breakfast. A piece of bread might settle his stomach.

A woman and two men were talking earnestly just in front of the registration desk. He thought he knew the woman. She looked very familiar. Not wanting to ignore somebody he ought to know, he walked toward her.

"Um—I think—" he began.

"Are you all right?" she said.

"Don't I know you?"

She smiled.

One of the men said, "She's Gabrielle Coulter."

"Uh..." He knew that meant something. But what? *Oh! The TV reporter!*

She said, smiling, "Are you really okay? I know it's rude, but frankly you look terrible. And since you're a fellow American, we feel responsible for you."

"Some of us do," joked the other man.

Dooley said, "I'm not sick. Once I get some breakfast, I'll be fine."

"Worst case of jet lag *I* ever saw," said the first man.

Gabrielle Coulter pointed at his watch. Dooley said, "Seven A.M. give or take, isn't it?"

"Seven P.M.," she said.

# 6

"We couldn't have let you eat at the Metropole," she said, when they had settled into chairs at the restaurant. "Not in your condition."

The Café Kranzle was in the Hotel Baltschug, a well-known hotel located on the Moskva River, not far from the famous Gum department store. Actually within sight of the Kremlin, it was much more expensive than the Metropole and, of course, many miles from the orphanage. Getting there had not been easy. Light snow had started to fall. Like anyplace else Dooley had ever been, when the weather got bad the taxis got scarce.

"Nor any condition," said the first man, whose name turned out to be Sam Bielski. Dooley thought Sam didn't look well. He was pasty-faced but dark under the eyes and had a yellowish skin color. The second man, however, was as husky as the day was long. His shoulders were twice as wide as Gabrielle's. His neck was thicker than Dooley's thigh. He was probably just under six feet, so he'd weigh maybe two hundred and ten, and not a bit of it fat.

This man had been introduced to him in the cab as Gordo Malman, but they called him Gorilla. "Gorilla is our photographer," Gabrielle said. She added affectionately, "He carries heavy stuff all the time." She must realize that people saw Gordo's build first and his other probably fine characteristics later. Gabrielle seemed very sensitive to people.

"Well, thank you for rescuing me," Dooley said.

"Don't worry about it," Sam said. "CNN is paying."

The waiter proved to speak excellent English. Gordo said to him, "Vodka in those really neato thin glasses in a bucket of ice like"—he pointed to a set being served to a couple two tables away—"like that. And caviar. And black bread."

*"Po-Russki,"* said Bielski.

"Sam knows things," Gabrielle said, joking but with fondness. "That's why we keep him around."

The glasses resembled test tubes with a bulge at the bottom and arrived in less than two minutes. Even though there were four people at their table, six glasses stood in a glass bowl filled with crushed ice. "Your health!" said Gordo, first handing one to Gabrielle, then grabbing and downing his in a single gulp.

"You don't want any?" Gabrielle said to Dooley.

"Um—no, thank you."

"I knew it!" Gordo said. "Bit of overindulgence on the plane?"

"Quite a bit."

"No problem. I'll have yours." And he did, reaching a hairy wrist across the table.

"I'm embarrassed that I didn't know where I'd seen you," Dooley said to Gabrielle. "I realized as soon as Sam said your name, I've watched you lots of times."

The caviar arrived, also in a dish set in ice. For a cold country, Dooley thought, they went in for a lot of ice. With it were the chopped whites and yolks of hard-boiled eggs, some cream, and chopped parsley. The waiter asked whether they wanted capers, onions, and lemon, but Sam said, "Only if Dooley does," in such a disapproving tone of voice that Dooley decided he didn't. Gabrielle laughed and shook her head.

"So what are you here for, Ms. Coulter?" Dooley said.

"Call me Gabrielle. I was here a month ago and my tapes were destroyed, so we're reshooting. I'm making a documentary—my own personal project, for a change."

Dooley thought her wide mouth and large eyes were much prettier in person than on the television screen. He said, "Tell me about it."

"It's about orphans." As she talked, Gordo ordered another round of vodka and Sam said something in Russian to the waiter that in a few minutes resulted in the arrival of shredded cheese with garlic accompanied by black bread, a separate dish of mushrooms and dill, and a large dish of a spicy kidney bean salad. Dooley found his queasiness disappearing. He ate eagerly and listened to Gabrielle talk about North Africa, Romania, and the other places she'd visited to tape her documentary.

"How did you lose the tapes you shot here before?" he asked when she stopped.

"Oh, my room at the hotel was broken into. Hooligans, they said."

"Doesn't happen very often, even in Russia," said Sam.

"And what are you doing here, Dooley?" Gabrielle asked.

"I'm trying to trace the medical history of our adopted Russian baby," he said, and left it at that. He turned the topic to how people put together a documentary.

He wondered why she looked so sad. He didn't know she was wondering the same about him.

# CHAPTER EIGHTEEN

Until the 1920s, in the Chicago Nursery and Half-Orphan Asylum, children were not permitted to speak during meals. Breakfast, lunch, and dinner passed in silence except for the clicking of spoons on bowls.

*—Favorite Facts,* vol. 5

## 1

### New York City
### Mid-December

"You will recall that we've had a very large bid for three years now from a couple who want to adopt twin golden-haired girls with blue eyes," the Boss said.

"And we decided not—" Jean Sippoline began.

"Our Internet scout has now located a pair born just ten days ago in Arlington, Texas."

"Stop!" Sigmund Rutgauer said. "Bad idea. It's too dangerous." He raised his nose in the air, as if he had just tasted wine gone bad. "We can afford to be careful. Possible target children are born all the time."

"Not twins."

"The money would certainly be good for our bottom line," said Gordon Ridley.

"Our bottom line is just fine," said Rutgauer. "In fact, if I remember correctly, a meeting or two back, you"—he gestured at the Boss—"said our success was so great it placed us in danger of attracting too much notice."

The Boss took over, firmly. "I said that, and it's true, but we only need to be careful."

"Which is exactly what I mean," said Rutgauer, in a still firmer voice. "We included certain safeguards in our policies. Our guidelines, if you will. The first"—he raised one finger—"was never to acquire any especially unusual material. Which this is. It attracts too much attention."

"Absolutely," said Sippolene.

"The second was never to acquire material from anybody famous or powerful." He raised a second finger.

"And we haven't."

"Always get material from the middle or lower-middle class or even below, assuming the material is in good health. And never to acquire material under attention-getting conditions," Sippolene continued. "Not from the White House lawn for instance—"

"As if we would!" said Gordon Ridley.

"That was a pleasantry. And never two in the same geographical area in a short period of time—" He raised a third finger.

"Give it a rest, Sigmund. And give your fingers a rest," the Boss said. "We know all that."

Rutgauer continued, "But in the last year, we've broken several of our basic rules. Take the rule that we would obtain material primarily from single parents, or parents who were separated from each other."

"In fact," Sippolene said, "the best background condition of all is a situation where one parent is not in the home but wants custody."

"Exactly," Rutgauer said. "The police always think the other parent took the child. Even if he's got a perfect alibi, even if he's at dinner with the chief of police—"

Ridley huffed, "If he even *knows* the chief of police, we shouldn't—"

"I know that, Gordon! It's a *joke*. I'm making a point. No matter how provably he's elsewhere, if there's a jealous parent out there somewhere, he gets blamed first. Even if he's totally alibied, they'll think he hired somebody."

"The cops will follow him to the ends of the earth," Sippolene said, smiling. "They are really slow to put out all-calls if they think they know who has the kid."

The Boss stood up. It was time to stop the quibbling. "We had serious clients for the three or four units we made exceptions for. Serious clients with serious money."

"Like?"

"Two hundred and fifty thousand dollars. You can hire a lot of courier cutouts for that."

"True."

"I'm still of two minds about some of the other guidelines," Rutgauer said. "They aren't the word from the Mount. For instance, I agree that rural abductions give us the longest lead time, by and large. The country sheriffs don't respond as fast as city cops. Less tech assistance. Plus, rural parents always think the kid has been taken for a stroller ride by some other kid. They search the woods first and drainage ditches and things like that. In cities they panic immediately. But still, strange cars get noticed in the countryside. In the city nobody expects every car to belong to somebody they know."

"Suburbs are the worst," Sippolene said.

The Boss said, "Hold it! Let's get back to the subject at hand. We've been offered a million dollars for twin girls in perfect health, with blue eyes and blond hair. We have an easily aquirable pair. I say we go with it. Split them up for the flight abroad, of course. Route one child through Scandinavia and one through some sort of missionary place in, say, Addis Ababa."

"It's still too dangerous," Sippolene said. "Sooner or later, when they're with the new family, somebody will get suspicious. They'll be noticed."

"I didn't tell you the best part."

"What is it?"

"This couple is multinational. The wife is from Denmark and the husband is from the U.K. They live in the U.S. right now, but they have no particular sentimental attachment to the States. They're willing to spend the rest of their lives abroad if they can get these children."

"That does make it safer," Sigmund Rutgauer said.

"Oh, like we can enforce that," Sippolene said. "Three years, five years down the road? Suppose they want to come back? Please!"

Rutgauer said, "If they're willing to spend a million dollars, why don't they just kidnap the twins themselves? Hire a SWAT team."

"Deniability. They know they can claim they had no idea the children weren't legitimate orphans."

"They keep their hands clean and we take the risks," Rutgauer said.

"That's why they pay us the big bucks."

Rutgauer sat forward. "Wait a minute! What do they know about us? This sounds too much like this couple knows how we operate."

"No. They've only heard we're good."

Sippolene said, "I say we don't do this one."

The Boss said, "I'm setting up surveillance. We'll make the final decision to go ahead or abort in two weeks. But I'm planning to go ahead. We won't have merchandise this good very soon again."

There was a minute of uneasy silence.

"On another matter," said Sigmund Rutgauer.

"Yes?"

"Gabrielle Coulter. She's just gone back there."

"Back there?" said the Boss. "To Moscow? Why the *hell*?"

"She says she needs to reshoot her tape."

"That's plausible—"

"I don't trust it. She's pretty, but she's not a dimwit."

"Well, then, you'll just have to keep an eye on her, won't you?"

# 2

As the others left, the Boss said to Rutgauer, "Hang on a minute."

"What now?"

"My son-in-law has gone to Moscow too."

"Why?"

"He says to find the boy's genetic history to anticipate future health problems."

"You don't believe that, do you?"

"No. We're going to have to make a decision about this."

HIGH POINT PUBLIC LIBRARY
HIGH POINT, NORTH CAROLINA

# CHAPTER NINETEEN

... To establish safeguards to ensure that
intercountry adoptions take place in the best
interests of the child and with respect for his or her
fundamental rights as recognized in international
law ...

—The Hague Convention on the Protection of
Children and Cooperation in Respect of Intercountry
Adoption of 1993

## 1

### Moscow
### Mid-December

Through her U.N. connections, Claudia had found the names of
two doctors in Russia who would be sympathetic with Dooley's
request and could help him. One was an official in the Russian equiv-
alent of the surgeon general's office. Since a visitor needs an inviting
organization, and because Dooley had told her not to tell Windsor
House about it or ask their help, giving her the reason that they might
want to whitewash a medical history, she had looked for a sponsoring
agency through her contacts. The medical society official agreed to
sponsor.

Wanting your child's medical ancestry was reasonable, even
though Russians might argue they didn't have the resources to help

out everybody who had adopted a Russian orphan. As it turned out, Dooley had already met the second one of the two men who were on Claudia's list. Dooley and Dr. Alexandre Kempski, who was now a surgeon, had come to know and like each other when both were doing graduate work in pathology at NYU.

Kempski had warned Dooley in an e-mail before Dooley left New York that the upheaval which fractured the Soviet Union had also ended a lot of the old Soviet-style careful record-keeping. Less money was available for the secretarial work, for ordinary filing. There was no guarantee that the adoption authorities could trace his son's father. In addition to Teddy's Russian medical records, Dooley had the mother's signature on a piece of paper, all papers validated by the Russian government. He had had to have a statement from the country he was adopting the baby from, or the U.S. would not recognize the adoption. The statement had to verify that the parents either were dead, had abandoned the child, or were unknown. In the case of Teddy's father, he had been named but his address was marked as unknown.

Dooley expected bureaucratic delays at every point. The Russian penchant for making everything take forever also had him worried.

Moscow would be intimidating; just finding his way around would be a problem. The metro area alone had a population of twenty-two million. Economically, Russia was in near chaos. After a short burst of enthusiasm at the end of Soviet rule in 1991 and some good financial times in 1993, the country sank into a spiral of currency devaluations and increasing reliance on foreign imports for most consumer goods. Much of Moscow was worn and drab, and many of the people were disheartened.

Kempski met Dooley for coffee and cake in the morning, and

they spent two hours eating and reliving old times. Ordinarily Dooley would have loved this. Now, any delay made him feel like he was dying.

Finally, Kempski sent him over to a functionary to help him get around. This man, Dmitri Nabok, spoke English and had various permission papers that must have required hours and hours to obtain from the state. He also had the work and home address of Teddy's birth mother. Teddy's *supposed* birth mother—but Dooley had not told Kempski anything about his doubts.

Dooley was surprised to find that Dmitri Nabok was actually in the office at the time Dooley had been told he would be, and was willing to take him to the woman who had given birth to Teddy. Still, his basic fear remained. Would they just palm off a woman on him who would claim to be Teddy's mother? He very much *wanted* her to be Teddy's mother. Then he could go home happy and forget the whole horrible nightmare.

## 2

The woman worked in a long line of startlingly similar women. They wore gray smocks and dark scarves over their hair, the tails of the scarves tied behind their necks. Dooley told himself that it was only because their clothes were so similar that they looked to him like clones. But their faces were very much alike too. They all looked hungry.

And they were all making the same motions. A conveyor belt moved white cone-shaped plastic pieces along in front of the women. At Masha's place in the line, eight or ten women each plucked a threaded, gold-colored plastic ring from a barrel next to her, removed one of the cone-shaped plastic pieces from the conveyor belt, and screwed their threaded gold piece onto the threaded base of the cone. Then they replaced the combination onto the conveyor belt.

"She is very lucky to have a job," Nabok said.

Farther along the line, other women picked one of the assemblages from the conveyor belt and snapped a round white piece onto the gold ring on the bottom of the cone. They managed to assemble these two additions to most of the cone-shaped pieces that passed by. Dooley thought that the few that escaped them would be removed somewhere else in the factory and would return again on the conveyor belt.

"What are they making?" he asked Nabok.

"I don't know. Flasks, maybe?"

"Toy rocket ships?"

"They break for lunch in about ten minutes," Nabok said.

He and Dooley simply stood and watched the line. At noon a whistle blew and all the women stopped in midmove, turned, and walked away. The conveyor belt stopped several seconds later. A large number of the cones had gone on past.

Masha looked around, hanging back behind the other women.

"Does she know we're coming?"

"Yes. Of course."

"Does she know who I am?" Dooley asked. "I mean, Teddy and all?"

"Yes, they told her. She had to get permission for an extra-long lunch."

Feeling extremely awkward, Dooley gestured for Nabok to lead the way. The man stepped forward immediately, probably aware of Dooley's uneasiness.

Masha turned. Dooley saw her face for the first time. She was actually a beautiful young woman, possibly twenty-five, with a very pale complexion, like Teddy's. But her skin had the paleness of ill health or undernourishment.

"Miss Lemontov," Nabok said, being especially courteous to her, "this is Dr. McSweeney." Dooley had been told that unlike many Russians she did not speak English. She followed the obvious gestures of introduction and responded in Russian. Nabok added, to Dooley, "She says, 'Welcome to Russia.'"

"Thank you."

Masha had brown eyes. That didn't rule her out as Teddy's mother. He wanted so much for her to be Teddy's mother. It would solve everything. All of his agony would simply go away.

She took a coat from a line of pegs and Nabok ushered them out into the cold. Nabok's agency car stood at the curb. There were few other cars in this part of town, which appeared entirely industrial. Masha Lemontov raised her eyebrows at the car, but got in when Dooley opened the door. They were going to take her to lunch, probably an unusual experience for her, Dooley thought. He knew nothing about Moscow beyond what little he'd seen during his earlier visit, so he'd asked Nabok to find "someplace nice." He doubted that Nabok would interpret that as someplace fancy. More likely someplace nourishing and filling.

He was right. It was a big, hot, noisy restaurant, full of people. The front windows, facing the street, were fogged with moisture and little rivulets ran down the glass. There were Christmas decorations up in the window, including figures of St. Nicholas. The Russians loved St. Nicholas, and the feast of St. Nicholas Day, December 6, was just past. The celebration had been suppressed under the Soviets. Now Muscovites were having fun with St. Nicholas again.

Dooley helped Masha to take her coat off. She smiled at him, then laughed out loud. Being helped off with her coat was probably an unusual thing too. Actually, a lot of the American women he knew thought the gesture was pretty archaic. He hadn't planned to do it. It had just happened.

There was a heavy fog of cigarette smoke. That smell had become unfamiliar for Dooley. Years ago, back home, every restaurant you went into smelled of cigarettes. This was stronger than he remembered. Russian buildings were notoriously badly ventilated. You didn't want to let in the Russian winter.

Masha showed absolutely no sign of being dismayed at wearing her work clothes to a restaurant where most of the people were dressed in business suits. She looked around her and sat down, perfectly self-possessed.

Then she took off her head scarf. Her hair was brown and straight. Dooley sighed inwardly. She might be Teddy's mother, but nothing so far suggested that she was.

They ordered lots of food, including herring for starters, pepper steak, and beet salad. The waiter delivered a big basket of dark bread. Masha tore up a piece and began to eat.

Sensible woman, Dooley thought. If somebody's willing to feed you, eat first, talk later.

After she'd drunk some coffee and eaten a piece of cheese from a sampler plate the waiter brought, Dooley said, "You know why I'm here."

He waited while Nabok translated.

Masha nodded and spoke and Nabok said, "You are here because you adopted my son. I am glad that he is in America. I am not certain why you want to see me. Possibly you want to know that I am happy about it."

Dooley said, "Yes, we'd like to know that. Can I show you pictures of him?"

When she agreed he pulled photos from his pocket. While the waiter put down dishes of olives and the herring, she studied the photos. To Dooley's eye, she looked interested, but not sad or nostalgic.

Aware of his scrutiny, she said, "I will tell you what happened." Nabok translated again, following her smoothly, much like a simultaneous translation at the U.N.

"My little boy was born when I was twenty-one. But he was my third child. I was not married. There was no one to support me. It seemed to me that I should care for the two children I already had, which was hard enough to do of itself. So the day after he was born I told the hospital that I would put him up for adoption. As you probably know, here we must wait several months for finalizing. They want to know whether I will change my mind. Also, in Russia, sometimes the grandmother comes and claims the child. But my mother is dead. So my baby resided in the baby home until he was freed for adoption."

"I think in Russia the father has no claim if he's not married to the mother?"

Nabok said, "That's right," then translated for Masha. After she spoke, he responded, then she responded. It was cumbersome but it gave Dooley a chance to think about what he would say next. Nabok said to Dooley, "I mentioned that in most states in the U.S. the father has rights to the child even if they aren't married. She said, 'Why?'"

"I can't answer that."

Masha was chatting very freely. Possibly she felt she must pay for her big lunch by giving Dooley his money's worth in explanation. If so, he welcomed it. He was glad too that she had made no suggestion of wanting Teddy back.

But then, she might not be Teddy's mother. She might even be a well-coached actor. Well, not actor, exactly. He believed she was who she seemed to be, actually worked in the factory, and had actually given a baby up for adoption. He just didn't believe she was Teddy's birth mother.

"What do you make at your factory?" he asked.

"Children's toys."

"What was that thing with the white and gold parts?"

"A play samovar. For tea parties."

Masha worked her way through a spicy mixture of mashed potatoes and turnips, a Wiener schnitzel, and a sort of sweet and sour red cabbage, while Dooley worried. They waited for more coffee and a dessert that Nabok explained "involves lots of whipped cream" and Masha told him more about herself. She would say a sentence and then watch Nabok translate as he retold the story to Dooley or sometimes she'd just go on talking and let Nabok talk over her.

"I was in school, planning to attend college, when I became pregnant the first time. I was seventeen. The father was a student also, and he didn't want anything to do with the baby. I became sick, and couldn't go to school anymore. After my daughter was born, I worked in a factory that made automobile parts. Then I became pregnant again. The baby was a boy. But I couldn't stand on my feet all day, so I worked as a seamstress in a clothing factory. Sitting down, you see. It paid very little. And as you know, the economic condition of the Russian Federation is very precarious. So when I became pregnant a third time, I decided I could not keep the child."

"Were you ill with the third pregnancy?"

"I had swollen legs. It was very uncomfortable."

Dooley had to know whether she had taken tetracycline while she was pregnant. After all, Rumpelstiltskin *could* be wrong. *Couldn't he? Please let it be.*

"What medicine did you take for the swollen legs?"

"Medicine?" She smiled.

"Like a diuretic, or—"

"I do not have the money for medicines."

"Isn't there a clinic?"

"Not unless one's illness is very serious. And sometimes not even then."

"You had no medicines your whole pregnancy?"

"No. No medicine." She thought a moment and said, "Why do you ask? Is there a problem? Is the boy sick?"

"No." Dooley sagged a little in disappointment and then masked it by crossing and uncrossing his legs. "Nothing for infection?"

"I did not have infection."

"And the child wasn't born with any infection that they'd have to treat?" Syphilis was a possibility, he thought, an illness that an antibiotic could have been given for. It hadn't been in the medical records, but who knew what might have been omitted intentionally or accidentally?

"No. The baby was well."

"Never an antibiotic?"

"I saw him only a few hours."

He sighed. Well, that was that. The orphanage took over after she gave him up and they had no record of any tetracycline.

She was clearly puzzled by his reaction. His disappointment was far too obvious.

Better ask what he had claimed to come for, even though his heart wasn't in it. "I had wondered about your family medical history. You understand—so many illnesses are inherited."

"Yes, I understand." She explained what little she knew about her parents and grandparents. Heart disease. Both parents. A grandfather who died of kidney failure. A cousin who was diabetic. Several male relatives dead in war and two great-aunts dead of hunger or disease during World War II.

"And the father?" Dooley asked. "What was his health history?"

*Please let her say he was an Irish tourist. An Irish immigrant!*

"He comes from a healthy family. His mother is still living. I don't know anything more."

"Who is he?"

"Just a young man from Moscow," said Masha. "He lived on my block. His parents knew my uncle. I don't see him anymore. I think his father had heart disease."

"A Russian?"

"Belarus."

Another hope gone. Dooley hardly heard her, though he nodded. Now he needed to get a DNA sample. But how? He had worried about this for days. One plan had been to take her out and buy her a few items of food or clothing, among them to include a new, beautiful scarf. He would then pocket her old one, pretend to throw it away, maybe, and then pocket it. There would be hairs on a scarf. Another plan was that he would hold her coat and, while she wasn't looking, pick hairs off the collar. The lunch with Sunny Bakeley had given him the idea of gum, and he had brought along a package in his pocket. It would be easy enough to offer her some, but tricky getting hold of it later. He thought he could offer her gum, then take her somewhere to buy candy. She would have to get rid of the gum in order to taste the candy. He'd hold out a tissue for her. Or maybe he could get saliva from her drinking glass or coffee cup. He could wipe the edge of the glass with a tissue.

She did not have any visible cuts. There would be no Band-Aids to find in wastebaskets. He could hardly pull hairs out of her head. Well, he'd have to decide soon.

She wound down, explaining that her two children were fortunately very healthy, especially fortunate because medicine was too expensive. She ate all the whipped cream cake. Dooley sighed again. She was thin probably because she gave her children most of the food she could afford to buy.

The whole nightmare suddenly became too much for him. Too much misery, too much doubt, too many orphans. He couldn't stand another minute of this.

"Could you give me a blood sample?" he asked.

"Now?" Dooley had heard the surprise in Nabok's voice, as he translated the question.

"Well, yes. I just need a smear. I wish I had a slide. A piece of plastic might do. I just need to air dry it."

"Why not?"

## 3

So in the end, Dooley wiped her finger with vodka, and she gave herself a stab with a safety pin they had also dipped in vodka. Dooley mumbled something about checking for some genetic markers, which seemed to convince both Masha and Nabok.

They dripped two or three drops of blood in a narrow shot glass, which Dooley stoppered with a small amount of Kleenex tissue. He would dry the whole thing out when he got to his hotel. If you let blood stay wet many hours, the DNA would degrade. But he believed the effort was pointless. He could not see how Masha could be Teddy's mother, which meant Teddy's mother was still out there somewhere in the world, probably grieving. Like Dooley was grieving. He tried to put on a cheerful, interested, neutral face and knew he failed.

Even though he now had his blood sample, he asked Masha Lemontov whether he could take her to Gum and buy her some clothes or housewares or whatever she liked. He hoped this offer wouldn't offend her. In the matter-of-fact manner she had shown all along she said, "Certainly yes. Some pots and pans. Clothes for the children."

Heartsick with the conviction that Masha was not Teddy's mother, Dooley bought her everything she wanted, then arranged for Nabok and the car to take Masha and her purchases to her home after work.

The man who had sat watching them in the restaurant had been fascinated when Dooley took the blood sample. He did not even bother to follow them to the store.

4

Gabrielle Coulter stood in the entry corridor of the orphanage. She was feeling as heartsick as Dooley, but she was far more skilled in covering up. She knew how to keep her face bright, interested, and impersonal in front of cameras and could keep a pleasant face for governmental officials too. She had kept a calm face during shelling in Afghanistan, and standing in freezing rain in Oslo, and once when she had broken her wrist and had to go on camera, even though the wrist couldn't be set until the crew got out of Uganda.

She missed Justin.

Gorilla carried the cameras and batteries this time, which only made her long even more for Justin. Gorilla was a perfectly good cameraman, but not brilliant like Justin. And Justin had been so sweet.

At least Sam Bielski was with them, as well as two representatives from the Ministry of Education, two doctors, the orphanage director, and Vlasta again to translate. Even though the cadre of attendants was smaller than last time, it was all essentially so similar that she could almost see Justin standing among them, just beyond sight. If she turned her head quickly, would she catch a glimpse of him?

Gabrielle had convinced CNN that there was a story behind the two men with different names, a story she had to pursue. She had built it up as a possible black market in toys and baby formula. The idea of a large gang stealing food from the mouths of babies sounded like a real human interest story to CNN. She was more honest with Sam Bielski, admitting that she had no idea what the men were up to, but she hoped to find a clear connection with Justin's murder. She was surprised to learn that Sam actually thought there was a major story in there somewhere. "Mainly because the impersonation involves two different countries, not two areas of one country," he said.

They had a perfect pretext to go back. Their tapes had been destroyed. CNN had argued to the Russians that since Russia had given them permission the first time, there should be no problem in just repeating the visit. It worked.

There was no way for the Russian government to know that the tapes had not been destroyed. The Moscow cops surely had looked at the tapes in her shoulder bag, but they couldn't know what the destroyed tapes had been, so they did not know they were identical to the ones she had, the ones they had already seen.

Gabrielle had not wanted to go back to Russia ever again. She was scared. At the same time, she felt she had to. Justin's ghost needed revenge. Or justice.

And maybe she could help the children. Help them how, she

didn't know, but if there was a scam going on, it was certainly not designed to benefit the children.

Now she and the group walked through the dingy greenish corridor into the large room for infants. Here again were the children in their white-painted iron cribs. Once again, Gabrielle did a stand-up for the camera.

"Under the former laws, an abandoned child was listed for adoption by Russians for three months. After that, foreign applicants might adopt. In 1998 the waiting period was increased to four months. A child is considered abandoned if his parents have signed relinquishment papers. If the parents have disappeared or are considered unfit, six months have to go by now before the child is legally considered an orphan."

Gabrielle terminated the stand-up to let Gorilla get on with his photography.

Gorilla wanted to catch each child in the cribs, but Gabrielle could tell from the sweeps of his camera that he was not framing the shots as Justin would have. When they viewed the results later, they'd have too much panning and not enough focus on any one subject.

The babies had a few toys, like last time. These included a set of wooden blocks, appropriate for toddlers, maybe, not infants, a football, and, of all things, three Barbie dolls.

Gabrielle looked for the tiny blond girl she had seen before. She was still there, still in the same crib, still staring at the ceiling, apathetic.

After the infant room, Gabrielle, Sam, Gorilla, and the Russians traipsed back into the hall. A janitor was mopping busily in front of the door to the older children's lying-down room. The floor he was mopping was perfectly clean and the baseboards around it were already wet. The orphanage wasn't going to let her get in there again.

"I wonder if I might interview you personally on the matter of your philosophy of the care of infants in orphanages," Gabrielle said to the director. He nodded as if eager to get rid of her. She was looking at him, but of course Vlasta translated her words.

The director looked pleased and a bit puffed up. Probably he got more criticism than compliments. He spoke Russian to Vlasta, who translated, "I believe that could be arranged. I must get permission. How long will you be in Moscow?"

"We planned for a week," Gabrielle said.

"I will try."

"And I would like to interview perhaps one of the doctors here. On the question of medication and nutrition."

When this was translated the director was slightly less cordial. Nevertheless, Vlasta translated to Gabrielle, "Yes, I'm certain you will find our arrangements for the infants most humane."

"I'm sure I will," Gabrielle responded. "And I would like to talk also with some people from the Ministry of Education. Perhaps Mr. Krysigin and Mr. Lupov, whom we met last time we were here, would be available."

Vlasta's eyebrows flicked up just a bit. Gabrielle exchanged a gaze with her, but only for a fraction of a second.

Before Vlasta was able to translate, even at the sound of the names, the director's smile disappeared. He barely let Vlasta come to the end of the sentence before he barked his words.

Vlasta translated, "It will be impossible."

# 5

Vlasta walked with them to their hired car, as before. Gabrielle said, "You looked as if you wanted to say something back there, Vlasta."

"No, not really."

"Do you know Mr. Krysigin and Mr. Lupov?"

"No. I only see them here. I know them only to introduce them."

"Does anybody, I mean anybody, other than the director, know who they are? Is there anybody I could ask?"

"Oh no." Vlasta shook her head fiercely. They had reached the car. Gabrielle held out her hand.

"Well, goodbye, Vlasta. I think we're done here. I don't suppose we'll meet again. We go back in a few days."

Gorilla stowed the camera gear in the car. Vlasta hesitated. "I wish I could help you. But I can't."

As the car pulled away into falling snow and Vlasta disappeared in the whiteness, Sam said, "That girl was scared."

"I know. I was right! Something is going on."

Sam said, "I can see that. Well, tomorrow we go interview Stover at the embassy."

# 6

Dooley staggered into the Metropole at five o'clock amid wind and thickening snow. His body felt like gravity had doubled. Even keeping his eyelids up was a struggle.

Gabrielle, along with her two companions, sat in the bar, just visible from the entryway. They saw him and Gabrielle called out, "Dooley! You look frozen. Come on in here."

Gorilla said, "Have a drink to warm you from the inside."

"No hot toddies available," Sam added. "No hot buttered rum. Plenty of vodka."

Dooley filled a mug with tea from the electric samovar, then walked over and sat with them. "I'm just going to have this. It's hot. Then I'd better get into drier clothes." He had the blood sample in his pocket and he wanted to dry it. Gloomily, he reflected that the blood was probably useless anyway. It didn't belong to Teddy's real mother. Old habit, though, commanded him to treat a specimen properly. His job was to keep it dry and uncontaminated, even if it only proved a negative.

"Hard day?" Gabrielle asked.

"Very hard."

"Have dinner with us? Eight P.M."

"You're extremely nice."

"How long are you going to be in town, Dooley?" Sam asked.

"I was planning to stay for a week or more in case getting documents took a long time. But they had the papers all ready, so I think I'll try to get something on standby tomorrow."

"We'll be sorry to see you go," Gabrielle said.

"I've pretty much finished what I came here for."

# 7

Gabrielle had never been under any illusion that the orphanage director would simply roll over and gasp out what Mr. Krysigin and Mr. Lupov were up to just because she asked him. She had been a reporter much too long to think it was as easy as that. But she had watched faces from Stockholm to Tienanmen Square and expected to surprise some reaction from him, and there she had succeeded. She was satisfied, even gloating a little. However doubtful she had been about finding out the whole story, she knew you could always learn more than the people who were afraid to ask.

Her next step would be to visit the United States Embassy. Sam Bielski had scheduled the meeting with Mr. Stover for tomorrow morning at ten. Sam had also inquired about whether her team could visit the ambassador himself. Stover was doubtful, but he went so far as to check whether the ambassador would be in Moscow. Yes, he was planning to be. Since Sam did not tell Stover what they wanted to chat about, Stover could hardly decide whether it was important enough for the ambassador. Personally, Gabrielle thought the suspicions they had so far were too vague for somebody that important. She also thought, if there was a serious scam going on that would embarrass the Russians, the ambassador would not help them until he had checked with Washington.

She had tried to decide whether it was better to go to the Moscow police before or after Stover. If the police detective was tied in with the scam, he could put out a warning that somebody should block her, and word might reach the embassy before she had a chance to explain. On the other hand, if Stover considered her story a threat to amicable U.S. relations with the Russians, more important than ever since 9/11, he could order her to stop investigating. She would have to obey. The government had a say in whether she got permission to enter foreign countries. In addition, her rights in these nations were different from rights at home. In the United States, Stover could not have hobbled the press unless there were a gag order in an active legal case or a national emergency. Here, her protections were not quite the same. Much of Russia worked on the conventional wisdom of the old Soviet Union. Keep everybody quiet, tell nothing, arrest and detain anybody who blabs. The problem was, now that some of the rules had liberalized, you could still be in prison for weeks before they realized a rule didn't apply to you. You'd probably get out, but you had lost and they had won.

# 8

Dooley forced himself to appear in the lobby at eight, as he had promised. He knew he had to eat, and sitting in his room sunk in gloom wasn't going to help. Somehow he had to get himself straightened up.

He found Gordo at the bar and Sam and Gabrielle talking near the front desk.

"We can't go out, Dooley," Sam said.

"Why not?"

"The snow's getting worse. They think if we went out we might not be able to get back to the hotel."

Dooley thought, Isn't Russia used to snow? But given the economic chaos, maybe they didn't have enough plows if it started coming down hard.

"Sure. Let's not take chances."

Gabrielle smiled at him. She said, "Come on, Gorilla. You've wrapped yourself around enough vodka. Get some food in you."

"If you can call it food," Sam said to Dooley.

At a big round table, Gordo ordered vodka for the bunch. Sam grabbed the menu and said, "I'll order."

"Better let him," Gabrielle said.

Two women were dining together at a table near Dooley's group.

He recognized them as the wives of two men who were still at the bar. Apparently the men weren't planning to eat. One of the women was a Mrs. Pilchard. He had met her at the samovar earlier.

Mrs. Pilchard said to the other woman, "Do you know how long I stood in line at the INS for fingerprinting? Six hours!"

"They were supposed to tell us where to go for fingerprinting right after we filed our I-600A. It took them seven weeks."

"Somebody told me that a few years ago you could go to your local police station to get fingerprinted."

"Yeah. But they got so many botched prints they gave it up. That's why you have to go to an INS official fingerprinter. Then they send them to some office in Nebraska. And then *they* send them to the FBI."

"Yeah. They lost mine. Not Ed's. Just mine."

"I mean, I understand that they want to know that you're not a serial killer before they give you a child. But why do they need to fingerprint my husband's son by his first wife?"

"If he's over eighteen and lives in your house—"

"Yeah, yeah, I know. He could be a ravening child molester."

Dooley pushed around a serving of beets and an underdone potato.

At a table on the other side of Dooley's group sat an American couple, the man in his late thirties and the woman a few years younger. Their nationality had been obvious just from the short snatches of conversation Dooley had overheard. They didn't talk to each other a whole lot, Dooley noticed. Probably worried. Now the wife leaned over and asked Dooley's party, "Is this good Russian food that we're having?"

Dooley's whole table laughed.

"This is the Metropole," Gordo said. "They don't really *do* food."

"We were told not to go back out in the snow to look for a restaurant," the wife said.

Sam said, "Very sensible."

"Oh, Gabrielle Coulter!" said the wife. "The *reporter!*" she told her husband, who just smiled and nodded.

Gabrielle said, "Let me introduce my friends here. Gordo Malman, Dr. Dooley McSweeney, Sam Bielski."

"Gabrielle doesn't like a lot of fuss made about her," Sam said.

"Oh. Of course. I'm Sylvia Carroll and this is my husband George. Dr. George Carroll. He's a cardiologist."

"We got into Moscow last night," George Carroll said. "Saw an orphanage this morning and another one this afternoon. The one near here."

"We didn't see an *orphanage*, George," his wife said. "We saw babies."

"Sure. That's what I meant." George lifted his eyebrows at Dooley and Sam. It was one of those "women are like that" gestures. Dooley wondered whether George wanted a baby quite as much as his wife did.

"Did you see any baby you—"

It was very awkward to ask whether they saw a baby they wanted. It sounded so much like did you find a suit that was a good fit. Nice fabric? Nice color? He decided to ask straight out. "I know when we adopted it was important to Claudia to find a baby she bonded with. It makes you feel terrible, because you're turning down the other babies as if they aren't quite acceptable in some way."

"Yes, that's exactly how I felt," Sylvia said. "But you have to realize you're going to spending the rest of your life with the child."

"Yes."

Gabrielle said, "So you're looking to adopt?"

"Yes."

Dooley asked, "Are you with an agency?"

"Yes." Sylvia Carroll looked young and eager. She said, "Windsor House. They're wonderful. They're going to help us adopt a baby!"

Dooley said, "Don't."

# 9

"What an odd thing to say, Dr. McSweeney," Sylvia said.

"I'm sorry. That was silly of me." He was horrified at himself.

"But what did you mean?"

"Nothing really. I guess just that they're very expensive."

"I've heard of them," one of the guests at a nearby table said, leaning over to be better heard. "They're fairly new."

Dooley said, "New?"

"Four or five years old, I think. But they've got a great reputation."

George Carroll said, "Was that the agency you went with, Dr. McSweeney?"

"Um, yes, it was."

"How did they do for you?"

"Fine."

George Carroll said, "It sounds like you have reservations."

"No. They did fine for us." Dooley picked up his fork and attacked the hard potato.

"Did you get a baby?"

"Yes."

"Did the baby turn out to be everything you hoped for? Mentally and physically?"

"Yes."

"Because you do hear horror stories," Sylvia said. She glanced at George, probably thinking he was being too pushy.

"Our baby is just fine." Dooley filled his mouth with potato, chewed, and hoped George would shut up. He heard the gossipy, worried voices of the two women, laughing voices from the men at the bar. His head ached.

The big front door of the Metropole slammed back against the wall. A woman ran in, trailing snow. She was screaming at the top of her lungs. She stopped, hyperventilating and gasping, and gabbled out a few words.

Dooley had already risen to his feet. He was a doctor, after all. He recognized her clothes as those one of the cleaning staff might wear, ragged wool coat, scarf, and clumsy boots.

"Are you sick?" Dooley asked, hurrying forward. She wouldn't understand his words, but she might understand the tone.

Sam had followed him. "She seems to be saying there's a person outside frozen in the snow."

Dooley rushed out, coatless, into a blizzard. He looked around in confusion. The lights at the front double doors of the Metropole were bright enough, but they were worse than nothing in the howling swirl of whiteout. The bright light caused the snow nearby to shimmer like a cotton wall, making it more difficult to see than if there had been no porch light at all. Dooley shouted, "Where?" back into the lobby. Two hotel employees, plus Sam, Gabrielle, and George Carroll, all came out behind him. The hotel bellboy spoke in Russian. Sam said something to the man in which one of the words sounded like "doctor." Then Sam said to Dooley, "Near the walk. Look to the right."

Near the walkway lay a woman, partly hidden by small evergreens. Dooley knelt beside her. There was snow on her coat. She lay on her side. Her eyelashes were white with snow. Her eyes were open and staring, which might mean death, but Dooley knew that hypothermia was unpredictable. "Gabrielle—please hold the doors open! George and Sam, help me carry her."

"Sure thing," Carroll said. Sam knelt down near Dooley.

Dooley said, "We'll get her inside where it's warm. Then I can tell more."

They picked her up. Dooley felt beneath her as they did and made a mental note that the underside of her body was warm, though the top was cold.

"Gabrielle, have somebody get pillows and blankets!"

They staggered the few yards to the door, sliding in the snow and ice. None of them was wearing boots. Sam fell once. He wasn't well, Dooley remembered, regretting getting him involved.

Going up the steps, Sam fell again to one knee, but bounded up and kept going. By the time they got the woman inside, Gabrielle and the hotel staff had laid pillows on the floor with a blanket over them and piled two more folded blankets near the makeshift bed.

"Come on. A little farther," Dooley said.

They put the woman down gently onto the bedding. Sam drew a deep breath and straightened up. Dooley went to his knees next to the woman and moved her flat on her back, brushing hair from her face to check the pupils of her eyes.

Gabrielle gasped. "Oh, my God!"

"What?"

"It's Vlasta!"

# CHAPTER TWENTY

My little daughter is five months old. She is sweet,
sleeps through the night, and smiles a lot. I have
multiple sclerosis. I thought it was in remission, but a
few weeks after Tracey was born, it became suddenly
much worse. My right eye is completely blind and I
can't walk. My doctor thinks I'll be permanently
bedridden soon. My parents are both dead and my
baby's father and his parents don't want to deal with a
child. I want to find an adoptive couple before I die.
Please write to me. By the way, my doctor says
multiple sclerosis in the mother doesn't hurt the baby
or pass on to the baby. God be with you.

Write Box 233

## 1

Dooley lifted one of the woman's ice-crusted eyelids. The iris was
wide open, making the eye appear unusually dark. He repeated with
the other eye. It was equally dilated, and both were fixed. More to
delay the bad news than to find out anything further, he checked her
carotid pulse. There was none.

The hotel manager, Mr. Gabovitch, had come rushing to Dooley's side, but now stood slightly back, away from the woman. "I have
telephoned to emergency medical services," he said.

"That's good." Dooley stood up. "Can we talk?" he said to Mr.

Gabovitch, walking toward the desk to pull him away from the staff and guests gathered around.

The manager realized immediately what this meant. "It is too late for doctors?"

"Yes."

"Oh. This is bad."

"It's worse, actually."

"How do you mean?"

"She was strangled. You'll need to call the police."

# 2

They covered the young woman with a sheet.

The police were delayed by the blizzard, which was now sweeping the snow into deep drifts at road intersections. As the first minutes of shock turned into an hour, the hotel manager, Gabovitch, grew fidgety and shiny with sweat. Finally, he gave his staff orders to move the body to the hall behind the offices, out of the main lobby. Dooley did not understand the Russian words, but when the two kitchen hands bent over and picked up the draped form of the dead woman, he started to say, "You shouldn't move—"

Then he stopped. This wasn't his country. He couldn't give orders here. Besides, where the woman now lay was not where she had been attacked, nor where she died. It wasn't really a crime scene. Dooley sank into one of the overstuffed but uncomfortable chairs in the lounge end of the lobby and waited grimly for the arrival of the police.

# 3

It took an hour and a half for the police to appear. They came into the lobby, four of them, slapping at the snow on their shoulders and talking loudly. They were speaking Russian, but Dooley knew they were talking about fighting their way through the weather.

He watched plump Mr. Gabovitch answer their questions. The man's body language was a schizoid mixture of haughty manager and a bone-deep Russian fear of police. He held himself erect, head up, but he was sweaty and his hands kept seeking each other out to twist together. Finally, Gabovitch called for the cleaning woman who had found the body.

The police were more abrupt with her. They barked questions, raised their eyebrows, shook their heads, and in fifteen minutes reduced the woman to tears. At this point two of them went with the manager to see the body, something Dooley thought they should have done in the first place. Then the manager pointed at Dooley.

With Dooley they were courteous. The apparent leader, a police officer with a barrel shape and a very red face, even favored Dooley with a rattrap smile. Gabovitch translated for Dooley. There was not a great deal Dooley could tell them, beyond the diagnosis of death. No, he had not heard any commotion outdoors. No, he had heard no screams until the cleaning woman screamed. No, no suspicious person had entered the hotel, but he wasn't sure what a suspicious person would be. One or two people had come in during the ten minutes or so before the cleaning lady screamed. He had assumed they were hotel guests. No, he had never seen the dead woman before. No, he didn't know who she was. He was about to say that Gabrielle recognized her, but he held his tongue.

They waved him away. The manager thanked him for his help.

Fifteen minutes more went by while the two who had looked at the body came back to report.

Gordo and Sam sat chatting, hunched over a table at the side of the lobby. Gabrielle was near them but not looking at them, not speaking. She had her hands folded in her lap and stared into the middle distance. To Dooley, she looked scared. That was quite remarkable. He knew next to nothing about reporting, but it was obvious that if you were sending reports from trouble zones all over the world, you'd get yourself into tight spots quite often. He walked over to her and sat in the closest chair.

"Gabrielle?"

"I'm sorry. I can't talk now."

"Then just listen. I can see you're scared about something."

She didn't answer.

"I didn't tell the police that you used the dead woman's name."

Gabrielle raised her head and looked at him.

"Why not?"

"I thought it was up to you. It's not like she'll go unidentified. Everybody carries I.D. around here. I felt a wallet in her pocket when I examined her. At least I assume it was a wallet." He paused. "Who was she, Gabby?"

"Her name was Vlasta. She was a translator. She translated for us at the orphanage."

"Today?"

"Yes. Both times."

"Both times meaning—"

"Today and the last time I was here."

"So you believe she was coming to the hotel to translate for a guest here?"

She didn't answer.

"You believe she was coming to see you, don't you." It wasn't a question. "Why, Gabby?"

"I can't say."

"You're a reporter. You asked her something. She was coming to tell you more than she had revealed when you and she talked before."

"She hadn't told me anything before."

"And now you feel responsible."

"Dooley, how did she die? Did she just freeze? At first I thought she died because she tried to get here in the blizzard and got exhausted and froze. But there are too many police for that."

"No, she was killed. She was strangled."

There were tears in Gabrielle's eyes. Dooley put his hand over hers, just for two seconds, then got up. "It hasn't been a good day for any of us. And I've got an afternoon flight home tomorrow. Good night. I'm going to turn in."

To Dooley's amazement, she said, "Lock your room door. Not just the automatic lock, the inside bolt. Don't let anybody in."

# 4

Past midnight.

The room was black. There was very little sky glow, since Dooley's window faced the street but away from the center of Moscow. He was wakened by a scraping sound and sat upright, thinking someone was inside the room.

Dooley listened. The sound was more of a subdued sigh, as of metal sliding on metal, but it wasn't near the bed. He slipped out of the covers, the adrenaline in his blood overriding the cold.

He listened again. The sound was coming from the door. From outside the door. He padded softly to it and listened again. With one finger, he touched the doorknob lightly. It turned, brushing his fingertip.

*Fling the door open suddenly and see who it is? No, the bolt's locked. If I unlock it, they'll hear.*

Dooley took hold of the knob on the bolt. Slowly, slowly, he turned it. He was fighting the snap he knew would come when the bolt kicked back. Slowly he turned it.

But it unlocked with a sudden snick.

He grabbed the doorknob and flung the door open.

He was too slow. He barely caught a glimpse of an overcoat trailing behind as a man fled down the fire stairs.

Dooley knew he'd never catch him. Besides, Dooley was in pajamas. He did what you were supposed to do. In the absence of an in-room telephone, he dressed, now high on fear and anger. Then he marched down to the lobby and asked at the desk who had gone out.

The night manager knew very little English. Enough though, to make it clear: he had seen no one and heard nothing.

When Dooley woke up the next morning, at first he had no memory of the incident. His body was cold all the way through. There was no real light, but everything around him had a gray, directionless glow, like lighting in a funeral home. As if he were in a coffin, when he tried to move his arms, they felt locked in place. Most disorienting for a person from New York, there was no sound. The world was utterly hushed. With his eyes wide open, he saw very little but a gray square overhead, and he heard nothing at all. He was in a box, yes, but not a coffin. His box was his room: fifteen by twenty feet. He was trapped only in his own misery and three heavy blankets.

The elements of his life came back to him slowly. Memory of the threat facing Teddy seeped over him as a trembling ache. Soon after that, he realized he was in the Metropole Hotel in Moscow. It must be early morning, early enough so that the sky was still half-lit. When he checked his watch, though, it was 9:45. Still, it might be just about dawn. He was no expert in Moscow sunrise time. He knew that the days were very short in midwinter this far north.

Then he remembered the attempted intrusion. Was this what Gabrielle had warned him about? Possibly there were thugs that went around Moscow slipping into hotel rooms and stealing money or jewelry while the guests slept. He'd heard of that happening in New York.

Lowering his feet to the floor, Dooley gasped at the cold. But he put up with it long enough to get to the small window.

All the world was white. The windowsill outside was several inches deep in snow. The ground was an undulating field of cotton, with no features. The view of the buildings beyond, which he had seen clearly yesterday, had vanished behind a slow sifting of snowflakes.

What about his flight home? Did the Russians cancel flights when there was snow? His flight wasn't until late afternoon, but he always got antsy when he was catching a plane.

Dooley got his clothes on fast. He was still cold. He wanted to get his blood moving, so he headed downstairs for breakfast.

In the lobby of the Metropole three or four people sat slumped in chairs. Dooley got a mug and filled it with hot tea from the samovar, then, since there was no one at the front desk, walked through the bar toward the arch that led to the dining room.

Gabrielle sat at a table with Sam Bielski. Gordo was nowhere to be seen. Too much vodka last night.

The ground floor of the Metropole Hotel was a huge square, divided into four large square quarters. One square was the dining room, one was the bar with stools and bar tables, which opened into the dining room through a big open arch on one side and into the lobby through a big open arch on the adjacent wall. The arches were a cosmetic retrofit, done after the army base had stopped using the building. The remodeling had been cheaply accomplished, and the curves of the arches were not quite symmetrically cut.

One quarter of the ground floor was the lobby desk and check-in area, with offices behind dividers to the rear of the desk, and a few chairs scattered on the guest side. The last quarter was a sitting room, also accessible through an arch from the lobby, with chairs, writing desks, and even a fireplace. For the Metropole, this lounge was luxury.

In the dining room, one of the adopting couples sat glumly sipping coffee at a round table. Dooley paused at Gabrielle and Sam's table. "How are you this morning?" he asked them both.

Gabrielle said, "Well enough, I guess."

"I think somebody tried to get into my room last night. I want to thank you for warning me." He didn't notice that she held her breath when he said this. Dooley went on, "Did you hear any more about what happened to the translator?"

"No. The police aren't saying."

"Why is everybody looking so gloomy around here? The murder?"

"We're snowed in."

"We can't be. I have a flight today."

"You said it was an afternoon flight. Maybe we'll be plowed out by then."

"I'd better go ask at the desk."

# 5

"We don't know when the streets will open, doctor," Mr. Gabovitch said.

"But we have to do our OVIR registration within three days of arrival. How do we do that?"

"We will accommodate that for you."

"In this weather?"

"We have telephoned the agency and they are extending the period of—what is word?—of grace?"

Visa registration was a must. You could get into huge problems if you didn't do it. When he and Claudia had been here before, Windsor House with its corresponding inviting organization had done it for them, but Dooley knew this time he must be sure to cover the bases himself.

"I guess there must be snowplows out," he said.

"Many, many snowplows. But look." The manager pointed at the small window near the door. "It is snowing still."

It certainly was. Dooley pressed his face against the window. It wasn't just snowing, it was a whiteout. Gales of snow whipped against the window. Occasional strong gusts of wind opened gaps in the whiteout, but the momentary clearing served mainly to show Dooley how fast the wind was blowing and how dense the snow was when it made the world disappear again.

"Mr. Gabovitch, do they say whether Sheremetevo Two is open?"

Gabovitch clapped his hands to his face. "If it should be open, sir, would you wish to fly in this?"

Gabby had not mentioned Justin's murder to people here. At the Metropole, of course, a couple of employees and the manager knew about it. But they wouldn't mention it to the new people. The manager would not want to say anything that would make his hotel look bad.

She had asked Gordo and Sam Bielski to keep it to themselves. It wasn't that she especially wanted it to be secret so much as that she hoped to avoid getting into a discussion of what had happened and why. If she was to have a chance of finding out what was behind his death, the people involved must have no suspicion of her motives in coming here. They should not worry that she might be investigating them. She hoped she was presenting the perfect front: a reporter who had come back to retape what she had lost.

She hadn't liked coming back to the Metropole, but there was no choice if she was to learn more. One of the main goals was to get a look at the guest records.

Dooley sat down at a table in the dining room. He smiled at Sam and Gabrielle, even though he didn't feel like smiling. Gabrielle and Sam had their heads together.

Sam spoke to the waiter. Unlike the waiters at the best restaurants, this one had only a smattering of English, but Sam knew a smattering of Russian. The waiter left on whatever errand Sam had given him. Dooley sat on, tired and cold.

As soon as the waiter left, Gabrielle got up. Nodding at Dooley, she left the dining room, and went into the lounge. Oddly, she hadn't said anything to Sam. Usually people said things like, "I'll be right back," or "I'm going to the rest room."

Mr. Gabovitch came in from the bar and walked to Sam Bielski. "Yes, Mr. Bielski?"

# 8

Gabrielle slipped from the lounge into the back of the lobby and behind the front desk. She had thought of several lame reasons to explain being in the offices if she was caught: "Where are the rest rooms?" "I need to talk to the manager." "There was a rat in the dining room!" But none of them appealed to her. She'd wing it. Counting on the fact that the Metropole was not overstaffed, she moved with authority. Inside, she was nervous. And determined.

The reverse side of the front desk held shelves. They were filled with stacks of paper, forms, pens, ink cartridges for the printers, several credit card machines, boxes of throat lozenges, half a dozen bottles of vodka, mostly empty, and a bottle of schnapps, unopened. There were no files. The sign-in book was there, but she had looked carefully at it when she signed in and knew there were only a couple of used pages before the one she had signed on. It was a new book.

Swiftly, Gabrielle moved to the back offices. There were only two. She picked the larger one, deciding that it would be the manager's personal space.

She was right. There was a good-sized but cheap desk, all the usual computer gear, a dead plant, and several filing cabinets. She didn't read Russian and couldn't guess what the labels on the cabinets meant. That didn't matter. The hotel used old-fashioned ledgers as sign-in books in addition to computerized records, apparently wanting an ink signature from all the guests. Unlike hotels in the U.S., the

Metropole asked each guest to check in individually, not just the person whose credit card was paying for the room.

Gabrielle swiftly pulled out drawer after drawer of the filing cabinets until she found the cache of sign-in books. They were ordinary eleven-by-thirteen ledgers, stored spine-up in a file drawer. She couldn't read what was on the spines. Her goal was simple enough: without any knowledge of Russian, she need only find the one she had Justin had signed a month earlier, then note down all the names of people who checked in for the several days before them and a day or so after. Gabby reached in and removed the first one.

# 9

Dooley's chair faced Gabrielle's with Sam's back to Dooley. Gabrielle had not returned and Sam was talking with the manager. Since Sam's back was to Dooley, what he was saying wasn't always audible.

"But just a general idea," Dooley heard Sam say.

"Sir, we just don't know." Dooley could hear the manager clearly, since he was facing toward him. The man sounded impatient.

"—of the Kremlin. We call them beauty shots—"

"The streets are not plowed. It is impossible."

"Not impossible, surely—"

Dooley listened bemused. This went on for several minutes. Finally, Gabovitch said, turning, "I will check for you."

Sam said, "No, no. Don't bother now. Let me ask this—"

The manager made going-away noises and edged away.

Sam said, "We have a lot of photography to do—"

Gabovitch kept moving. Sam said, "Well, can you let me know?"

"Oh absolutely, sir."

Gabrielle arrived suddenly at the table. Her lips were pressed together. The manager said to Sam, "I will notify you immediately."

"No problem," Sam said, cutting the conversation short.

Dooley was careful not to look at Sam or Gabrielle. He heard Gabrielle's chair being pulled out, then a deeper scrape as she drew it toward the table.

"Nothing!" she said softly to Sam.

Mumble from Sam.

"No, but almost. I heard somebody in the hall but he was going to a storeroom, I guess."

Another mumble from Sam.

"I copied out all the names, even the Russian ones. But I didn't recognize any of them. So we've learned something. Assuming that anybody registering has to show a passport and visa, they probably didn't stay here."

"Assumed name?" Sam asked.

"Gotta show something. I would think they'd use the passport in the names they used at the orphanage. We can have somebody translate the Cyrillic. I wrote it as carefully as I could."

Mumble from Sam.

She answered, "Exactly. If they didn't stay here, then somebody here is passing them information."

# 10

During the long morning, something happened to Dooley. He sat in the lobby, watching the other hotel guests walk to the desk, ask whether there was any news, and walk slowly away. A very few people arrived from outside—people from the neighborhood, possibly, since none of them checked in. All of them had apparently walked a good distance. They were covered with snow, and stamped their feet and slapped at their clothes in the entryway. The manager would engage them in short conversations that involved a great deal of shaking of heads. Dooley concluded that they were residents from the area who thought a big hotel would have more news than they had. They usually downed a couple of vodkas before leaving.

Meanwhile, Dooley was turning into somebody different. He could see the future and it was bad. He would lose his son. Sooner or later he would find Teddy's parents. Teddy had been stolen from them. Dooley would tell the parents about Teddy and they would come for him and take him away. With proper verification, of course. With proper safeguards. But eventually, no matter how it destroyed Dooley and Claudia, they would take him. He and Claudia would never see Teddy again.

Dooley would have made it happen. Claudia would hate him. She'd mourn for Teddy, her son lost after more than ten years of wanting him. Six, seven, eight years of wishing for him and four years of having him in her arms. Gone because of Dooley. Claudia would be destroyed and Dooley would have made it happen.

Or Claudia would take Teddy and run away.

Or—

Dooley would go home, tell nobody anything, and keep Teddy. He would do anything and everything he had to in order to cover up Teddy's origins. He would lie if anybody came near the truth. He would move if he had to, out of New York, out of the country if necessary. He would tell Claudia what he had learned because, of course, she had to be in on the deception and ready to move at a moment's notice. They would both have to stop talking about the agency that found Teddy for them. There was clearly something evil there. Maybe they had better stop talking about Teddy being adopted at all.

And he would completely forget about the fact that Windsor House would go on stealing children. If they stole one, they would steal more. He would let that happen. *Let that happen?*

No, wait. He couldn't do that.

Could he and Claudia flee with Teddy and then send an anonymous message to the FBI about Windsor House?

Dooley actually felt his mind pulling apart. It wasn't frightening. He thought it seemed quite reasonable, all things considered. It had simply become too painful to hold two entirely different necessary views of the future in the same mind. So somewhere there were now two minds. He remembered vaguely learning about the Kubler-Ross stages in adjusting to one's impending death. Something like anger, denial, bargaining, something, something, then acceptance. He'd gone through several of them in the last weeks. But not acceptance. Never acceptance.

He sat in his chair in the dining room, quiet, outwardly composed. His skin ached, as if he had the flu. He didn't believe he could move, so he simply observed the hotel guests, wondering what made people look so troubled when they didn't have his terrible problem.

Of the forty or fifty hotel guests, about half were here to visit the big orphanage nearby. The rest were commercial travelers looking for a moderate-price hotel, and a few were visiting the remnants of the military base, where equipment was still stored. Dooley suspected these of being black marketers. Except for George and Sylvia Carroll, the other hotel guests wanting to adopt had been brought in by a dozen or so other agencies, not Windsor House. One of these couples had been here five weeks and complained that their agency wasn't helping enough. Windsor House was clearly upscale. Dooley and Claudia had been in Moscow only three weeks before they had seen "their" baby, finished the paperwork, and been permitted to leave with Teddy.

Adoption talk swirled around the lobby as people whiled away the storm.

Mrs. Pilchard said, "Our agency told us to put down on the I-600A and the home study that we were going to adopt two children even if we only wanted one, so if we wanted to adopt again in a year or two we wouldn't have to go through that paperwork all over."

One of the men, Mr. Zeeks, told another couple, "You can't *talk* to anybody at the INS. I mean, you can call them as often as you want but nobody knows anything."

"We found that out," Mr. Pilchard said. "And every INS office around the country is different. Some of them charge just one four-hundred-dollar fee no matter how many children—"

"Ours doesn't. They charge a separate fee for each child *and* a separate I-600A."

"Ours just charges once. Where are you from?" Mrs. Pilchard asked.

"Portland."

"Oh, jeez. Everybody says the Portland office is the worst."

"Yeah," Zeeks said. "It's famous. Lucky us."

Pilchard said, "They say San Jose and Denver are just as bad. They'll sit on paperwork half a year. Like nobody's lives are passing by. I'm really lucky to be in the Baltimore area. Everybody on the Net says Baltimore's the best."

It was all like sandpaper on burned skin to Dooley. He had to get home! Sure, and when he did, what would Claudia do? Would she want to adopt again? Or would that be unthinkable? Would he? Would it matter what he thought? Was this the end of his marriage too?

He had to get home.

## 11

A huge front of warm moist air had stalled, in a comma-shaped line reaching roughly from Warsaw through Moscow, almost to Archangel. As it shouldered against the frigid Russian winter, it rose, overrunning the cold air and forming a low-pressure system the Europeans called a cyclonic system. Hour after hour, cold temperatures condensed the moisture out of the air. A snowbelt a hundred and fifty miles wide hung over all of western Russia. It snowed without letup, the new snow falling on an existing foot-deep blanket deposited by normal December precipitation.

Airlines all over Eastern Europe canceled flights. Governments prepared for airlifts of food and medicine to outlying communities. All television channels broadcast bulletins to people to stay home. They said no one should attempt to travel on foot or by car, particularly not on small or remote roads. Schools canceled classes. Hospitals hunkered down, keeping all staff that happened to be on the premises. The army and the police canceled leave and prepared to mount ski patrols. The forecast was for a twenty-year storm, possibly an epic storm.

Then the cold back end of the storm swept in. Winds reached forty miles an hour over the area, temperatures dropped, drifts of snow grew to twenty, then thirty feet deep, and a blizzard became a weather catastrophe.

Around noon Mr. Gabovitch entered the lobby and called for attention.

"It is bad news that I have. All transportation is shut down. All airports, all railways. Automobiles do not move in the streets. We are said to have suffered twenty-nine inches of snow, but it continues to snow. With it are drifts. It is expected well more than a meter and a half by tomorrow morning."

The guests began to groan.

"However, it is important to remember that the city of Moscow is well prepared for snow. Twenty-five thousand workers will be on streets to clear roadways. Also our snowplows that place snow into trucks to carry away. Also salt spreaders."

"But how long will it take?"

"I cannot tell you at this time. We are requested by the government to conserve food. So the dining room at our Metropole Hotel will be serving a more limited menu."

"Be grateful for small blessings," Sam mumbled, sotto voce.

The smell of boiling cabbage was already wafting from the kitchens.

"Fortunately," the manager continued, flicking just one puzzled glance at Sam, "we have a perfectly adequate supply of vodka."

Weak cheers. Most of the guests had already taken on a certain amount of antifreeze.

"I will inform all guests as soon as information comes to me."

## 12

By late afternoon the hotel guests had divided into interest groups. The seven or so men who were in the area to look at army surplus huddled in a sullen bunch at the bar. They were in competition with each other for equipment, Dooley supposed, and appeared to dislike each other, arguing constantly in surly Russian. Still they had nothing in common with anybody else and stuck together by default. The adoption group was a party in full swing, even though it was composed of very different individuals.

One woman, named Mrs. Monk and wearing a monklike dress of brown wool with a white collar, was advising the others. "Now, if you're going to adopt again, do it within eighteen months, or they'll put you through all the paperwork all over again."

Mrs. Pilchard confided to Sylvia Carroll, "When I got my 171-H in the mail I felt like I found the pot of gold at the end of the rainbow."

"It's 797-C now, I think. But I know exactly how you felt."

"Yes," said Mrs. Pilchard. "I felt good too, until I discovered they forgot to cable the Moscow embassy."

"That's the government for you," Mrs. Monk said. "Make you jump through every hoop they can, send you back to do it over if you have one thing wrong, and then they can't do the only job they're supposed to do."

Sylvia Carroll said to Mrs. Pilchard, "You didn't come all the way here before you found out, did you?"

"No, thank God. I had faxed Moscow to be sure everything was ready. That's when I found out they'd never heard of us, so I had to go back and jog the INS again."

Mrs. Monk snorted. "They say the FBI and the INS hardly talk to each other. They say they lose each other's paperwork on purpose."

"I think it's just sloppiness," Mrs. Pilchard said. "Not malice."

"My, you are a kindly sort."

"I'm getting less kindly every time one of them screws up."

George Carroll said, "Why didn't your adoption agency check everything for you?"

"They should have."

"Do you have Windsor House like we do?"

"No, Fokker Adoptions."

Mrs. Pilchard asked, "So when we get the child and head back to the U.S., the INS gives us an IR3?"

George Carroll said, "Yeah. An IR3 just certifies you and your husband were both here. An IR4 means only one adopting parent was here, so you have to go through a whole 'nother adoption in the States." He scratched at his short, dark beard.

"But I thought Russian law said both parents had to be here or they wouldn't let you adopt."

"That's true."

"Then what's the IR4 for?"

George laughed. "I don't have a clue."

Dooley finally went to his room, walking like an old man. Frantic to get home, he couldn't stay downstairs in indecision any longer. He lay down on a cold bed. He dragged all the blankets in the room over himself. For two hours he tried to sleep. Then he decided that was pointless and he went back downstairs to the lobby.

# 13

By early evening guests at the Metropole were beginning to act like strangers trapped in an elevator.

Mrs. Monk said, "You know, that Mrs. Shevardnadze, whatever her name is, makes me so mad I could just spit nails! I mean, I'm sorry. I know her husband's out of power and she can't hurt people anymore, but still!"

Sylvia Carroll said, "Why?"

"Cutting off adoptions! You remember. She said people from other countries shouldn't be allowed to adopt Russian orphans."

Sylvia said, "Oh, right. I remember hearing about that. She thought it was giving away their birthright. Their genetic patrimony."

"No, no, no. Depleting the Russian gene pool is what she said. She got the Russian Parliament Committee on Women and the Family to declare that adoption by foreigners was cultural genocide."

"Well, I know it sounds kind of stupid, but you can imagine being upset if American children were being drained away to other countries."

"No, I can*not*! The children were orphans! They had out-country adoption or nothing!"

Sylvia said, "Well, but they *would* lose their cultural heritage, wouldn't they? They wouldn't grow up speaking Russian for instance."

"Oh, bull! There's no cultural heritage for a dead baby!"

"I know you're right theoretically, but—"

"It's not theoretical! They practically canceled adoptions! But they did absolutely nothing to take care of the orphans. Do you want to guess how many babies died in that time? Real babies, not theoretical babies?"

"No, I don't think I do."

"She was a self-important bitch! I say thank goodness for Putin!"

"Putin! He was KGB. Think of what he must have done in the old days."

Somebody at the bar called out, "Didn't he freeze adoptions for a while too?"

"We've got entirely too many adopting couples here," Sam said in an aside to Dooley.

"Putin was director of the KGB, you know," Mrs. Monk said.

"I know," Gordo said to Sam. "We'll call this the heir port."

"Did you get hit up for huge fees, Mrs. Monk?" George Carroll asked.

To Dooley, George Carroll seemed subtly different tonight. He even looked different. Dooley had thought of him as one of those husbands who went along with "the adoption thing" because their wives wanted it very badly. He had seemed a little bit bored. But as the day wore on, he had asked increasing numbers of questions about the various agencies the adopting hotel guests were using. He appeared to be less bored all the time, while the other people in the lobby, dining room, and lounge were getting crabby with tedium.

In the early evening, Dooley, who had been pacing around tensely, managed to get one of the chairs in the lounge when the commercial traveler who had hogged it all afternoon gave it up and went to the bar. A couple of minutes later, one of the military surplus buyers who had been sleeping in the chair next to Dooley woke up with a start, looked around, and left the room.

George Carroll slipped quickly into the vacated chair. Carroll apparently had had the foresight to load up on two bottles of vodka and a glass. He leaned back in apparent comfort, even though the chairs were not particularly comfortable, overstuffed but hard. His wife, Sylvia, sat in the lobby chatting with Gabrielle.

About a dozen people had scattered themselves around the rest of the room, most in the overstuffed chairs, a few on the even less comfortable benches or desk chairs.

Carroll placed the two bottles of vodka on a table between himself and Dooley. Both bottles were open. Carroll's glass had just a few drops left inside. A drinker who didn't want to get caught short, Dooley thought. Or maybe he was less enthusiastic about adopting a Russian orphan than his wife was. Or he was bored to tears. Or maybe he was just a guy who was scared of being trapped by a deadly snowstorm while in a foreign country. In which case Dooley could hardly blame him.

Carroll saw Dooley staring at him. "Want a bit of this?" Carroll asked. "Just get yourself a glass."

"No. Thanks anyway. Been there, done that. Too recently, as a matter of fact."

"I get it." Carroll poured himself a generous shot in his squat glass and downed it in one gulp. He blinked a couple of times. He poured the stuff down as if it were water, Dooley thought. "Gonna be a long couple more days if the plows don't come."

"That's for sure."

"So, Dr. McSweeney of New York City, you're not here to adopt a baby, right?"

"No." Dooley wished Carroll hadn't brought the subject up.

"So what are you in this part of the world for, Dr. McSweeney?"

"I wanted to find the parents of the baby we adopted."

"Uh-huh. Why?" Carroll leaned slightly to one side, then straightened and poured another shot.

"Medical history. A lot of diseases are the result of genetic predispositions. We needed to know what our son's family history was."

"At this time of year?"

Dooley raised his head. "What?"

"You come to this part of the world at this time of year for that? I mean we're talking Russia in winter. What's the rush?"

"No rush." Even to himself, Dooley didn't sound convincing. "We figured the parents were probably poor. Maybe without the best medical care. They could get lost in the—the vastness of Russia. Or they could die. We might never find them."

"And did you?"

"Uh—I found the mother. She has no idea where the father is."

"How do you know she's the mother?"

Dooley took a deep breath. He felt like he'd been slapped. "Because she says so. And the documents say so."

"I see. Well, you have to excuse my caution, but seeing as we're planning to adopt too, I need to ask. Suppose they just showed you some woman and had her say she's the mother. How would you know?"

Dooley said nothing.

George Carroll went on. "Did she look like your child?"

"Physically? Not too much. I don't look exactly like my parents."

"Sure you don't want a drink? You look like you could use one. No? See, what would worry me—actually, I mean what does worry me is how little we know about these children. Of course, you're a doctor, so you can assess basic health, can't you?"

"Well, I'm not a pediatrician. But yes, basically." Dooley wiped his forehead.

"But me, I'd have to take what I was told. Although, of course, they get a Russian doctor for you to give an opinion."

"But you're a cardiologist, aren't you?"

"Yeah, sure. But it's been a long time since med school." He laughed. "Once you specialize you never use some of that stuff again. I could tell generally what was what, I suppose."

"Yes. They do tests, of course."

"Blood tests. A bit of stuff like TB tests, I'm told. AIDS and hepatitis. But the tests are analyzed here and it's a Russian doctor, so who knows whose side he's on? For that matter, even if he's a Windsor House doctor, who knows? Put it more frankly, we *do* know. We know Windsor wants to make the sale."

"Sale?"

"Oh, let's be honest here. They're in the business to make money, aren't they? I mean, how much did you pay?"

"Ah—"

"That was a rude question. I apologize. But *I* don't mind being frank. We're looking at about a hundred and fifty to two hundred thousand, if all goes well. Because, see, we want a hard-to-get type of child. Blond, blue-eyed, like Pep—Sylvia. My peppy wife."

"It's natural enough to want a child who resembles you."

"So you got one too, then? Well, my point is, how do we know where they got it? Sure, I can ask to meet the mother, but suppose they just show me some woman who's been paid to say, 'Yes, I'm the mother'? How would I know otherwise?" George Carroll, eyebrows raised, fixed his gaze on Dooley.

"I don't really know."

"This is just me, probably being overly suspicious, but I wonder. They could perfectly well have a baby farm somewhere in Russia where blond women make their living giving birth to blond children. Or for all I know, they could go about the Russian hinterlands kidnapping children to order."

Dooley turned hot, then cold. *He knows.*

"Or at prices like that, they could range all over the world, picking up children to order."

Dooley stared.

"After all," Carroll said, "just me again, being skeptical, but nobody from the outside is going to search Russia for babies, are they? Even if you couldn't find the mother of your child. You assume people in Russia just disappear anyway. Just like you think the father of your child disappeared."

Dooley reached for the vodka bottle, then thought better of it and brought his hand back. *I can't show any fear. I have to be perfectly calm.*

"And in a way, if that's what's going on," Carroll said, "wouldn't I be equally guilty? The person who makes it happen by paying big money is just as guilty as the man who steals the child. Just like the man who pays big money for ivory is just as guilty as the man who shoots the elephant. Wouldn't you say I'd be just as guilty, if so?"

"I don't know," Dooley said in a high-pitched voice. "You might be if you really knew for sure."

"*Exactly!* If I knew for sure, it would be just like handing somebody two hundred thousand dollars and saying, 'Go out and steal me a baby.'" He corked the vodka bottles.

Dooley tried not to faint. He could hardly hear Carroll saying, "I'd better get to the men's room. I may have had one too many of those. Save my chair for me. Or if you can't save the chair, save the vodka." He laughed loudly, sprang up, and walked a little lopsidedly around the far side of the room to the rest rooms beyond the bar.

Dooley sat unmoving. *He knows. He doesn't just know what Windsor House is doing, he knows about me! How could he have found out? But it doesn't matter. Or maybe he doesn't know. Is he baiting me, to see what I'll do? But he's too drunk for that. I hope he didn't see me react. How would I know whether he was trying to get a reaction out of me? Maybe he won't remember all this when he sobers up.*

Suddenly, Dooley reached for the bottle of vodka to take a slug. He was too anxious. His hand knocked the bottle to the floor. He picked it up, backed into the table, knocked the other bottle off. Fortunately, the tops were on tightly enough so neither spilled. By the time he got both back on the table, he just picked one and unstoppered it, took a deep drink. It was the one George Carroll had been drinking from although he didn't know that.

He tasted pure water.

# 14

And the snow continued to fall, swirling into tornadoes in the stiff wind.

The phone lines were clogged with people, all trying to call home. Dooley tried several times to telephone New York and got through after more than twenty attempts. He told Claudia they didn't know whether they'd get out tomorrow or next week.

"How's Teddy?" he asked.

"Want to talk to him?" Dooley was about to say people were waiting for the phone. It was too painful to talk with Teddy now. But Claudia had already put the phone down and the next voice he heard said, "Daddy? Where aw you?"

"Hi, Tedder. I'm thousands of miles away."

"Why?"

"Oh, it's a long story, pal. I'll tell you all about it when I get home."

"Coming home soon?"

"Soon, Teddy. As soon as I can."

# 15

After a while, the staff started coming to the bar to drink. The first five or six times, Mr. Gabovitch reprimanded them and sent them back to their posts. Then a couple of the higher-level employees, office clerks, reminded him that they were only supposed to work eight hours. They were professionals, they said, trained in operating the computerized reservation system, sending e-mails, sending and receiving faxes and such, and they were off duty. Since by governmental decree they could not go anyplace else, and since they were on their own when not on the job, they were entitled to normal behavior and normal refreshment.

Which of course meant that the cleaning women, busboys, kitchen staff, secretaries, and so on, a group that was essentially marooned at the Metropole until the emergency was over, decided they could drink too.

A large, varied, and jolly population filled the bar, growing jollier as the hours went by.

# 16

"What's wrong, Dooley?" Gabrielle asked, taking an overstuffed chair next to him, just vacated by Mrs. Monk. Outside the window, snow blew past.

"I can't get home."

She tilted her head and looked at him. "Doctor, you're not the type of person who's going to look *that* bereft just because your flight's delayed."

"Um." Dooley rubbed his face with his hands. "I really do have to get home. It's Christmas in two weeks. I have presents to buy. Claudia's going to want help with decorating the tree. I took a leave from work, but if this goes on, people will have to fill in for me. And that isn't fair—" He stopped because Gabby was laughing. "What?"

"I do interviews for a living. I know when people are blowing smoke."

Dooley was suddenly overcome with a desire to tell her what was wrong, the whole horrible story. He believed she would listen and be sympathetic. She seemed like a person who had heard everything and still kept her balance and sensitivity.

Wait a minute. What was he thinking? Good God, she was a *reporter*! For all he knew, the next thing that happened, he'd be hearing about himself on CNN.

"Your thoughts are practically playing tag across your face, Dooley."

"I'm sorry. It's just too hard to talk about."

"It looks like it's pretty hard not to talk about too."

He was going to answer, if he could only think of an answer, when he saw headlights against the snow. He jumped up to look out the window. "It's a snowplow! Halfway down the block, and coming this way!"

"Hey! Maybe we'll get out of here."

Dooley and Gabrielle dashed to the front door. Jacketless, they ran down the walk to look. The snowplow passed directly in front of them, foaming breakers of snow rolling away from its blade. It was closely followed by an automobile that looked like a humvee. The plow was making no effort to clean snow from the street. It was clearing a path for the car.

It had to be somebody important. Or somebody who could pay a lot. Dooley tried to see into the car. There was a dim dashboard light and a streetlight near the end of the Metropole walkway. It passed under the streetlight before disappearing away into the night. He saw who it was, and he reeled back.

Then Gabrielle said, "Mr. Lupov!"

Dooley didn't speak. He had been about to say, *"Sigmund Rutgauer?"*

Dooley spun around. He walked rapidly into the hotel lobby and bolted up the three flights to his room. Once inside, he paced across the small room, confused by the implications of what he had seen. Bits of information came hurtling together in his mind.

There was a knock at the door.

Opening it, he saw Gabrielle.

"This isn't a good time," he said.

"Let me come in."

He stood aside.

"You need to talk to somebody," Gabrielle said. "This isn't just travel trouble, Dooley. You look like death." She sat on the room's only chair and Dooley sank down onto the edge of his bed.

He told her. He told her about adopting Teddy, about taking him home almost four years ago from this very hotel, after leaving the orphanage down the street. He told her about the leukemia scare and the tetracycline and the fact that he was virtually sure that Teddy was not a Russian orphan. He did not tell her he had recognized the man in the humvee. That part of it affected another person and led to terrifying questions he needed answers to immediately. It shouldn't be shared. He said, "I think Teddy might have been moved illegally from some other country, where maybe he was in foster care."

"Could you find out where?"

"I've been trying."

"Government agencies could do it for you."

"Yes. Maybe. Maybe they'd take him away from us before even starting to look for where he came from."

Gabrielle had been a reporter too long to be fooled. "Haven't you tried asking the agencies?"

"No."

"Why not? Even if he had been in foster care they'd probably let you keep him after all this time."

"I don't know that."

She wouldn't let up. "Have you tried to find out what the policies of different foster care systems are?"

"No."

"Why not?"

He took a breath. "I think the probability is that he was abducted."

"Good God, Dooley! Kidnapped?"

"He's a type of child that would be valuable."

"How valuable?"

"Certain types of children, if they're in perfect health, can go for two hundred thousand dollars."

Gabrielle looked stunned. "Really? I knew there was baby selling," she said. "I never realized *that* much money was involved."

"There's always been a black market in babies. The price has gone up more and more every year. Maybe because of birth control. Unwanted babies are scarce commodities," he said. "Also, today the black market is much better organized."

"Dooley—did *you* pay that much?"

"My wife took care of the paperwork. She's a lawyer."

"You mean you don't know what she paid."

"She said twenty-five thousand."

Gabrielle persisted. "You don't believe her?"

"I do, but she said thirty once and twelve once too. I assumed sometimes she was adding some charges and other times not. I don't want to talk about what she may have paid."

"You can afford to pay that?"

"I can't. She has family money. You have to realize, Gabby. She was desperate for a baby."

"I do understand that. What I can't understand so well is why not adopt a *really* needy baby. I've seen so many." When he didn't answer, she said, "I'm sorry. I haven't walked a mile in your shoes. I have no business criticizing."

She studied him some more. Then she rose, went over, and sat next to him on the edge of the bed.

"You would have, wouldn't you? Adopted a needy baby?"

He didn't answer.

After a time, she reached out and touched his shoulder. "You're a good person, Dooley. This isn't your fault."

"What will you do with what I told you?" he asked abruptly.

Gabrielle frowned. "You think I'm going to use it for a story."

"I don't know, Gabrielle. How could I? I don't know you well enough."

"Do you think I would put your little boy on CNN?"

"I think if Windsor House is selling stolen babies it's one hell of a story."

"It is. You're right about that."

"And?"

"And let me ask you something. If they're actually *stealing* babies, don't you want them exposed?"

"I want them stopped, Gabrielle. I don't want Teddy exposed."

"But what about the other babies?"

"I've thought and thought about that. If Teddy isn't the only one—and why would he be?—there are other families with missing

BARBARA D'AMATO

children. They're going through hell every day their child is gone. But the families who have those children would go through hell if they were taken away."

She wouldn't let him escape so easily. "And if Windsor House isn't stopped, they'll kidnap more children."

"I know."

They were both silent for several minutes. Finally, Gabrielle said, "Let me give you two assurances. First, I'm not going to do any 'story' on Windsor House right now. I'm in the middle of something I have to finish. Second, even if I did, I wouldn't use specific cases without the adopting parents' permission. The children shouldn't be pictured anyway, and if the parents are willing to be interviewed they could be seen from the back. Nobody's at fault here, except Windsor House."

"What would you do if I asked you not to do a story on this at all?"

"I don't know. I don't know."

"What if I claimed I had told you in confidence? Not for attribution?"

"Then I would leave you out of the story, even if I did it."

"But if you bring down Windsor House, all its adoptions would come apart."

"I doubt that. My guess is most of their children are legitimate adoptees. Nobody could snatch infants on a large scale. They probably only take children when they have a special request and adopting parents willing to pay big money."

Dooley groaned.

"Dooley, you adopted in all innocence. You didn't do anything wrong."

"I'm doing something wrong right now."

"By keeping Teddy?"

"Of course."

"Well, that was what I was thinking when you asked whether I would sit on the story. Assuming there is a story and assuming I can verify it. I was thinking—my sitting on it doesn't alter the fact that you have to make a decision."

"Oh God. I know."

"If you're right, you know what they're doing? They're laundering babies."

"Like laundering money?"

"Exactly. You launder money by passing hot money through a legitimate business. They're laundering babies by passing stolen babies through Russia."

He couldn't speak. The silence drew out.

Gabrielle looked so good to him. It was sheer luck, amid all the horrors of the last few weeks, that he had met somebody who was honest. She was smart and beautiful, but she was also kind, and that was far more important to him right now.

"How much longer are you staying?" he asked.

"We planned five days more. But we lost all day yesterday, as far as getting any work done."

He walked Gabrielle to her room and went back to his. He wanted to touch her. Hug her. He thought her touch would comfort him, and, oh God, did he ever need comfort right now.

In his room, alone, he burrowed under the scratchy blankets.

# CHAPTER TWENTY-ONE

Recognizing that intercountry adoption may offer the
advantage of a permanent family to a child for whom
a suitable family cannot be found in his or her State
of origin . . .
> —The Hague Convention on the Protection of
> Children and Cooperation in Respect of
> Intercountry Adoption of 1993

## 1

When they came, it was with a roar. Dawn was four hours away, but everybody on the street side of the Metropole heard them come. Dooley jumped out of bed and looked out his window. The snowplows muscled forward in a wedge, shooting snow into large trucks that accompanied them. As Gabovitch had said the night before, when they came it would be "Three chest-to-chest."

"Side-by-side," Sam had said.

It was five A.M. Dooley was in his clothes and downstairs in twenty minutes.

An hour later, there was talk of taxis and the possibility that the airport was open. Dooley called the airlines and got two maybes, a yes, and a no. By now Gabrielle was downstairs too, awakened by all the running around in the hallways.

"I wanted to catch you before you left," she said.

"I'm going to the airport right away," he told her.

"It's important for you to get home, isn't it?"

"Very."

Drawing a slow breath, Gabrielle said, "You need to know something for your own safety. Probably I should have told you earlier. I came back to Russia to find out who killed my partner."

"You said a relationship with a man had just ended."

"Yes. Ended in the most horrible way possible. Justin was a wonderful, kind person. And the best cameraman I had ever worked with. We were such a team, such a great team, Dooley. I can't describe him in a way that would make you see him, but I could show you his work sometime, and you'd understand."

"Why was he killed?"

"That's the question. I came back to try to find out."

"What happened to him? Is it too painful to talk about?"

"No." She told him the events of the morning she came back to the hotel to find Justin drenched in his own blood. She didn't spare Dooley any details. He was a doctor, after all, and it helped her to go over it. The telling didn't diminish Justin or the unfairness of what had happened to him, but telling it over and over smoothed some of the rough edges, like polishing a stone. Telling it also clarified her thinking.

She told him about the two men in the tapes from Romania and Russia, and how they had different names in the two places.

"It was the tapes they came to destroy, must have been, but I think they had planned to kill Justin too. I wasn't sure at first, but the more I thought about it, they must have believed he knew they were the same men, because he pointed the camera at them. He could check the tapes against each other when he got back to New York. He was a photographer, therefore, he was a visual person. Anyway, I think they took the chance to get rid of a possibly aware witness and the tapes at the same time. And make it look like some kind of ultrapatriotic hooliganism.

"I knew when I found the pictures of the men that something was going on. They were passing themselves off as officials of different government agencies in two different countries under two different names. I need to know whether the orphanage officials in Romania and Russia are in on the scam. Whatever the scam is. I think Vlasta was coming to tell me what she knew about them. I'll go to our embassy when the snow stops and ask them to tell me whatever they knew about these two men. I have names for the men, although they're probably false. And pictures. An embassy often knows about Americans running illegal businesses, and often knows their aliases. After all, people like that can embarrass the United States. It makes sense to keep tabs on them."

Gabrielle was in a rush of urgency, trying to communicate everything. She didn't notice that Dooley wasn't responding.

"Sam and Gorilla and I think we can find out who these two men are. Whether they are Mr. Krysigin and Mr. Lupov or Mr. Anatole and Mr. Bassable, they are doing something, probably something criminal. Maybe it has to do with the money that goes to the orphanages. These places look to us as if they operate on a shoestring, but they don't. There are a lot of costs, so there must be ways people can skim money. It's horrible to think of people sneaking money from babies who have almost nothing, but there are people that cruel. Or they're doing something having to do with the babies themselves. I don't know just what. Finagling who can adopt, maybe. They're making enough money to get a snowplow to drive in front of their car."

Dooley just nodded.

"But the more I think about it, the most likely thing is that Lupov and Krysigin are involved in the adoption horror that you fell into."

Dooley nodded again.

"Otherwise we'd have to suppose there were two scams related to one orphanage going on at the same time. It's not impossible that they're separate. It's not even terribly unlikely, given the condition Russia is in right now. But it's way more likely that they're connected. Don't you think?" When he didn't answer, she went on. "You realize it was Lupov I saw last night?"

"Mm-mm."

"I think I could get to the truth if I could just figure out who Mr. Lupov really is."

"Maybe," he said noncommittally. "If you could find out."

## 2

If Sheremetevo 2 was claustrophobic in ordinary weather, tonight, with water, ice, and mud tracked in, it was cavelike. Many passengers had been stranded there for two or three days, having flown in and not been able to get either into Moscow or out on another flight. Now too, travelers who had been marooned in Moscow two days past their flight times were arriving at the airport irritable and loud. The place smelled of damp wool, damp fur, wet floors, and unwashed people.

Long lines stretched from every check-in. Dooley got in one, stood two hours, his body buzzing with urgency, and was told he could take standby on a flight for an hour later.

# 3

At the Metropole, Mr. Gabovitch telephoned the man he knew as Lupov.

"Dr. McSweeney has left, sir," he said.

"Left for where?"

"The airport. For America."

# 4

Flights were called. Flights departed. His first standby flight took off without him. There was a flight direct to New York at 10:17, but it was full. He was on standby for the 12:12 flight, but nobody canceled and he wasn't surprised.

Finally, the logjam began to clear. The 1:27 direct flight to Kennedy allowed him to board. He was very grateful.

Dooley did not notice the tall, thin man who boarded shortly after him. The man wore an astrakhan hat that covered all of his hair and most of his forehead. The fur collar of his thick wool coat muffled his mouth. There was nothing to notice. Most of the passengers on the plane were dressed similarly.

Dooley belted in, watched the acceleration over ground that was still bordered by mountainous snowdrifts, felt the lift, and tried very hard to relax. After half an hour in the air, he realized he had not called Claudia. In the airport, he had intentionally waited because the airline could easily have told him he'd be on a flight and then cancel him at the last minute. He and Claudia usually did not meet each other at the New York airports. Often flights didn't get in on time and getting to and from the airports was so time-consuming.

Fortunately, he was able to call from the airphone on the seat ahead of him.

"It's me," he said.

"Are you all right?"

"Oh, sure. Tired. But I'm airborne."

"That's a relief."

He told her the flight number and arrival time.

Claudia said, "Did you find out anything?"

"About the medical history? Not much."

"Well, you can always say you tried." She sounded somewhat pleased.

"I'll tell you more when I get there."

"Be safe."

"Sure. 'Bye."

Dooley settled back in his seat, more troubled than ever. He reflected that he was probably the only person on the plane who wouldn't especially mind crashing.

# CHAPTER TWENTY-TWO

A leading intercountry adoption agency made a
million dollars profit last year on four million in
revenues, a profit of twenty-five percent. Owners of
such businesses can make $200,000 a year.
By contrast, McDonald's Corporation had a very
good year this year, making $1,780,200,000 on
total sales of $14,357,700,000, a profit of 12.4
percent.

*—Favorite Facts,* vol. 11

## 1

## New York City
## Mid-December

Claudia McSweeney had been alarmed at Dooley's voice on the
phone from the air. There was something seriously wrong. For a few
minutes she told herself that airphones always make you sound funny.
But it wasn't a matter of sounds and tones; it was a matter of his
words and mood. There was something very wrong.

It was going to be about Teddy, of course.

## 2

The taxi into midtown passed block after block of Christmas decorations, Santas with kettles and bells, store windows filled with products and strewn with glitter glowing in the twilight. The outdoor theater advertising included Christmas specials. *The Nutcracker* was playing at Lincoln Center. The Big Apple Circus was open for children who were out of school for Christmas vacation.

Compared to Russia, it was an indecent riot of consumer goods. Toys, mittens, and scarves in every color, Christmas cakes and green-and-red ice cream. Compared to Dooley's expectations for his son six weeks ago, it was all a reproach. Would he ever take Teddy to a circus?

Where would they all be next Christmas?

## 3

He let himself into the apartment, the "Merry Christmas, Dr. McSweeney!" from the doorman still ringing in his ears.

"Dooley! You're back early." Claudia put her arms around him and hugged him. He didn't hug back.

"I'm not early. I'm on time."

"Well, in international travel, that *is* early." She laughed.

"Daddy! Daddy! Daddydaddydaddydaddydaddy!"

"Tedder!" Dooley swung Teddy up in his arms and held the child to his aching heart. "I got you something."

"What? Whatwhat?"

He took a gold-wrapped box out of his suitcase and handed it to Teddy. "Can you take it in your room to open it, big guy? It's a secret."

BARBARA D'AMATO

302

"Yes, Daddy." Teddy ran away fast. Whenever he ran, he ran fast. Dooley closed the living room door.

"Claudia, we've got to talk."

"What is it? You're scaring me."

"It's scary all right." She sank into the sofa. Dooley remained standing. "Claudia, when we first thought of trying to adopt, it was after you'd had some fertility treatments."

"Not *some*. A lot."

"But they weren't working, and you started to investigate adoption in the U.S. You were still having fertility treatments while you looked. We applied to adopt, but it took forever. After a while we were a little older than what was preferred, which made it harder. And you wanted a red-haired, green-eyed baby, which made it harder yet. Everything looked grim."

"It certainly did."

"Then suddenly you got onto Windsor House."

"Yes. It was a godsend."

"Maybe. How did you hear about it?"

"On the Net, I think. Or maybe somebody told me. I don't remember."

He knew that she was lying. Claudia remembered everything. "Okay. Why did you decide to go with them?"

"They had a wonderful reputation. They could find the child you wanted and get you through the foreign paperwork in record time."

" 'A wonderful reputation.' How long had they been in business?"

For a moment she said nothing. Then, "Uh—I don't remember. Ten years, maybe?"

"Teddy is four. We got him three and a half years ago. Would it surprise you to learn that Windsor House is just four years old itself?"

"Yes. Yes, that would surprise me."

"How could it have a reputation? How could it have a track record?"

"It must have. I heard about it."

"I also discovered that babies like Teddy are selling for a hundred thousand to two hundred thousand dollars. You told me twelve thousand once. And I think you said twenty-five thousand once, all fees considered, you said. But Windsor House sells babies for hundreds of thousands of dollars. You never said you paid that kind of money. I don't think you have that much to throw around."

"Throw around! This is our *son* you're talking about."

"Spare me. He's somebody's son, that's for sure. Whose child is he, Claudia?"

"What do you mean? That woman in Russia."

"No, he is not the child of that woman in Russia." He stepped toward her, bent over, and took hold of her shoulders. "Claudia, you tell me now. No more lying. Are you and Sigmund Rutgauer and the rest of your U.N. cronies running an adoption ring?"

"What?"

"Are you selling bootleg babies?"

"Of course not!"

"Prove it."

"Why are you doing this to me? How could I possibly prove it?"

"If you aren't part of Windsor House, tell me who is."

"I don't know."

"Who put you onto them in the first place?"

He could almost see the struggle in her mind. For just a few seconds he saw her decide not to tell him. Then she wilted a little.

"All right," she said.

"Who, Claudia?"

"My father."

Dooley took a breath. "How did he know about them?"

"Dooley, I think my father founded Windsor House. My . . . bad experience showed him the need."

Dooley sank into a chair. It made sense, God help them all. "Windsor House kidnaps babies to order, Claudia. And I think they kill people."

Tears were running down her face. "No. I don't believe it."

So he told her. Everything he'd found out about Teddy, everything he'd found out about Windsor House. He described the murder of Justin Craig and what Gabrielle suspected was the reason. And he told her about seeing Rutgauer in Moscow.

When he finished, he said, "I'll call Annalise. We need her over here right away."

# 4

"Well, look who's here," Daniel Tarkington said. "At this hour of the night. And all unannounced."

Ruth Tarkington appeared in the doorway behind him. "Claudia! Dooley! Is there something the matter with Teddy?"

"Not exactly, Ruth," Dooley said. He pushed his way in, trailed by Claudia.

"Not exactly? Is he sick? You never just pop in without—"

Dooley said, "Claudia, maybe you and your mother could go wait upstairs."

Claudia said, "No." She had not uttered a word in the car during the forty-minute drive. Dooley had no idea what she was thinking.

"I'll stay too," Ruth said.

"Isn't this nice? Family time." Daniel walked to his bar and poured a Laphroaig scotch. He didn't offer any to Dooley. "Have fun on your trip?"

"It wasn't supposed to be a fun trip."

"I guess not, since you're back so soon. Did you find out what you wanted, Drooley?"

"No."

"Not even from that nice Russian mother, Drooley?"

"No."

"Not even with that nice blood sample, Drooley?"

*He knows. He had somebody watching me. Maybe it's not such a bad thing that he's willing to own up to it. Maybe that will make this easier to do.*

"No, Daniel. I didn't find out what I wanted. I found out what I didn't want."

"Oho! Wordplay. My favorite game."

"This is no game, Daniel. Ruth, I really wish you'd leave us alone for just a few minutes." She held her fists to her chest, but didn't back away, and Dooley decided to go ahead. She was an adult; they'd been wrong for a long time in treating her like she was half-child, half-woman.

"Daniel, you and Sigmund Rutgauer and certainly several others have been running a baby-selling ring called Windsor House. You're selling 'special' babies for whopping sums of money."

"Oh, that's a news flash, Drooley."

"That's bad enough, and illegal in several states including New York, I believe. What is really vicious is this. You've been stealing specific babies to order, transporting them to Russia and Romania, and selling them to Americans from there as genuine orphans."

Dooley heard Ruth breathe, "Kidnapping?"

Daniel said, "And you're upset because——?"

Dooley stared at him. "How can you ask that? What sort of a monster are you?"

"Oh, basically the kind that makes money. We do our work for it. It took three weeks to get him thinned down."

"You starved Teddy?"

"Not starved. Simple rations."

"I don't get you, Daniel. I can't break through to you." Dooley stole a look at Claudia, but she stood near Ruth, rigid and angry. "I'll go further. Windsor House has been killing people, two that I know of in Russia. I hold you directly responsible."

Daniel poured another two fingers of scotch. "And that and a dollar will get you ten cents' worth of gum, Drooley." He swirled his scotch, admiring the color.

"What is this attitude, Daniel? I could as easily be telling you there's a flat tire on your car. You'll go to prison, Daniel. For the rest of your life!"

"Only if you tell, Drooley."

"Of course I'll tell. The FBI needs to come in on this right away. God only knows how many kidnapped children are out there!"

"Ah, but you won't tell, you see"—Daniel paused and smiled happily at Claudia, Ruth, and Dooley—"because you would lose Teddy."

Sound ceased. Dooley couldn't hear Claudia so much as breathe, and Ruth stared at Daniel with big, pleading eyes.

"Well, that's it, then," Dooley said. "You're wrong. You gambled and misjudged me." He walked over to the hall phone.

"What are you doing?"

"Dialing 911," Dooley said, over his shoulder.

"Don't, Dooley!" Claudia said.

More firmly, Daniel said, "Don't do it." Dooley looked back and there was a gun in Daniel's hand where the glass of scotch had been.

*I should never, never have agreed when Claudia begged me to give him a chance to explain. I should have called the FBI immediately. God, I'm going to be killed because of my pity for her. Killed by kindness. What a bad joke!*

"You can't shoot me," Dooley said. "People would know I was missing. Ruth and Claudia are witnesses."

"Ruth and Claudia will be able to keep Teddy if I kill you. You've been despondent. You went for a walk. We couldn't understand why you didn't come back, so tomorrow we call the police. So puzzling. I think I'll just pop over to Tarrytown with the body. If I remember rightly there's a nice deserted stretch of waterfront between Tarrytown and the Sleepy Hollow cemetery. The body ought to wash right on down the Hudson. Just to be on the safe side, I'll try to put the bullet into soft tissue. The fish'll eat that first and if the skeleton is ever found nobody will know what killed you."

As he spoke, he walked slowly toward Dooley. While still not close enough for Dooley to grab the gun before Daniel could fire, he lowered the muzzle enough to aim directly at Dooley's abdomen.

Dooley said, "Daniel, stop! You need to know that I've told people about Windsor House. You can't get out of it this way."

"I don't believe you. Who did you tell?"

"People who were staying at the Metropole Hotel. I'm not going to give you their names."

"Wouldn't matter. Let the cops close Windsor House if they want."

"They'll get you if they do."

"Nope. There's nothing in my name at the office. Not even fingerprints. Only one of the employees knows who I am, and I can take care of him before he gets wind of this. The rest will just be running for their lives anyhow. I'll hang back in the shadows and let it blow over. I'm bulletproof. I'm completely air-gapped."

Claudia said, "But they'd still take Teddy away from me, Daddy."

"Don't worry about it."

"Daddy, *please, Daddy!* You can't let them!"

"Claudia! Stop it. You're being whiny. Just like when you were a little child."

"But Daddy, I can't lose Teddy."

"If you have to give him back, *I'll buy you another.*"

# 5

Daniel Tarkington pointed the automatic carefully so that it would fire diagonally through Dooley's abdomen from front left to rear right. Abstractedly, Dooley thought it would take out his kidney after plowing through his intestines and some major arteries. He tensed to jump Daniel. His only chance was to get there ahead of the bullet.

A *clunk!* A gunshot. Glass breaking. And a scream. Daniel's eyes went out of focus. He dropped to the floor.

Ruth Tarkington stood next to the limp form. She held the neck of the scotch bottle. The rest of the bottle lay next to Daniel's head, pouring the last of its liquor into his hair.

On the floor where it had bounced, a couple of feet away from Daniel, lay the automatic. The bullet had struck the wall beyond Dooley and ricocheted into the ceiling. Daniel groaned but did not move.

"I'll call 911 now," Dooley said.

# 6

"No, actually you won't."

A shadow on the living room wall moved and a man came into the hallway.

"Sigmund!" Claudia said.

"See, what Tarkington was saying—that's not exactly the scenario we're going to be able to use." Rutgauer spoke lazily. He carried a revolver, a Colt whose wild west style contrasted with his European manner and clothing.

Drawling, he continued, "It's not very pleasant of Tarkington to be willing to involve me and keep himself clean, is it?"

"Does it matter?" Dooley said. "There's plenty of evidence against you."

"Of course it matters. If I neutralize all of you, I'll have quite some time to sanitize the office and get over to Europe to clean up the rest. I hardly think anybody is going to look for you sooner than twelve hours from now. Could be longer."

"Other people know."

"They may know something. They don't know me."

Horrified, Dooley realized that even Gabrielle did not have Rutgauer's real name. In his eagerness to protect Claudia, he had withheld vital information. If he died, no one might make the connection.

"When I stop to think about it," Rutgauer said, "the best way to sanitize the office is to set a fire. The New York cops wouldn't connect a fire in an adoption agency to me. Or to Tarkington, for that matter, since he left himself air-gapped so nicely. I don't think even that dimwit Blandford knows who he is."

"Sigmund, please!" Claudia begged. "Leave us alone. We won't say anything."

"Excuse me? Really? What we need here is a convincing picture. There was a burglary—no, I'm sure the proper term is 'armed robbery.' Daniel"—he kicked Daniel, who blinked briefly—"tried to attack the robber but was shot. The robber then shot everyone else. I'll have to take a few trinkets, of course." Sigmund looked around the hall and into the dining room, where a silver tea service stood on a sideboard. "I'm sure there will be plenty of trinkets."

"Rutgauer," Dooley said, "you can let Ruth and Claudia go. They'll take an oath not to reveal anything."

"I'm going to start with Daniel. It's important to get the angle of the bullet path right, so it won't look like he was lying down when he was shot. Okay, you. Old lady. Back away. Claudia—the other way. Dooley, hold Daniel up at a sitting angle."

Dooley didn't move.

"Dooley, if you're very good about this, I just might let Claudia go. Hold Daniel up."

Dooley dove at Rutgauer, hitting with both fists as hard as he could in the middle of the man's chest, the whole weight of Dooley's body behind the blow. Rutgauer sailed back in the air a couple of feet and crashed to the floor, his head striking the marble with a hollow crack. Dooley stared. He hadn't meant to kill him. But the blood leaking from his ears and nose signaled mortal injury. Dooley knelt and tried for a pulse. He didn't find any.

The revolver had not even fired.

Dooley heard a grunting roar. He turned and saw Daniel Tarkington on his knees, reaching for his automatic. His hand scrabbled for it, scratching at the floor. Claudia leaned toward him.

"Claudia, stop him," Dooley called.

Claudia still watched. Tarkington's hand closed on the gun.

Claudia stepped on his fingers.

"Daddy, I can't let you shoot Dooley."

# Chapter Twenty-three

Senator Garrison:     I don't see why you can't enforce this.

Special Agent Cates:  Well, you see, Senator, some states allow
women wanting their child to be adopted
to advertise. Some allow pretty much any
sort of advertising. Some have restrictions.
In some states it's criminal to advertise. Of
course, the Internet is awash in ads.

## 1
## New York City
## Mid-December

It was four A.M. when they got to their apartment. They had
hardly spoken to each other on the long drive back from Chappaqua.
Ruth Tarkington was in the back seat. They dropped her at a hotel in
Manhattan. They asked if she needed someone with her, but she said,
"Maybe tomorrow. I want to be alone right now."

Dooley had called the FBI, and then the Chappaqua police. On
the advice of the FBI, as well as the statements of Ruth and Claudia,
the local police took Daniel into custody. They interviewed Dooley
intensively for three and a half hours, putting him through his shoot-

ing of Sigmund Rutgauer over and over again. Ruth and Claudia gave shorter statements and then waited while the police exhausted their questions for Dooley. The FBI and police let the three go at three-thirty A.M., promising more interviews the next day.

Teddy woke up when they got to the apartment and Dooley went in to tell Annalise they were home.

"You're back, you're back. Daddy! Daddydaddydaddy!"

Dooley hugged Teddy and told him a little story about Christmas in Russia, how they celebrated it at a different time and how they had processions with the archbishop and Franciscan friars and in the procession would be goats, sheep, and a donkey from the manger scene.

"Real-live donkeys?" Teddy asked.

"One live donkey," said Dooley who hadn't actually seen the procession. It wouldn't be held until December 24. "And they ring bells and play big brass trumpets."

"Don't the crumpets scare the donkey?"

"I suppose they do, Tedder. I'm not sure. Now go back to sleep."

# 2

Claudia was waiting for him when he closed Teddy's bedroom door. He followed her to the kitchen.

"We have to talk about how we're going to save Teddy," she said.

"Don't, Claudia. It's just too late."

"Too late for what?" Her voice quavered.

"Too late for us. We can't keep Teddy. He was stolen—kidnapped—from someone."

"No."

"I'm afraid it's yes."

"We won't lose him if you don't tell anybody."

"You don't mean that. God, Claudia, we can't keep him."

"Nobody needs to know."

"*We* know. Besides, the evidence is in the Windsor House offices."

"They may not have incriminating records, like where the child really came from. Why should they?"

He shook his head but it didn't clear the buzzing. "Claudia, suppose our child had been kidnapped? The FBI needs to stop these criminals."

"We're the only parents Teddy's ever known. You can't do this to him."

"We have no choice."

"Dooley! Please! You can't take my baby away. You can't. It took so long to get him. All those years I went through all the medical horrors."

"I know you did." He wanted to put his arm around her shoulder, at least *try* to comfort her, but she wouldn't stand for it right now and he couldn't do it anyway. He was too angry at her, even while he felt great pity.

She said, "All the pain. You know about pain—it's what you doctors call 'discomfort.' "

"I tried to help."

"Oh, you tried to help. All the drugs that make you sick. All the tests. There's one where they lay you down and blow gas up into your fallopian tubes. They do that in case you've had PID. That's what you doctors call pelvic inflammatory disease, as if it were some cute little friend. And if they think you had it, they look at you like you caught a sexually transmitted disease."

"They shouldn't, and anyway if they did, you hadn't had any PID."

"No. Then they tried to harvest eggs. They stimulate your ovaries and then they go in through your abdomen and try to suck out some eggs. That one is particularly painful."

"You told me."

"I told you. And you had the *discomfort* of listening."

"I took all the tests they wanted me to take too."

"And that's another thing. When they proved that you could father a child, but I couldn't get pregnant then what did you feel? You felt that if you'd married somebody else you could have *your own* children."

"Teddy *is* my own child." Quickly, he said, "And if we adopt another, he or she will be my own child."

"Oh, easy to say. But do you really mean it? Don't answer that. You'll tell me you mean it. How would I ever know?"

"Claudia, nobody knows anything about something that didn't happen. It's all hypothetical. What if I had been sterile and you could have children? How would you have felt about me?"

She didn't answer. And he thought that meant he had his answer.

# 3

The call from the doorman came first thing the next morning.

"There's a Mr. Sexton and Ms. Smith from the FBI, Dr. McSweeney."

"Send them up."

When Dooley opened the door, he said, "George and Sylvia Carroll. I'm not really surprised."

# 4

Claudia was absolutely silent through all the FBI questioning. When Walter Sexton turned to her and asked her specific questions, she answered only yes, no, or I don't know. Exasperated, he finally said, "Mrs. McSweeney, did you have any idea your child might have been kidnapped from another family?"

"No."

"You realize we're searching all kidnapping records. Teddy may turn out to have been a victim."

"I didn't know it then, and I don't know it now," she said, breaking into speech. She "went lawyer" as Dooley called it. "I want to warn you, Agent Sexton, that making any assumption that Teddy isn't legally our child would be very unwise. Windsor House may have traded in adopted children, although I don't know that for a fact. But I would assume most of their children were perfectly legal adoptees, and their success may have been primarily the result of good scouting for healthy Romanian and Russian children. Any public announcement that Teddy's adoption is questionable would constitute defamation of Teddy and us. Most important, there is to be no attempt to take Teddy away from us. That *would* be kidnapping."

# CHAPTER TWENTY-FOUR

We have the largest number of baby
photos on the Net! Full physical
descriptions! Health of both
parents included at your request!

**CLICK HERE [ ]**

## 1

"You need to face this," Dooley said to Claudia after the FBI left.
Annalise had gone to the park with Teddy, trailed by a rent-a-cop
Dooley had hired, just to be on the safe side. Daniel was in custody,
but there were others in the Windsor House gang, and Dooley wasn't
taking any chances.

"It's cold out," he said. "They could be back any time. We have to
talk *now.*"

"There's nothing to talk about."

"All right. I'll sit here and talk to you. You can listen."

"Why should I? You believed I could kidnap children and sell
them to the highest bidder."

"Claudia, what was I going to think? You lied to me about Teddy."

"When? When did I ever lie?"

"You said you paid the agency thirty thousand. Then once you
said twelve. Once I think you said twenty-five. I fooled myself into

thinking you were just adding in some fees at one point and leaving some out at others. But I know now it was all a lie."

She looked away, smoothed her skirt.

"Claudia?"

"Daddy got him for me. He didn't charge anything. He said my fertility problems had given him the wonderful idea to develop Windsor House Adoptions just when he needed money and I deserved to be the beneficiary."

"Did you know he was stealing children?"

"Of course not! I would never have allowed that to go on! You can be damn sure he didn't tell *me.* For that matter, I didn't know it then and I don't know it now."

"You're going to have to face this."

"Do you care what I went through? I wanted a baby!"

"Do you care what Teddy's real mother went through? And what she's still going through?"

"*I'm* his real mother. Who got up and walked him at night when he was teething? Who took him to the pediatrician? Who changed his diapers? Who wiped his tears when some child pushed him down on the playground? You told me once that being a parent isn't just who gave birth, it's who nurtured the child."

"I was talking about voluntary adoption."

"Well, have you thought at all about what's best for Teddy? What's best for him is not to disrupt his life. He needs to stay right here, in the only home he knows, with parents who love him."

"If you could ask Teddy right now, I'm sure he'd agree. But he can't. He has parents someplace."

"The courts are giving more weight to the best interests of the child these days. *And they're right!*"

"Claudia, you're not serious. Listen to yourself! You sound delusional. Are you telling me you believe the courts would approve of kidnapping?"

"There's no kidnapping! There's no kidnapping! There's no kidnapping!" Claudia fell down onto the floor on her knees, sobbing and gulping. "There's no kidnapping. Dooley, really there isn't. He's my baby! He's my *baby.*"

Dooley wanted to pick her up and hold her. At the same time, he wanted to scream at her. That her obsession had caused this. That her blindness had ruined his life. And Teddy's life. That she had been wrong. That she was still blind to the pain of Teddy's birth parents. It was one thing to want something badly. Even to want something reasonable. To want a baby was reasonable. But now look.

*Goddammit! I'm losing my son too!*

He held out a hand to touch her shoulder. Then he pulled the hand back and walked out of the room. He went into his office, his half of the office, with tears running down his cheeks. All he could think of was getting himself back together before Annalise came back with Teddy.

They must not upset Teddy. Dooley resolved that he would be strong for Teddy. He would no longer fool himself that Teddy's parents would turn out to be dead or unfit. He and Claudia were going to lose Teddy. Sweet, chubby, happy, funny Teddy. Poor Teddy. The most innocent one of all in all of this. He'd have enough unhappiness to deal with soon.

# 2

And then they passed into limbo.

Claudia's mother stayed in Manhattan rather than be in the Chappaqua house alone. Daniel Tarkington was denied bail, even though his lawyer argued all the usual things—he had ties to the community, he was an established businessman, he had no history of arrest or even brushes with the law. The prosecution argued that he had contacts abroad, knew how to obtain false passports and other I.D., and that his crimes were unusually heinous. Dooley thought it was not these arguments that kept his father-in-law in the federal lockup. He thought the judge read the file carefully and decided that Daniel Tarkington was a man who would not hesitate to leave his family in the lurch, a man with no conscience.

Dooley knew that the FBI was working on the missing children, trying to match adoptees with kidnap victims. He had given them permission to sample Teddy's DNA again, which they did by swabbing the inside of his cheek. After all the needles he'd had to face during the leukemia scare, Teddy was fearful of this, but he had to admit afterward that "it was nuffing."

Dooley had waking nightmares thinking of other adoptive parents around the country who would soon be hit with the news that their child would be taken away.

Christmas got closer and felt like an execution date. Grimly, Claudia and Dooley decorated a tree. Each went to a few stores, separately, and bought presents for Teddy and for Ruth. Dooley believed that a present from him to Claudia would seem like a slap in the face. He was quite sure she felt the same.

Claudia and Dooley went to work each day. Dooley was especially careful not to make mistakes when reading tissue slides; he knew his mind wasn't quite right.

Then one afternoon, five days before Christmas, Dooley got a letter from the lab that analyzed DNA for him. He received reports from them frequently, as the blood, skin, hair, and saliva samples were analyzed. Still, he opened this one with hands that trembled more than usual.

He said, "Oh, my God! Sunny Bakeley!"

# 3

They sat around a table in the courthouse. Walter Sexton and Pepper Smith were there from the FBI "to observe, not to throw our weight around."

There was a social worker from Child Services, a young male social worker, which was unusual. Also a local Teaneck police officer, the cop who had responded to the kidnapping report in the first place, nearly four years earlier. His face was very solemn. And there were Claudia, Dooley, and Sunny Bakeley. Claudia sat as far away from Sunny as she could.

Teddy was at home, his New York home, with Annalise and the guard.

"You lied to me, Dr. McSweeney," Sunny Bakeley said. "You pretended you were looking for a housekeeper."

"I'm sorry."

"Let's bear in mind, Ms. Bakeley," the social worker said, "that Dr. McSweeney was also the person who found you. Not the FBI or the police, but Dr. McSweeney."

"That's true."

The social worker's job, Dooley thought, was to try to bring the parties together in the interests of the child. And while Sunny Bakeley sounded sad, as if regretful to accuse him of lying, she did not sound angry. When he had talked with her on the phone, she had been thrilled and weepy at the thought that her son had been found.

Claudia was angry. She and Dooley had scarcely spoken for a week now. Teddy knew there was something wrong, even though they maintained a good front around him. He felt the tension in the air. He cried more often, for less reason than he usually did. He wanted attention and woke up in the night worried about monsters under the bed.

Annalise knew something was wrong too. First the guard, then the silence between Dooley and Claudia. She had just said, "Tell me when you can."

Dooley observed Sunny Bakeley, who sat across the table from him. There were similarities between her and Teddy beyond their red curly hair and wonderful green eyes. She was reflective, thinking, and quiet. Teddy was like that. Some of the children he played with were mercurial, but not Teddy. He was often a peacemaker in a group of four-year-olds.

The social worker said, "We usually advise the person who will be taking the child to make several unthreatening visits to the present custodial home. Play with the child. Let him get to know you. Then the child should visit your home a few times, but return to his present home."

"Won't that confuse him more?" Claudia said.

"No. It should ease the transition."

"That's hard to believe."

"It's like going to Grandma's house. Or a friend's for a sleepover."

"It will be hard on everybody."

"Mrs. McSweeney, all of this will be hard on everybody. But taking it one unthreatening step at a time should make it somewhat easier on Teddy."

Dooley knew that Claudia didn't want to spend that much time with Sunny. On one of the rare occasions when she talked with him,

BARBARA D'AMATO

324

PROPERTY OF
HIGH POINT PUBLIC LIBRARY
HIGH POINT, NORTH CAROLINA

she said, "This woman has nothing. She's a dog groomer. No, not even that. An *assistant* dog groomer."

"She's a nice person."

"Why do we try to give children attention and an enriched environment? Why do we give them good schools? Because we think it makes them happier and more successful in life. Does she have a nice house, or even a good apartment? No. Does she have any education? No. Can she give him extras like skating lessons or piano lessons? No. She doesn't even live in a safe neighborhood. She can barely provide for him. And where's the father? For all we know she's promiscuous."

She was getting into her lawyer voice again. Finally Dooley said, "Claudia, don't start some legal argument that Sunny is unable to care adequately for a child. We're not going to fight this. She's the mother and that's that."

He studied Sunny now, with increasing acceptance.

Sunny opened her purse and took out a bag of peppermints. She held them out to the others. The cop and Dooley each took one. Sunny put one in her mouth.

The social worker said, "When Teddy visits Ms. Bakeley, he should take along a few toys. He should leave one or two at her place so that he has something to come back to."

"And maybe I can buy a toy for him to take back to the McSweeneys' too," Sunny said. "That way he can think of me when he's there."

Claudia groaned.

"Tell me something, Ms. Bakeley," Dooley said.

Sunny said, "Yes, doctor?"

"Was Teddy ever prescribed tetracycline?"

"Mm-mm. He had some kind of infection. He started teething

early, and the new tooth in the bottom got infected. They tried penicillin, but it didn't work so they changed."

"I see."

The social worker pulled out a calendar. "Well," he said, "let's
plan out the transition process."

Claudia slumped in her chair. She said, "Ms. Bakeley. Can I ask
you for just one thing?"

"Please tell me what it is."

"Will you go on calling him Teddy. Please?"

# CHAPTER TWENTY-FIVE

In March 1994, President Clinton signed the
Convention on the Protection of Children in Respect
of Intercountry Adoption drafted at the Hague.
So far, Congress has not ratified the signature.

## 1

### New York City
### January

Daniel Tarkington was arraigned and bound over for trial. Jean Sippolene vanished. Gordon Ridley turned himself in when he heard of the arrests. He offered his testimony to the feds in exchange for a favorable disposition of his case.

Russia opened a fresh investigation of the murders in Moscow. Walter Sexton and Pepper Smith's DNA evidence, collected from seventeen babies at the orphanage, proved that three of them had been abducted from outside Russia. His photos identified one of the two men who had appeared in Justin Craig's tapes. That man was arrested. He confirmed that Sigmund Rutgauer was the other killer. The director of the orphanage has been arrested as well. Mr. Gabovitch was connected to Vlasta's murder as an accomplice.

With Walter and Pepper's recordings of being advised to take large amounts of cash out of the United States illegally, the FBI got a warrant to search the Windsor House offices. In addition to records on the babies, they found pollen in the rug that had come from a plant native to an area of New Mexico where a baby had recently been kidnapped. That baby was traced to Russia and returned to her parents. Mr. Blandford was arrested.

Dooley had believed since he met her that Masha had really given birth to a child. He was terrified that that child might have been killed to make a documentable place for Teddy. The Russians traced the birth and found that Masha's child had died just a few days after birth of a strep infection. It wasn't good news, but it ended that particular fear.

## 2

After the last of the conspirators still in the United States had been caught, Pepper Smith requested an interview with Mr. Bettenhausen.

"Was Walter Sexton sent to Russia to do anything illegal?"

"Yes, in a way. He was out there in the wind, without any legal justification. He was an undisclosed agent operating in Russia illegally."

"Then so was I."

"Ah, actually, that's true."

"Can you tell me now why I was assigned to watch Walter? He seemed very professional to me."

"Walter is the unguided missile we launch when there are children involved."

"Unguided? He behaved very well, I thought."

"I'm glad to hear it."

"How did you get him to go to Russia? I assume he knew the dangers."

"Walter Sexton is a fine FBI agent, but with a troubled history. He's one of the Sextons, you see."

"*The* Sextons?"

"All right. You're too young to remember. In the late 1960s and early 1970s, there was a baby mill operating in southern Ohio. You need to know there have been a fair number of baby mills in this country's history. But in those days we ran about one adoptive couple for every baby available for adoption, so it was a much more—ah— buyers' market. Today we've got maybe a million couples who want a baby and fifty thousand babies available."

"Yes, sir."

"Yes. There were homes that took in young pregnant women from good families. It was a terrible stigma to be pregnant in those days, if your family was middle class, so you went 'to stay with your sickly aunt who needed help.' You came back a few months later, no longer pregnant. And the babies went to good families."

"Yes, I've heard this, sir."

"I'm sure you have, but it's hard to appreciate the power of that disapproval. Anyway, his parents ran a baby farm. A 'home.' Good, healthy babies came from that home."

"So what was the problem?"

"The first was they were selling the babies. We don't know when Walter first became aware that his parents were charging money for healthy white babies, but they were probably doing it before he was born. Because the prices were lower then they needed a big turnover. Many of the women they took in felt they were tricked or pressured into giving up their babies."

"But would Walter have known that?"

"Walter's problem was this. He lived in the house, of course. It was in rural Ohio, forty miles from the nearest hospital. With approximately thirty to forty women at any time, in different months of pregnancy, they had about two or three deliveries a month."

"What do you mean? You mean there at the house?"

"Yes. In those days, uncomplicated deliveries often happened in local med centers or clinics. Anyway, the Sexton clinic had registered nurses on the premises and an obstetrician on call. My point is, the babies were delivered there."

"Okay."

"When he was a child, little Walter Sexton's bedroom was right above the labor and delivery rooms. A first baby takes about sixteen hours of labor and a lot go longer. Walter lived and slept with the screams and moans of women in labor in his ears. He could go to school and come home and the woman was still screaming. And when they were moved to the delivery rooms he heard shrieks of incredible agony."

"Why did his parents allow that?"

"They were making a profit. They were arrested a few years later for selling the babies."

"Did the doctors withhold anesthetic?"

"Not really. These were the days before epidurals and after it was discovered that inhaled anesthetic during birth damaged the baby. Actually, for the time, it was rather good obstetrical care."

Pepper took a few seconds to think. "And so what did that do to him?"

"Of course, that kind of trauma could go either way. He could've grown up hating babies, I suppose. Or never wanting to impose birth on any woman he loved. And he hasn't ever married or had any children as far as I know."

Pepper said, "Well, how do *you* think it affected him?"

"He has an unnaturally enlarged view of how valuable babies are."

"Unnatural like unreasonable?"

Bettenhausen halted a moment. Then he said, "I don't mean unreasonable. It's just that babies are his hot button. Like with some people it's dogs."

"Yes, sir," said Pepper. "And I think Walter is right."

# 3

Two weeks after Christmas, the time came for Dooley and Claudia to turn Teddy over to Sunny. Sunny had every right to demand him sooner. Dooley thought it was generous of her to let them have this last holiday time with their child. On January seventh they drove him to her place in Teaneck.

In a last-ditch frenzy, Claudia had begged Dooley to suggest Sunny come live with them as an au pair and Teddy would stay in their home. Dooley forbade her even to suggest it, and while he couldn't really forbid anything, Claudia gave up the idea when she saw what he thought of it. He did suggest, however, that they offer Sunny a down payment on a small condo apartment in a better area of town. At first Sunny was doubtful. After a few days she agreed, understanding that they were right to be worried about Teddy's safety.

Sunny had moved into the new condo a few days earlier, and two visits had familiarized Teddy with the place. He was picking up on the mood of the adults, though, as they walked toward the door with his suitcase. He started to cry.

Dooley hugged Sunny. Claudia didn't.

Teddy kept crying.

Sunny picked him up and held him. He kept on crying.

Claudia said, "See, Dooley?"

Dooley shook his head.

Sunny said to Teddy, "I know what, honey." Teddy stopped crying long enough to listen. "How about if Mommy Claudia comes to visit you on Sunday, and Mommy Sunny and Mommy Claudia will take you for ice cream?"

"Good," said Teddy, smiling, his face wet with tears.

# 4

The next day Dooley met Gabrielle at noon for lunch. He was working seven A.M. to three P.M., and only had an hour. She was planning to tape voice-overs for her documentary later in the day. The documentary would be dedicated to Justin's memory and was almost finished. Dooley had talked with her on the phone a few times, but had not met her since they got back from Russia.

"I saw your news report on Windsor House, Gabby," Dooley said. "It was very fine."

"Thanks."

"I appreciate your keeping Teddy out of it."

Gabrielle studied his face. "There were other parents who really wanted to talk."

They fiddled with coffee for a few minutes. There was a great deal unspoken between them. Finally Gabrielle asked, "What has happened with Teddy?"

Dooley's eyes filled with tears, which he refused to let spill over.

"Tell me, Dooley."

"He's with his mother. His *birth* mother. We've lost him, Gabrielle."

"I'm so sorry. For what it's worth, I think you made the right decision."

"Would I have made the right decision if I hadn't been forced into it by talking with you?"

"You already had. I knew even when you told me about everything, his leukemia scare, and the tetracycline and all, that you had made a decision. You wouldn't have told me otherwise."

Dooley sighed. "I hope I had."

"How is Claudia taking it?"

"She hates me."

"Oh, Dooley."

"She hates me now, but she may not hate me next month. Or next year. Things have been sad. Claudia is a woman who has lost her child, and she needs me. Even if she hates me, she needs me."

"I understand."

"I don't approve of everything she did. But she was under the influence of a lot of fertility drugs that really do alter mood, and she was desperate."

"You don't have to explain."

"She hasn't been the Claudia I married for quite a while. But I owe her. In time, I'll see what happens. I'd like to make her well again."

"Dooley, really, you don't have to explain."

"If it hadn't been for you, I'm not sure what I would have done. When you say you knew I had made the decision, that's not all of it. I think I had made the decision because of you. You're honest. You're a whole person. I don't think I could have faced you if I had tried to keep Teddy."

"I'm happy for that."

"I'm not happy. But I'm content."